I0574427

DEEPLY DEVOTED TO HIM

DEEPLY DEVOTED TO HIM

Eskay Kabba

4 Horsemen
Publications, Inc.

Deeply Devoted To Him
Hidden Love Series Book 4
Copyright © 2023 Eskay Kabba. All rights reserved.

4 Horsemen
Publications, Inc.

4 Horsemen Publications, Inc.
1497 Main St. Suite 169
Dunedin, FL 34698
4horsemenpublications.com
info@4horsemenpublications.com

Cover and Typesetting by Autumn Skye
Edited by Blair Parke

All rights to the work within are reserved to the author and publisher. No part of this publication may be reproduced, stored in a retrieval system, or transmitted in any form or by any means, electronic, mechanical, photocopying, recording, scanning, or otherwise, except as permitted under Section 107 or 108 of the 1976 International Copyright Act, without prior written permission except in brief quotations embodied in critical articles and reviews. Please contact either the Publisher or Author to gain permission.

All characters, organizations, and events portrayed in this novel are either products of the author's imagination or are used fictitiously. All brands, quotes, and cited work respectfully belong to the original rights holders and bear no affiliation to the authors or publisher.

Library of Congress Control Number: 2022951388

Paperback ISBN-13: 978-1-64450-770-4
Hardcover ISBN-13: 978-1-64450-917-3
Audiobook ISBN-13: 978-1-64450-772-8
Ebook ISBN-13: 978-1-64450-771-1

DEDICATION

To the LGBTQ+ military community, especially to those who served
before 2011. You are seen, and you
are valued. Thank you for your service and sacrifice.

This book contains scenes of attempted suicide and homophobic slurs. Please consider your triggers before reading.

If you or a veteran you know is suffering from depression, anxiety, and/or post-traumatic stress disorder, or just need to talk, please reach out for help. Go to https://www.veteranscrisisline.net/ or Text 838255.

CONTENTS

PROLOGUE

"**W**hat's wrong?" Connor asked him at dinner. He could tell Jamel's mind was elsewhere.

"Nothing, just that the premium for Obamacare is going up, again." Jamel sighed. "It's like paying a car note. But what can I do? Especially since that asshole in the White House is trying to get rid of it altogether. If I didn't have a family history of heart disease, then I would just let it go but I need annual check-ups, including cardiology."

"I know," said Connor. "But I told you I would just put you on my insurance. It allows for domestic partnership, which we are."

Jamel smiled. "I might just take you up on that now. But that would be more money coming out of your paycheck."

Connor rolled his eyes. "I can afford it, Mel. It's fine. I just got my open enrollment package so it will start next month."

"Okay."

They were quietly eating, but Connor was thoughtful. "Also in my enrollment package are questions about beneficiaries and accidental death stuff. Stuff I never bothered to fill out in the last couple of years. But I can fill it out now.

And maybe put together a living will, giving you permission to pull the plug."

Jamel chuckled a bit. "I had one, a living will," he told him. "My parents are the beneficiaries. It's probably still active."

Connor gave him a look. "So, if something were to happen to you, your parents would be making the decision for you?"

He shrugged. "Yeah. We should probably change that."

Jamel chuckled, but Connor was serious when he said, "Yeah, we should. We need to. And I need one too. One that says you and only you should be making decisions for me."

"I agree. We can write it up and get it notarized. But it might not be legally binding, in case someone from our family would want to challenge it."

"Because we aren't married?"

"Yeah, because I think they look to the closest living relative to make those kinds of decisions. But let's draw up all the paperwork anyway, have Ethan's lawyer look at it, and seal it air-tight. It will be fine," Jamel said nonchalantly.

He didn't think much of the conversation until Connor's next words made his heart beat faster. "Or. We could just. You know. Get married. And then there will be no question."

Connor's eyes didn't meet his as he spoke, his head spinning. Even he couldn't believe what he just said, but it seemed logical. And his partner, who rarely had a reaction to things, definitely reacted to that. Jamel slowed down his chewing to avoid choking, completely surprised at Connor's suggestion. He swallowed his food first, then put his spoon down, took a sip of wine and smiled with a closed mouth at his partner.

"What?" Connor asked, trying to be casual.

"Nothing. I'm just listening to you explain the best way to ensure I be the one to pull the plug," Jamel said amusingly.

"Ugh, Jameeeellll," Connor whined.

He laughed, but he was quietly waiting for Connor to continue the conversation. So, Connor turned to face him as he spoke. "Okay, I'm just saying, instead of going through the rigmarole of getting papers drawn up, if we have a marriage certificate, then everything I have, including my pension, goes to you. As spouses, you'll be my closest living relative so you can make decisions for me if I can't. And vice versa. It just makes sense."

Jamel blinked at him. "To get married."

"Yes."

"So, you want to get married." It was more of a statement than a question.

"If you think ... it's a good idea, then yeah, sure."

"Actually, this is your idea." Jamel raised one eyebrow. "All yours."

Connor rolled his eyes at him. "Okay Mel, fine. My idea. But you're on board, right?"

Jamel smiled again. Was that a fucking joke? he thought incredulously. "On board with marrying you?"

"Yeeeeaaah...?" Connor drew the word out hesitantly.

He looked at Connor amusingly. Then he shrugged and picked up his spoon to start eating again. "Whatever you want to do, Con."

Connor looked at him for a moment. "Um ... okay. Well maybe tomorrow you can drive pass the Providence court-house on the way to work—"

"Oh no. I'm not doing any of that," Jamel said casually. "This is your idea. You go down to the courthouse, set everything up. Just tell me when and where."

Connor looked at him and pouted. "Why not?" he whined again.

Jamel put his spoon down again and looked at him seriously. "Because, Connor, when we made the decision to be together, it was me pursuing you, convincing you that we would be perfect together. When we decided to buy this house and move in together, it was my idea. I had to convince you that it would be a great decision. Two major decisions in our relationship and I did the work. This is your idea. Your major decision. It's your turn to do the work."

Connor sat there with his mouth opened. He had no idea Jamel felt that way. "Um ... okay," Connor said softly. Jamel nodded and continued to eat his dinner.

Connor was thoughtful again and then asked his lover, "Soooooo ... do you want me to, like, officially ask you?"

Jamel smiled into his plate. He hadn't expected it, but that would be awesome if he did give him an official marriage proposal.

"That's up to you, Connor," he said, in a low voice without looking up.

Connor didn't respond, but his heart was racing. It was finally catching up with him, this conversation they were having. They had already been together for eight years and committed to spending their lives together, so the wedding ceremony would just be a formality. But still. Married. On paper, yes but still... married. That's huge.

But because it was Jamel, he knew it would be okay.

They didn't talk about it again but made love passionately that night, and Jamel left early for work the next day.

He still couldn't believe Connor suggested they get married. He didn't know if they would actually do it, but just the fact that it came as a natural next step in his mind made him love Connor even more, if that was possible.

Connor took some time off from work that afternoon and went to the courthouse. First confirming that October 17th was open for a judge to do the ceremony, he signed the initial paperwork to seal the date and brought the papers back home for them to sign together. He didn't say anything at dinner, and Jamel was not going to bring up the conversation again. He meant what he told Connor the night before.

Connor waited until Jamel got into bed, then he crawled in after him and laid on his side to face him. Jamel was on his back, but he turned his head to look at his partner. Connor was staring at him, his eyes so full of love. It made Jamel want to give him all his attention, so Jamel slowly turned his whole body to him. He reached his hand out, running his fingers through the side of Connor's hair and down his arm.

Connor gave him a soft smile. "I love you, Jamel."

"I love you too, baby," he responded.

They were both nervous, but for different reasons. Connor's heart was pounding out of his chest. It was not like Jamel would say no but it still made him nervous to do it. But he knew what Jamel said was accurate. Every major decision regarding their relationship had been Jamel putting things in motion. It was his turn. Jamel still couldn't believe that Connor was ready for this next step in their lives.

Connor slid away from him and knelt on his side of the bed, and reached his hand out. Jamel smiled and reached out too. Connor took his hand, inhaled and exhaled, and then began.

"You've given so much of yourself to me and this relationship. It's solid and amazing because of you. You've never hesitated to show me how you feel about me, about us. Even when I'm feeling vulnerable and insecure, and I ask you not to leave me, you never fail to make me feel secure, assure me that you aren't going anywhere, ever. So, I guess this is my way of letting you know that I'm never leaving you. That I love you and want you in my life forever. And I guess the best way to do that is to, you know, give you permission to pull the plug."

Jamel smiled softly again but, inside, his heart was exploding with love for Connor and what he was about to do.

His partner continued. "So, if you're in agreement, I would love to marry you. Do you ... want to marry me?"

Mel leaned over and kissed both of Connor's hands, then leaned up and kissed his lips softly.

"Yes," he said. "I would love to marry you too."

CHAPTER 1

DESPITE THE ACHE IN MY HEART, I SMILED

Jamel

I woke up that August morning the same way I always do, with my husband snuggled against me. Whether on his back, his side, or his stomach, it didn't matter; his smooth, porcelain skin was always right up against my side. That morning he was on his side, his hands folded and tucked under his chin, while his face was against my rib and his leg right up against mine. I watched him for a moment, his pink, pouty lips slightly open as he breathed on me. He recently got a textured haircut with a short quiff right up at the front. I couldn't run my fingers through his blond mane anymore, but it looked good on him, made him look a little younger than his 35 years of age. I had been growing out my beard, which he liked too. He told me that he likes the gray strands growing in, because it made me look distinguished. I felt old at 38, but if a couple of grays have me looking distinguished to him, I will welcome the whole salt-and-pepper look. *Anything to make him happy.*

My arm was stuck above him and got numb overnight, but I didn't mind. I loved being close to him, and I loved how close he loves to be with me. He said to me once, "We're so close, we could be one person," and it's true. No matter how we fall asleep, his body always finds mine, even now almost ten years later. He just got back yesterday from a speaking engagement in Nebraska, talking to younger veterans about trauma and how to cope when you come home from war. He called the presentation, *Meet The New You.* Sometimes I went with him, but this time I didn't. My crew was in the middle of a renovation in Attleboro, an eight-week project with two more weeks to go. I had a team of eight guys, not including Tyrell, my brother and my foreman. I needed to get up soon and get there, but I hadn't seen my partner in almost a week, and it was hard to leave the bed. His body was so warm, and his skin was so soft. It was home to me.

I moved my numbed arm slightly and flexed my hand a few times. He stirred at the change in his comfort and opened up his eyes, looking up at me. Those hypnotizing, icy blue eyes still took my breath away. He didn't smile just yet, and we just stared at each other. He closed them again and moved away from me to stretch his arms, which were probably also numb. I turned my body sideways, and he moved back toward me to lay against my chest and draped his arm around me, as I did the same to him. He sighed in contentment, as I sighed with him. I kissed the top of his head.

"Good morning."

"Morning. What time is it?" Connor closed his eyes again.

"6:22 a.m.," I told him. "I gotta get going."

"Hmmm… 'kay. I gotta get up too," he said but did not move, and I didn't either. I had to be there by 8 a.m., and it was at least a forty-minute drive, without traffic. But instead, I continued to hold him. Then Connor flicked his tongue on my nipple, and my dick twitched.

"Mmmm ... Don't do it," I warned him. "Don't. We gotta get up, baby."

He pushed me over until I was on my back again, and he was on top of me. He smiled at me slyly, with eyes sparkling like jewels. "Connor..." I warned him again.

His sexual appetite was insatiable, especially those times when we hadn't been around each other in a few days. We sucked each other off as soon as he came home in the afternoon, then he fell asleep early after dinner, so we didn't make love last night. I knew that was what he was going for. But as much as I wanted to be inside of him, we didn't have the time. We typically do not have quickies, and he knew it. But he kissed my mouth over and over again, his pink lips teasing mine. *Fuck it.*

I pulled him against my body as our erections grinded together. He pushed his tongue in my mouth and licked mine, and when I returned the favor with my tongue, he sucked it hard. *Yep, that's it, he won this argument.* I sat up and took him with me. I flipped him backwards so that he was on his back at the bottom of the bed, and I was over him, making him laugh.

Because at least if I'm dominant, I have a chance at getting out of here by 7:30 a.m.

We kissed with our hot, bad breaths, and I turned him onto his stomach. He moaned as I licked my lips and kissed the back of his ear; that was his sweet spot. I left wet kisses all over his huge, colorful, phoenix rising tattoo with the fiery outline on his upper back, his present to himself when he turned 30. Its wings were spread out with reds, oranges, blues, and yellows like a sunrise. It was so symbolic of what he had been through: out of the ashes, he had risen to become this powerful being. Sometimes I still didn't think he knew how powerful he was.

I moved off him to grab the lube off the nightstand, then got back to him on the bed, slapping his ass as I straddled him. As I lubricated my cock, he said breathlessly, "Fuck me, Big Daddy."

And now I really want to fuck him.

I slid inside of him. I didn't take it slow or easy, and he knew I wouldn't. He held onto the bottom edge of the bed, and I pounded into him over and over again, slowing down to change up my stroke every once in a while, but I was on a mission: to get us both off as quickly as possible. Connor moaned and said a couple of things about how he missed my cock inside of him and called me Big Daddy until he started to tremble. I knew he was about to cum before he said it out loud. I closed my eyes, let my orgasm overwhelm me, and released inside of him, finding myself moaning with him as we came at the same time.

"Fuck," I said breathlessly and rolled off him onto my back, reaching my hand out to pull him closer. He did, moving half of his body on top of mine and laying his head on my chest right below my chin. We stayed like that for another full minute, then I lifted my head backward off the edge of the bed to look upside down at the digital clock. 7:09 a.m.

"I gotta go, baby," I told him softly.

"Okay," he said softly back.

Connor sat up, and I kissed him again before I ran to our en-suite bathroom and took a quick shower. So quick that by the time he came to join me, I was already making my way out. He pouted his bottom lip, and I kissed it as I left the bathroom. I was dressed, with shoes on, by the time he came out of the shower. I kissed that space between his neck and shoulder and ran out, texting Ty along the way to let him know I would be a few minutes late.

My phone rang as I was doing quality control checks on the first floor. When my dad ran Jones Maintenance and Construction LLC, he was very precise; not a nail was out of place or a sloping crown molding anywhere. And I give the same type of perfection. It annoyed the guys if I made them do a job all over again, but I took pride in our reputation, especially as an African American-owned construction company. So I gave no fucks about their feelings when it came down to these kinds of things.

"Yo Lane, whaddup?" I said, as I answered Henry Lane's call. Henry was an Army buddy and one of my best friends. We didn't speak every day, mostly texting, so it was nice to hear his voice.

"Jamel." He called me Jamel and not Jay, so I knew something was up before he said anything else. I waited for it. "He's… he's gone, man. Nick is gone."

My heart understood before my head did. My chest had already started to tighten. "Gone? Gone where?"

Henry was breathing hard on the phone, and I knew he was trying to hold it together. "He's dead. A building in a village sixteen kilometers outside of Kandahar fell on him. He saved a little boy but died later from internal bleeding. They're flying his body back today. I'm sorry, Mel."

It's like what he was saying didn't make sense. I spoke to Nick a couple of weeks ago, and he was fine. His usual cheery self. Ever since he got married four years ago, he had been extra cheery, like nothing in the world could ever get him down. He bought five acres of land in Johns Creek, Georgia, and put an 1,800 square foot mobile home on it for him and Josh. He was talking about all these plans they had for the land, and I was trying to help him decide if he wanted wild horses or wild chickens running around. Because to Nicky, it was all the same; a farm is a farm. *Nick Fedella can't be dead, because he needs to build his farm,* I thought stupidly.

"Jamel? You okay, man?"

I realized I hadn't spoken since I asked where Nick had gone. "I'm here." I didn't answer Henry's question exactly, but I don't think he expected me to respond.

"I'm at the house with Joshua. He's … he's not doing too well. I mean, none of us are. But he's laughing inappropriately and making jokes about joining him. Apparently, Nick was in that village getting a gift for him for their anniversary, so Josh keeps saying that he killed his husband. I'm worried about him so I'm staying over here, trying to get him focused enough to plan the funeral, which will be Friday. Will is driving down from North Carolina; he'll be here by tonight. You're coming, right?"

"I..." I was still trying to wrap my head around what he had just told me. *Nick is dead. Gone. Not coming back. No monthly, "Jay Jones, whaddup!" calls. How is this even possible?*

"Yeah... yeah. I'll be there."

"Okay. Jay, are you sure you're okay? I didn't even ask if you were driving or anything."

"I'm not driving; I'm working."

"Okay. Call me tonight if you need me. I'll be here for you. Let me know when you get to the ATL. You'll stay with me and Tosha and the kids. You and Connor."

Connor. I should call Connor.

"Yeah okay, we'll do that. I'll call you tonight with the travel arrangements."

Before ending the call, I remembered that Henry and Nick had been best friends since they were in grade school together. They were closer than brothers. "Henry, I'm so sorry. Are you okay?"

"I can't think about me right now," he said abruptly. "Josh is falling apart. Tosha and Katija are falling apart. The boys seem to be holding it together, but they just lost their uncle too. I'm literally running back and forth between my house and Nick's to make sure everyone else is okay. It just doesn't feel real to me just yet." I nodded, not that he could see me. "Just let me know when you're getting here, man. If I fall apart, you might be the only one I can count on to hold me up."

I nodded again. "I'll be there as soon as I can," I told him.

"Later, Jay. And I'm sorry too." He hung up before I could respond.

I stood there for a moment as Ty came into the room. "Hey, you never came back up to let them know if they need to redo the crown molding." He took one look at my face and said, "What happened?"

"I..." *How do I say the words out loud?* "Nick is dead."

His mouth opened in shock. "Your best friend Nick? What happened?"

I knew Henry told me, but I couldn't remember the details. "I don't know. Something about him saving a boy in Kandahar."

Ty came over and hugged me; I hugged him back halfheartedly. He said to me, "When is the funeral?"

"Friday."

"Okay. Don't worry about what's going on here. We got this. Go be with your friends."

I appreciated him. *Ty knows how important Nicky is to me. Was. Because he's gone now. What. The. Fuck.*

"Yeah, I'm going to make flight plans today."

"Did you tell Connor yet?" he asked.

Connor. I remembered him again. *I should call Connor.* "No not yet. I'm going to call him."

"Okay. But Mel, you can go home, you know. Go take care of you."

"Nah man. We … we have work to do." But even as I said it, I knew I would not be able to concentrate for the rest of the day.

"Go home, Mel. Go call Connor and go home," Ty said.

He pulled me back into a hug, and I gave him a real one, but I was still numb to the touch. Ty walked me out before I could protest and hugged me a third time in front of my truck.

"Don't worry; we got this," he told me again. "We'll finish on time."

I got in the car and realized I still had not called Connor. I started driving toward Rockville to the leasing office at the Starling Residence, where Connor had been the building manager for the last seven years.

I came in through the outside leasing entrance rather than the building entrance. I heard the music before I opened the door. Lauv was his favorite artist at the moment, and I could hear the base from the song "Adrenaline" playing loudly. Connor was at the desk, writing up something to add to a folder, and barely noticed when the door opened. He was moving his shoulders and mouthing the words strongly like he was at a concert as Lauv himself, raising his hands to pretend to blow the horn part of the song.

Jesus, he is so fucking cute. Despite the ache in my heart, I smiled.

He noticed me standing there and looked shocked, then smiled widely. "Heeeey!"

Connor turned the music down and got up as I came closer. "You missed me already?" He gave me a peck, and I pulled him closer, wrapping my arms around his waist and leaned into his neck.

"I love you," I said quietly to him.

He pulled his face back and looked me in the eyes. "What's wrong?"

How I managed to say the words again I don't know, but I did. "Nick. Nicky died."

His face mimicked Tyrell's when I told him. "Fedella? Oh my God, Jamel. I'm so, so sorry." He pulled me closer to him and hugged me tighter. *Connor also knows how important Nicky is to me. Was.*

We held each other for a moment, then Connor lifted his head up and said, "Let's go home."

It was only 2 p.m., and Connor had another hour and a half left of work. "No, it's okay," I told him. "I just wanted to tell you. I'm heading home now."

"*We're* headed home," Connor said.

He pulled out his cell phone to scroll through his contact list and pressed send, keeping one hand on my arm. "Ethan, yeah. Sooooo I know I just got back, but I need to head out early today."

I heard Ethan yell at him, "Come the fuck on, Connor!"

But I knew Ethan wasn't really mad as Connor had a tendency to do this. He only worked 32 hours a week as the building manager and managed his own schedule.

Connor knew too and smiled a little. "I know, I know, but now I have a family emergency. I'll give you back this hour later on in the week."

"Hour and a half!" Ethan corrected him loudly.

"Yeah yeah, sure sure. I got you," he said. "I scheduled the plumber for Mrs. Piori in 2E and the exterminator for the Christianson girls on the first floor. Also, Nathaniel Proctor is moving in on the 15th, apartment 1B. Everything was signed last month, and he has his keys, so you don't have to do anything. I was doing the accounts for Life Maid Easy cleaning service, but that can wait until tomorrow. I'm on it."

"This better be a real fucking emergency," his boss said sternly.

"It is, I promise. But I may be taking a few days off again; we had a death in the family, and we'll need to go to a funeral out of state." We had a death in the family, he told him. *Indeed, we did.*

"Well shit, Connor; you should have led with that. Get the fuck outta there!" Ethan said through the phone.

"Thanks E. I will call you later."

"Call Stacy, not me," Ethan said.

Stacy Ferguson was technically Connor's supervisor, but he constantly cut out the middle woman, much to her chagrin. Because despite being employer and employee, Ethan and Connor were also friends.

Connor rolled his eyes but said, "Okay, boss. I'll call her tomorrow." He hung up and looked at me. "Give me your keys. Let's go."

"I can drive, Connor."

"I know you know how to drive, Mel. Now give me your keys." He held his hand out.

I gave him the keys to my 13-year-old cherry red Ford F-150 pickup truck. He locked the door to his office and drove us home, leaving his newer white Toyota 4Runner in the parking space.

❤ ❤ ❤ CHAPTER 2 ❤ ❤ ❤

DON'T ASK DON'T TELL

Jamel

We stopped and picked up Olive Garden ToGo because he knew how much I love Italian food, even the cheap kind. Pasta was comfort food for me, ever since I spent three years with my family on a military base in Italy when my dad was still in the service. When we got home, Connor spread a blanket on the living room floor and set up the plates. We ate in silence. Even though we have a dining room table, when we want to be intimate, we sit on the floor and eat together, sometimes off the same plate.

He held up his fork every once in a while for me to eat some of his chicken Alfredo, and I did the same for him with my shrimp linguine. Sitting quietly with him was not new for us, but I knew he was waiting for me to talk, and honestly, I didn't know what to say. I was in my head about all these memories of Nick.

We always had so much fun together. When I left the Army, I knew the one thing I would miss more than anything was hanging out with Nick, when we were both on the base.

I didn't eat much for dinner, just picked at my noodles and let Connor feed me. Our dogs, Diesel and Maje, waited patiently for us to give them scraps, and they were rewarded with the breadsticks. Diesel, always the perceptive one, came over and put his head on my leg. He was getting old and had a heart condition that will end his life soon. We both knew it but didn't talk about it. I rubbed his ears, still lost in thought. I looked up to see Connor watching me.

"Let's take a shower," he said, breaking the silence. I nodded and followed him upstairs. We left the food on the floor in the living room.

He stripped my clothes off and turned on the shower in the hallway bathroom, because it was bigger than our bathroom shower. We stood under the shower head together, still not talking. He took my loofa and scrubbed every inch of my body. When I turned around to rinse off, he wrapped his arms around me and leaned into the back of my neck.

I heard him say, "I'm so, so sorry, Jamel."

I rubbed his arms and closed my eyes, waiting for the tears to fall but they never came. I was still numb to it all. So instead, I turned around and kissed my husband. He reached around my neck and kissed me back. Sweet, closed mouth kisses over and over again, as the water cascaded over our heads.

Connor McIntyre and I had been together for almost ten years and married for almost two, but we might as well have been married for twenty years. Connor was the most amazing and beautiful man I had ever met. He's such an empath, and only in the last couple of years had he seen his emotional intelligence as a strength rather than a burden. I told him that he needed to write a book about his life. But Connor said for him to write a book would be to reveal too many buried secrets that, if ever unearthed, would hurt a lot of people. He would be honest about his relationship with Vinnie, the love of his life that died in his arms in Iraq, and no one in his family knew he was gay, even after his death. He would be honest about his father's physical, mental, and emotional abuse, decades of beatings inflicted upon him, his mother, and his siblings by his homophobic father. His father was a respected Army veteran and Rockville citizen still because no one really knew their family secret of domestic violence. Connor had completely cut him off, but his sisters hadn't, and he didn't think it would be right for the rest of his family to reveal what they had yet to admit.

He would have to be completely honest and open about his sexuality, about being in the closet for 27 years and the countless men he slept with to avoid addressing his shame, guilt, and trauma. And even though he's out, he still was uncomfortable with it; Connor opted not to discuss his sexuality unless he was asked directly. Ethan joked that he had moved from the closet to the bedroom and liked to keep his bedroom door closed. I jokingly call him my Anderson Cooper on how mum he was about being gay and how good he looked in a black t-shirt. Ethan and I didn't say either of these things to Connor, as we knew he was still sensitive to the topic. But I do appreciate that if Connor was asked directly, he would never deny me, his love for me, or our marriage, whether I was standing next to him or not. That to me was more than enough.

I know he wants me to open up and lean on him and I will, but not yet. For now, I just need to hold it all in. And Connor seemed to understand it, understand me, because he was giving me the space I needed to process this devastating news without being distant. I loved that he just gets me, one of the countless things I love about this man that I married. Marriage wasn't even something I wanted or needed us to do, since we were already sharing our lives together. But I have to admit, it brought me so much joy to refer to him as my husband.

We kissed sweetly and held each other for a while, then he turned the shower off. "Come on, baby," he said to me.

We came out of the bathroom, and I sat on the bed. The aching in my chest was getting bigger, and I was feeling so heavy. And once again, my husband read my mood. Connor stood over me and put lotion on my body, starting with my chest and my back, massaging me along the way down to my feet. He took my waves pomade off the dresser and added it to my hair, then grabbed my hairbrush and brushed it down before putting on and tying my durag to it. I stood up and returned the favor and applied lotion to his body, the same chamomile-scented lotion we use at night. Both of us were semi- aroused: my dark brown penis laying against my leg at an angle instead of straight down and his peach-colored one with the dark pink head pointing straight out, but he ignored it and so did I.

He crawled up the bed, pulled the covers back, and patted it. It was only a little after 5 p.m., and the sun was as bright as ever but that didn't matter. I got in. He moved to lay against my chest, but I pushed him onto his back and laid my head on his chest instead, listening to his heartbeat and putting one leg over his. He stroked the nape of my neck with his soft fingertips.

Connor always talked about my gorgeous body, as he called it, because I'm bulkier than him, but his body was perfect. He was just about my height with long legs, solid calf muscles, and thighs leading up to a linear Adonis belt and inguinal crease. His torso was so sexy, down to the jaguar tattoo that covered the left side of his body. Sit-ups were his thing so his abdominal muscles were perfect too, an eight pack with that perfect symmetrical line going right down to his belly button. His chest was shapely and hard, with two dark pink circles surrounding his nipples. Even his collar bone was sexy; it looked like a bird in flight. And that was just his front side. His back was muscled and curved, and that groove in his lower back right before his crack was deep and enchanting. And his ass was like two melons, round and strong. So even when he laid on his stomach casually, it always looked like he was arching his back, waiting for me to enter him. And all of that was encased in the softest skin I'd ever touched. I was addicted to my husband's body.

Connor started talking, spending the next hour telling me about his trip. I listened and focused on him, putting all my attention onto him and the work that he was doing. His organization, Vinnie's Vet Buddies Incorporated, was doing more than just taking help-line and suicide calls. They had grown to creating events around the country from speaking engage-ments, mentoring services, financial resources to even speed dating events. They were connecting vets all over the country in so many different ways, and it was amazing. In Omaha, he and Benjin, the COO of Vinnie's Vet Buddies, had a TED talk–like event and panel on war trauma at a local VA hospital, and then a mix-and-matching event for mentorship. But those events always turn out to be a singles mixer. He had me laughing as he was talking about a young vet hitting on older women with pick-up lines like, "Does your father own a glass factory? Because I can see right through to your heart."

"Like, what the fuck does that even mean? I had to pull him aside and tell him to cool it. I'm like, 'You're sounding a bit stalkerish right now, like chill, little dude.'"

We laughed together, then fell quiet again for a moment. I loved his physical appearance, but Connor also made me laugh, all the time. I fell in love with his humor and wit too. Thinking about losing him the way Josh had lost Nick had me feeling sad all over again.

"Connor. Connor, I…." I trailed off. I didn't know why the words were getting stuck in my throat.

"I know, Mel. I love you too."

"Yes. But it's more than that. Henry said Josh isn't doing so well so he's staying with him for a while. He feels guilty because Nick was there in that village buying him a present for their anniversary. He's making jokes about dying to join him and hasn't attempted to make any funeral arrangements. Like he hasn't faced it yet. And I don't blame him. Because I don't know what I would do if I ever lost you. I don't know, man … I'm going to have to go first, because I don't think I can be on this earth without you."

I could hear the amusement in his voice as he said, "Like fucking hell you're leaving me here alone. You better let me go first or take me with you." We both chuckled.

Then he said seriously, "Tell Henry not to let Josh out of his sight. Josh is going to try to kill himself."

He said it so definitively that I had to ask, "Why do you say that?"

The one and only time Connor and Josh met was over video chat four years ago when Nick and Josh went to Mexico to get married, then called me afterward to tell me about it. Connor and Nick barely knew each other, and he knew Josh even less.

I said, "Josh is hurting but I don't see him as the type—"

Connor cut me off. "He's going to do it. He's going to make a serious attempt. Make sure Henry knows."

"I will. But why do you think he's going to do it?"

He was quiet for a long time. "Because I would if I was Josh. Because I did when I was Josh."

I didn't react at all but *holy shit! Connor tried to kill himself and he never told me!?*

"Because of Vinnie?" I asked calmly.

"Yes," he said simply.

"Connor—"

"I don't want to talk about it," he said abruptly. "It doesn't matter anyway. Just make sure that Henry is with him at all times. He just needs to make it to the other side of this. His pain needs to peak, but once he sees the other side, the new day, it might be better. Might."

"Shit, Connor," I said quietly. I wrapped my arms around him tighter. "Just once?"

"Just once."

I sighed. "Okay, baby."

I had so many questions and wanted to ask more, but I knew not to push him. If he hadn't told me in the nine years we had been together, then he wasn't going to start talking now. We got quiet again but that was okay. Being in his arms like that was more than enough. We laid together and watched the sun go down through the bedroom window.

Connor was the second white guy I had ever been with; Nick was the first. When I was just a few months past age 18, I met Henry Lane, an Army corporal at the time, and he introduced me to Nicholas Fedella, an Army Specialist and his best friend. I had no idea Nick was gay until he cornered me in his room one night. No one knew I was gay, not even Will Hernandez, my friend that I met on the first day of basic training. Will was so obviously gay in the way he would try not to gawk at the men, especially when their shirts were off. I never asked him; I just befriended him and stayed close to him to make sure no one tried to bully him. He was grateful for my silence around the issue and my friendship.

But Nick must have smelled it on me. After I had made a call home on his phone and was walking out of his room, he blocked my path. He looked at me right in the eyes and asked me plainly, "Are you gay, Jamel?"

I hadn't even come out to my family at that point. Dante, my best friend who was also gay— well, more like pansexual—made jokes and innuendos all the time about my sexuality, teased me about checking out boys and called me a future cocksucker. One night when I was 16, I asked him why he did that to me and Dante said, "To make it easier for you when you come out. I'm normalizing your sexuality for you!"

He laughed, but I told him right then and there, "I don't find girls attractive."

It was true. Girls wanted to date me, especially since I played football for Allendale High, but I didn't want a girlfriend. I kissed a few girls just because, but I really wanted to kiss Felix Brown, the half-black, half-Panamanian quarterback, with light brown skin, a tight ass, and a wide chest. I used to beat off watching him shower every day after practice from just a few stalls away. It was awful how bad I had it for him. I was pissed as shit when Dante told me Felix let him suck his dick in our junior year. I stopped talking to him for a month and never told him why. It was months later when we had that conversation on the front lawn of his house, staring at the night sky.

When I told him I didn't find girls attractive, Dante kissed me on my cheek and said to me, "And that, Jamel, is normal."

That was the first time I said it out loud. I had not admitted it to anyone that I was attracted to the same sex. So, when Nick asked me plainly, I didn't know what to say. I wasn't going to lie, but I was also in the beginning of my military career. So, I did the only thing I could do.

I smirked at him and said, "D.A.D.T." Don't ask, don't tell, the law of the land in 1998.

And Nick shocked the shit out of me when he stepped closer and said quietly, "Good. Don't tell."

He put his lips on mine, his tongue in my mouth, and massaged my penis through my Army fatigues. I almost passed out. No other person had touched my genitals in 18 years, other than my mother giving me baths when I was a child. He pulled back to look me in the eyes again, as he continued to stroke me outside of my pants.

"Yeah?" he asked questioningly.

"Fuck yeah." I told him and smashed my lips on his.

I got my first blow job that night, then gave my first blow job. He told me to come back in the morning when everyone went to breakfast. I did, and I gave my first rim job and fucked someone for the first time ever. The day after that, I lost my virginity, and it was the most amazing experience of my life. It was with such patience, ease, and concern for my well-being, as well as my sexual satisfaction. By day four, we were making love like old lovers. I cried real tears when he deployed out on day five.

Three days later, I found out he fucked Will a few weeks before me, and it broke my heart. I thought we had something real and special. But Willy, who knew all the gossip, informed me that this was his

M.O., breaking in new recruits and breaking hearts in the aftermath.

After a while, I tried not to be mad at him and focused on training. By the time his tour was up, and he was back on base, it was my turn to be deployed out, so we didn't talk for almost a year. When I got back, I didn't avoid him but I wouldn't find myself alone with him anymore. I knew he felt the chill I was giving him, and I probably shouldn't have been that upset about it, but it was something about knowing the connection we had, and to find out it wasn't as real as I thought was a little devastating. He cornered me one day anyway, out in the open on the benches, but still just the two of us. We talked it out, and he told me that it was never his intention to hurt me or lead me on, but that he was a "free bird" that enjoyed dipping his beak in many pools of water. However, he didn't want to lose me as a friend, that our friendship was important to him, and because of that admission, he would never dip his beak in my pool again. We maintained our friendship after that.

Three years later, when my first love Teddy broke up with me via SKYPE, on Nick's computer right before I deployed, I was devastated again. I just sat there, staring at the blank screen. Nick was one of my best friends by then. When I finally got up to leave, Nick had blocked my path like before. He held his arms open for me, but I scoffed and pushed him out of my way. Nick pulled me back, though, and held me tight until I broke down and cried on his shoulder. It was the one and only time I cried about Teddy leaving me the way he did.

When I got myself together, he held both my shoulders and looked me in the eyes and said, "Fuck him. Say it."

I nodded. "Fuck him." He nodded back. And that was the only conversation we had about Teddy.

Eight months after that, we were deployed at the same time in Afghanistan, getting wasted and talking about nothing in the empty barracks. I don't remember who started it because we were both drunk as shit, but we ended up with me fucking him on the tile floor. We started fucking around after that, every chance we got. My tour was up before his, but when he got back on base, he told me, "I didn't fuck another person the whole three months I was there without you; that's a world record. You're doing something to me, Jay Jones. And whatever it is, I don't want it to stop. I want to keep fucking you, and only you."

It was Nick's way of being endearing, and I loved it. And I loved him. So, we quietly made it official, only Henry and Willy knew. But it also lasted all of four months before he stuck his beak into another pool, repeatedly.

The first time I found out, it was Will who had told me absentmindedly. The second time it was a rumor mill that almost got him kicked out of the Army, as DADT was still the law of the land in 2002. He was more careful after that and stopped breaking in young recruits. The third time, he confessed to me about sleeping with townees in Junction City. That was when he convinced me to have an open relationship. Ironically, my willingness to accept his free bird status and still want to be with him made him fall deeper in love with me, while all it did for me was show me what else was out there. He was not happy when I told him I wanted to end it a year later, but he let me go. We remained close friends after that.

He saw me through my breakup with D'wayne, as well as my falling in love with Connor and all the drama that came with it. He confessed to me, even before he told Henry, that he found someone who made him feel the way I had made him feel all those years ago, like he wanted to be a better man; and this time, he wasn't going to fuck it up. They met in 2013; Joshua Zimmering was the one who refused to let him fuck him right away and when he did, he demanded exclusivity or nothing at all. I didn't even know this guy, but I knew he was the perfect one for my friend. Two years after that, they got impulsively married in Baja, Mexico, and called me on SKYPE to tell me about it. They lived on different Army bases—Josh was at Fort Irwin in California, Nick at Fort Riley in Kansas—and saw each other when they could, so last year, Nick bought land in the Atlanta suburbs, and they bought a mobile home together. Nick had been in the military almost thirty years, Joshua almost twenty, and it was where they were set to retire in another five years. *And now he's gone.*

Connor met Nicky in person only once, at our wedding ceremony last year in October 2018. Technically, we got married in 2017 in a courthouse but our mothers made us do an actual ceremony last year, so we did and invited them. Josh was overseas and couldn't make it, so Nicky came alone.

Nick looked at Connor and said, "Holy shit, it's a young me!"

They both have blond hair and blue eyes, but Nick's hair was darker blond, eyes darker blue, and his Italian heritage had his skin browning in the sun. Connor's hair was light blond, eyes light blue, and his Irish heritage made him paler naturally and redder in the sun without sunscreen.

Connor said to him, "A better-looking, more improved, less dick-wandering version of you, yeah sure."

Nick laughed loudly, grabbed Connor's face, kissed him on the lips, and said to me, "I like him. Keep this motherfucker."

We had been together nine years, at that point, and technically married so he was already kept, but I said to Nick, "I promise you I will."

Somewhere in the middle of remembering Nick, Connor started humming. It was a song I didn't know, but it didn't matter. He rubbed my back and hummed a song; then he began to sing it softly, and it was beautiful. Before I knew it, my eyes were stinging, and the tears were silently falling. Falling because my best friend of twenty years was gone. Falling because Connor's singing voice that he rarely uses was so sweet. Falling because the pain was unbearable, and yet I knew despite not seeing his face, Connor was crying and bearing it with me. Falling because my heart was aching for one man and so full of love with another.

CHAPTER 3

CORPORAL BIG BOY PANTIES

Connor

Jamel carried the bag with all our clothes and I carried our uniforms as we walked over to Terminal 4 at T. F. Green Airport. The airport in Providence was so small, there were no direct flights anywhere; it just connected you to bigger airports, like Bradley in Connecticut or JFK in New York. We had a 45-minute layover in D.C., before heading to Atlanta. Jamel and I found seats in the terminal near the window, and Jamel immediately grabbed his book, *The Twelve*, which was part two of an apocalyptic trilogy. He leaned back in his seat and started reading, so I put my earbuds in, closed my eyes, and listened to my favorite podcast, *Stuff You Should Know*. I did that as an act though; I wasn't really listening. I just needed something to do since Jamel stopped talking to me. We found out on

27

Monday that Nick died; it was Thursday. Jamel hadn't spoken to me in three days.

That's not fair. We said good morning if I caught him before he left really early to head to the 10,000-square-foot home his company was remodeling. And when I stayed awake long enough, he kissed me good night when he came home. At least he hadn't stopped doing that. I'm in love with his touch and kisses, and I didn't know what I would do if he stopped being affectionate with me completely. But I felt like he was avoiding me.

And I get it; Jamel was the stronger one in this relationship. He carried my emotional shit since the beginning of our relationship, and still does, keeping his inside, so being the vulnerable one was not something he was used to. But I was trying to show him that he could lean on me too. After crying on my chest for almost an hour Monday night, until he fell asleep from exhaustion, he hadn't really spoken to me since, let alone touched me, and it was killing me.

Not that I was looking for sex, because I knew that was not what he needed. If the tables were turned and I lost one of my first loves-turned-best friend, like Afia or Jack, suddenly, all I'd want to do is fuck and forget, just so I wouldn't lose my fucking mind. In fact, that was kinda what I did after I lost Vinnie. I fucked a lot and tried to forget. Jamel was the complete opposite of me in that way, so sex was off the table and touch will be minimal, as long as he wanted to be unemotional about Nicky's death. But I felt it, the lack of physical attention he had always given me so easily for almost ten years.

I whined to Afia last night on the phone, and she let me lament for a while. Then she put me in my place as only my Lovie could.

"Connor, I love you, but Ima need you to stop being a fucking dumb ass. He lost his best friend, and he needs you to be there for him. Even if he can't verbalize what he needs, you know him; you know what he needs. So put your big boy panties on, suck up your own feelings, and give him what he needs. Space when he needs it, closeness when he wants it. Either way, just be there." My Lovie, always the voice of reason.

Also, Afia was a bit edgier when she was breastfeeding. She hadn't called me a dumb ass in a while, so either I really was being a dumb ass, or she just wanted a reason to curse, as she rarely does it since she became a mom. Her 10-month-old son, Tyriq, was sleeping in her arms while she talked to me. The girls, soon-to-be 7-year-old Takeya and 4-year-old Tenille, were already in bed.

So here I am, putting on my big boy panties and giving him space. Dying to reach over and touch his arm or his face or stick my tongue down his throat, all the things I don't do in public. But I'm craving him like flies crave a fresh pile of shit. Okay, that is a terrible analogy, but fuck! I'm okay with his verbal silence, but it is the physical silence that is hard.

The airlines did the first call for the disabled, families with small children, and military personnel and veterans. We ignored the call for military, and when they called our group number, we ignored that too. We both liked to be the last ones on the plane and the last ones off, our innate way of still protecting civilians. As the last passengers were lining up, Mel stood up first, grabbed the bag, and walked ahead of me without looking back. I watched him for a moment, then followed. I stood directly behind him and moved with the line. Then I moved closer until my groin was right on his ass. He didn't push back, but he didn't pull away either. The next step he took, I was right on his heels. I couldn't help myself. I licked my lips and kissed the nape of his neck. I heard him inhale, but that was his only reaction.

"Sorry," I mumbled. "You just smell ... tasty." It was true; he used his coconut-scented oil on his skin that morning.

"It's okay," he said quietly. But his next step forward was slightly wider. Or maybe it wasn't, and I just felt like it was.

We got on the plane and walked down to our seats. Jamel stopped in the aisle and asked, "Do you want the window?"

"Yeah, okay."

I handed him our suits, which he folded in half and put in the overhead compartment before he took the seat next to me. He immediately opened his book to read, and I stared at his side profile. He got a haircut, and it was so low he was almost bald. He had a full, low-trimmed beard growing in, with individual strains of gray here and there. I loved his beard; it made him look distinguished.

I called his name, "Mel?"

"Yeah, Con," he said without looking up.

"Look at me."

He did; he looked at me with those gray eyes of his, and I forgot what I wanted to say. Ten years later, and he was still the most beautiful man in the world to me. But he also looked hauntingly sad.

I reached over and thumbed his cheek. He blinked slowly at me twice but didn't pull away. Instead, he took my hand, moved it to his mouth, and kissed it, without breaking eye contact. I did the same, pulling Jamel's hand to me, holding his gaze, and kissed the back of his hand. Then he let his book fall in his lap and pulled me close by my neck, with both hands to nuzzle his nose with mine, kissed my nose, then kissed my lips gently. I reached up to hold his wrists and kiss him back with more passion. I couldn't believe we were kissing on a plane! We had never done that before.

He stopped first. "Thanks for coming with me," he said softly on my lips.

"It was never a question," I told his lips. "You're my heart. And you need me."

"Connor..." He sighed. Then he pulled back and nodded at me. "Thanks."

Jamel stroked my face lovingly and slid his hands off my cheek, releasing my grip from him as well. Then he picked up his book and began to read again.

I stared at him, trying to control my emotions internally, hating these mixed messages, this yo-yo he had me on. He was pushing me away, pulling me close, and then pushing me away again. But Lovie was right; I knew who he was and being vulnerable was hard for him. I calmly put my earbuds in and looked out the window.

I'll do anything for him, give him whatever he needs for however long he needs it, but these big boy panties sure do give me jock itch.

♥

We got to Atlanta around 4 p.m., rented a car, and drove to Henry's house in Buckhead. Henry was still in Johns Creek and told Mel that Tosha was expecting us. I met Tosha a few years back when we first bought the house and had a barbecue. Tosha Lane was a beautiful African-American woman with the smoothest, prettiest dark skin I have ever seen. She's a nurse by trade, but she should have been a model. Last time we saw them both was at our wedding ceremony almost a year ago.

She was waiting on the front porch for us, wringing her hands, her eyes bloodshot from crying. When Jamel walked up, she fell into his arms sobbing. He held her and stroked her hair, letting her cry. I stood back and waited.

After a few minutes, she let him go and noticed me. "Oh Connor, thank you for coming." She pulled me into a hug too.

"Of course," I told her. "I'm so sorry for your loss, Tosha."

"Thank you. Come inside. We were just getting ready to sit down for dinner."

Tosha was baking like a million pies for the reception, so the whole house smelled like a bakery and the kitchen looked like one too. Jamel introduced me to Henry's children, their two grown sons Jermaine and Omar, and their 17-year-old daughter, Katija. His oldest son, Jermaine, lived with his girlfriend in South Carolina and came home for the funeral, but Omar and Katija still lived at home. Jermaine graduated from West Point and worked for the state department in South Carolina. Omar attended Clark Atlanta University, going for his MBA, and was currently in the Marine Corps Reserves, which naturally I loved. He was in the same fraternity as Jamel's brother Donny, Phi Beta Sigma. Katija was a JROTC cadet and was starting her senior year of high school in September. This was a military family if I ever saw one.

I got us settled in the room located in the finished basement, while Jamel helped set the table for dinner. The head of the table was left empty for Henry, but Tosha sat at the other head, which was nice to see. Jamel said grace for the family, and we ate Tosha's famous honey baked chicken, collard greens, and wild rice. The conversation naturally ended up about Nick, and the family lovingly traded stories about their beloved uncle:

Uncle Nicky, who gave Jermaine the sex talk after his dad did at 14, but his was way more graphic and included props. Uncle Nicky, who went down to the police station to curse everyone out and threaten bodily harm if they didn't release his nephew Omar from jail when he got into a fight over a parking space with a white guy, but only Omar was arrested. Uncle Nicky, who impulsively rented a van the day before Obama's inauguration for the whole family to drive to DC, walked all night in the cold until they were able to begin to camp out on the lawn so they could get as close as possible and witness history together, all to Tosha's annoyance. Uncle Nicky, who showed up unannounced just a few months ago to threaten Katija's boyfriend the day of her junior prom. Uncle Nicky, who Tosha thought was a big ass nuisance for most of her life but accepted his presence because Uncle Nicky was never going to go anywhere. This was his family, and now she wished she didn't yell at him so much.

Then Katija started crying suddenly. Her big brother Jermaine, who was sitting next to her, held her in his arms as his own tears fell. Tosha started crying, and Mel reached over and held her. Omar sat stone-faced, as Marines do. I reached across the table and took his hand and held it.

He looked at me as I said, "At ease, Private. It is okay to feel." He nodded, squeezed my hand tightly and didn't let go, but then turned away again to avoid my gaze. *He's a tough one, that one.*

Later that night, we put on our PJ bottoms and tank tops and got into bed together. Jamel laid on his back and stared at the ceiling. He hadn't pulled me close in days, which was completely unlike him; my loving man loved cuddles. I hesitated, then I moved closer to him. I put my head on his shoulder, threw my arm around his torso, and kissed his skin. He lifted up his arm, so I moved into his side. Jamel kissed the top of my head, then my forehead. I looked up at him. He kissed my lips gently, then kissed me again.

We stared at each other, then I smiled and said, "Are you gonna fuck me now?"

Our running joke from the early days when he wouldn't sleep with me. He laughed his big laugh, and it was nice to hear him laugh. It made me laugh too.

When it died down, he wrapped both arms around me and asked quietly, "Are you okay?"

"I'm fine, but it's not about how I feel. I just want to make sure you're okay." He was quiet, rubbing my back.

"I never asked, but why do they call you Jay Jones, not Jamel or Mel?"

"Because in my class coming in, there were four Jones: M. Jones, R. Jones, B. Jones and me, J. Jones. When Henry introduced me to Nick the first time, he said, 'This is Jay Jones.' And the name just stuck."

He went quiet again, but I was desperate to keep him talking to me. "How is Josh?"

"I don't know. I haven't spoken to Henry since we landed. I wanted to go over there, but he asked me to stay here and take care of his family for him. We'll stay there tomorrow though, after the funeral, if that's okay. Spend Saturday with Josh, Henry, and Willy."

"Okay."

He then asked, "Do you want to make love?"

Uuuuuugh, he's killing me. I really fucking do, but nope, that's not what he needs. He would only be doing it for me. Time to put on my big boy panties again.

I sat up on his chest and looked at him. "Only if you want to, Mel. If you really want to. Because I'm here for you. If you want to make love, we can make love. If you'd rather just lay here in silence, we can do that. If you want to share your favorite memory of Nick, we can do that too. Non-sexual ones though." I gave him a look of feigned disgust, and he chuckled quietly.

"Thank you." He said it so low that I barely heard him; it was more like reading his lips.

I kissed him softly and put my head on his right pec with his lion paw tattoo, my arm across his chest, my leg over his. We were silent for a long time, and I started falling asleep. Then he started talking.

"My favorite memory of him was two days before I left the base. Henry was leaving that year too, after fourteen years of service. He decided to leave after I put my papers in because I told him that as much as I loved being in the Army, family comes first, and he agreed with me. Katija was going on three and growing up without him, and he didn't want to miss not being around for his only daughter. Anyway, Nick was pissed and stopped talking to us. Pissed at Henry because they came in together and were supposed to die in the Army together. But Henry had a family, and Nicky didn't. Pissed at me because he didn't understand why I was resigning instead of taking a long leave and coming back. But again, I had a family to think of; Nicky didn't.

"So, one night, Willy invited us out, and it turned out he and Nick planned a going-away party for us at a local bar. Even some of the C.O.s made it out. He had a cake that said, 'Fuck you both, I'll be fine.'" We both laughed out loud.

"As always, it was just the four of us closing out the bar, at a table drinking Hennessy and eating cake. He said some things to Henry about him being his brother for the last twenty years of his life, and that will never change. No matter where in the world they were, Henry's family was his family too. Some other things, making us all tear up. Then he turned to me and said, 'Jamel'—he only calls me Jamel when he wants to be serious; otherwise, it's always Jay, or Jay Jones. He said, 'Jamel, I know I'm like your mentor and shit in all kinds of ways—.' I laughed at him, as they teased me for a moment. He said, 'But listen, don't end up like me, gay and alone. Be more like Henry. Find a partner, make some babies, and have a good life. This world is shit without having someone to love. You loved me, and I fucked it up with you. Don't fuck it up with someone else. Don't be like me.'"

I held him a little tighter because I knew he needed it. He continued.

"The day I left, Nicky said to me, 'I wasn't that drunk the other day. I meant what I said. Don't be like me. This world is shit without having someone to love. So fuck around, but don't just fuck around. Fall in love.' And I promised him I would." He was quiet after that.

I asked him, "Where is Nick's family?"

Jamel told me, "His mother still lives here in Atlanta. He never knew his birth father. His first stepfather sexually abused him, and his second stepfather physically abused him. It was Henry's family that gave him refuge from it all. Henry went into the army with Nick so Nick wouldn't be alone. Nicky does have a sister that's about ten years older than him, but she lives in Kentucky with her family, and they weren't close at all. She was most likely also physically and sexually abused too and ran away when she was 16, and he didn't see her for over twenty years.. So, if you were to ask Nicky who his family is, it's Henry and those people upstairs. Then he met Josh and started a new family."

Wow. My life growing up was shit but his life sounded like holy hell. Maybe Nick was more like me than I thought. Maybe he used sex to fuck and forget too.

I told him my thoughts. "I'm just glad he found someone to love in the end too. So, his life wasn't completely shit, you know? Even if it was just for a little while." Jamel squeezed me tighter but didn't respond. The sound of his heartbeat lulled me to sleep.

♥

Sometime in the middle of the night, the distinct feeling of something warm and wet surrounding my cock woke me up. I opened my eyes into pitch darkness, forgetting for a moment where I was, as my nerves were firing electric signals throughout my body. I moaned out loud and reached out, touching Jamel's head as he sucked and licked every inch of me. I didn't know how long he had been doing it, but I was already close.

"Oh God… oh God, don't stop, baby… I'm cumming," I told him quietly.

He pulled up to where only the head was in his mouth just in time for me to squirt super thick white cum in his mouth, as he twisted his lips around my cock. It felt so good to cum; my body spasmed a few times after nothing else came out. Jamel came up over me and must have swallowed most of it, leaving just enough for me to taste the remnants on his tongue when he kissed me. I reached for him below, but suddenly he jumped up and got out of the bed.

"Mel?" I called out. He ignored me, did not turn back, and left the room.

I laid there with one hand on my head. "What. The. Fuck?" I said out loud.

I must have fallen back asleep because the next thing I knew, Mel was tapping my thigh to wake me.

"Connor. It's a quarter past seven, and the service starts at nine o'clock. Get washed and dressed. I'm going to take Tosha and Tija over to the house to help drop off the desserts, then come back around to pick up you and the boys."

"Sir, yes sir," I said groggily.

Normally that got a smile out of him but not that day. He was completely stone-faced and all business.

"Get up," he ordered, then left the room again.

I sighed. *Corporal Big Boy Panties reporting for duty.*

♥ ♥ ♥ CHAPTER 4 ♥ ♥ ♥

NICK WOULD HAVE
HATED THIS SHIT

Connor

Nick bought five acres of land, put a house on one side near the creek, and had designated burial plots for him and Joshua half a mile away on the other side at the field's end. So, the field itself became the site for the ceremony. And good thing it was a huge field because there had to be at least 300 people in attendance, 90 percent service members: almost all Army, some Air Force and Navy, and a few like myself and Omar in Marine Corp uniforms, blue spots in the sea of green. And, of course, it was already 85 degrees in the baking sun on a mid-August morning, going up to the mid-90s by noon. There was a tarp covering the first two rows for the family, which included his mother, sister, sister's kids and grandkids, and Henry's family. And apparently also us.

We dropped off the boys, and I went with Mel to park the car, despite the annoyed look he gave me when I wouldn't get out of the rental. "Get up," were the last words he spoke to me about an hour and a half ago. He was trying to push me away, keep me at a distance, but I was determined not to let him. Not today. He needed me, whether he wanted to admit it or not.

We found parking closer to the house and ended up walking back down the hill to the field in silence, with me about a half step behind him. As we got closer, suddenly Jamel's hand reached out into thin air. I immediately took it and walked in step with him.

A few people saluted him, called out, "Sergeant Jones," as we walked to the front. I could tell he commanded respect with these people, some still in service that knew Jamel and Nick well, and others no longer in service but veterans who were there at the same time they were.

Halfway down the grassy aisle, a skinny, round and pretty-faced, curly haired Hispanic man jumped in front of us.

"Jameeeeellll!" he whined, then threw himself on my husband, sobbing dramatically.

Jamel wrapped his free arm around him. "It's okay, Willy. It's going to be okay."

Oooooh, okay. Now I know why every time he mentions Will, he would say he is "obviously" gay. How did this guy make it nine years without being called for Separation under the Honor Codes during the DADT era?

Will kept both arms around my husband, despite how close I was standing and Jamel still holding my hand. "Will you sit with me?" he pleaded, with tears falling out of his brown eyes. "Josh is sitting with Nick's mother and Henry is sitting with his family, and I don't have anybody anymore now that Nick is gone. I'm all alooooooone!" Fat tears rolled down his face.

I amusingly looked at Jamel, who did not turn to me, but I knew he saw my face through his peripheral vision. We try not to act jealous toward each other, but this was a bit much.

"Specialist Will Cardona, meet Marine Corporal Connor McIntyre, my husband," Jamel said.

SPC Will Cardona's mouth opened slightly, and he flipped his long, wet, dark eyelashes to look at me. "Soooorry," he kinda sang and slid his hands off my man's torso.

I smiled and let go of Mel's hand to shake his. "Nice to meet you, Willy. I've heard a lot about you." That made him smile widely. "You're welcome to sit with us," I told him sincerely.

"Thank you!" he said, relieved.

We started walking, and Jamel grabbed my hand again. Willy started talking nonstop as we walked the rest of the aisle, reminding me of Lovie. I knew Jamel kept in contact with Will, but only on social media, so they hadn't seen each other in person in years.

As we got to the front, more people saluted and shook the Sergeant's hand. He continued to introduce me by my title and as his husband, showing me off as if he was proud to have me by his side. We finally had an opportunity to introduce each other consistently as spouses like that, so it was a new experience. While it was slightly uncomfortable, it also made me proud and happy to be his military spouse. As usual, Jamel made me feel safe, no matter where we were. If people were shocked by his sexuality, they surely did hide it well. But there were other military service men and women and veterans with their same-sex partners, so I guess the military sure had changed since I left in December 2006. *Simon would be proud to see this. So would Vinnie.*

Henry came over to us. The first thing we both noticed was the fatigue all on his face. He walked up to us, and Jamel let my hand go to hold out his arms and give his brother-in-arms a hug. They held each other tightly and for a long time.

Jamel pulled back first and said, "You look tired, Henry." He touched his face.

"I haven't slept in a week. This is … a lot. A lot."

"I know," said Jamel. "But I'm here now. Do you need me to stay longer than Sunday?"

"I don't know man… I don't … I don't know."

"Okay. Whatever you need. Just say the word. I'll do what you need me to do."

"You're already doing it. Taking care of my family. So, thanks, Jay." Henry turned to me. "Thanks for coming too, Connor." He gave me a tight hug that I too returned.

"Of course. Nick was like family to Mel, so he's family to me too."

He patted my back. "C'mon, your seat is right behind us next to Tosha. I'll take you there; then Mel, follow me. Josh and the boys are waiting by the hearse. We're bringing him in."

Henry turned to start walking us under the covering when Willy whined, "What about meeee? You aren't gonna thank me for coming tooooo?"

Holy fucking hell, I thought, as Henry turned around and gave Willy the look that replicated my thoughts. He snapped at him quietly, his lips barely moving. "Will, I will beat the *shit* out of you in front of everyone here if you don't stop. This. Shit. I'm not taking care of you and Josh, so grow the *fuck* up."

Staff Sergeant Lane at your service. Willy immediately got himself together, stood up straighter, and walked with us without another word.

I sat between Tosha and Henry's seventy-year-old mother. I had heard that she was more of a mother to Nick than his own mother, who was quietly crying in her tissue. She hadn't laid eyes on her son in decades. I looked around at all the pomp and circumstance before the service began. I had actually never been to a military funeral; I was still in Iraq when they flew Vinnie's body home to his family and visited his grave months later. Everyone that was still part of my original unit is still alive, thank God for that. Taylor, Simon—who was the only female of our unit before he transitioned—Benjin, and Joe. So, all of this was new to me.

It carried on like a normal funeral at first. At exactly 900 hours, Josh, Henry, Jamel, Will, Jermaine, and Omar carried the flag-draped casket in, as we all stood up in respect. Josh technically should have been sitting with us, but apparently, he told them he was going to carry his husband's body and anyone that tried to stop him was getting shot in the neck. So, Henry gave in and had the honor guard stand down for the first part. It was so silent you could hear a pin drop, as the six of them walked in unison, stone-faced, carrying the body of the friend, brother, uncle, and husband that they loved the most.

They put the casket on the metal planks that would later lower Nicholas Fedella into the ground, then sat in the front row in the same order: Josh next to his mother-in-law, then Henry, Jamel, Willy, Jermaine, and Omar. My seat was directly behind Jamel's. I sat there watching and tried not to think about Vinnie. I was consciously trying not to rub the tattoo on my wrist with his initials, so I kept both hands on my thighs. I couldn't help it; my mind kept wandering back to if this was what Vinnie's funeral looked like. *Was it outside or in a church? Did this many people love him enough to come? Probably not, he was only 21 years old when he died. Vinnie wanted to have a military career too. Is this what his funeral would have looked like if he didn't die so young?*

Nick was not a religious guy, but his mother insisted on a Catholic priest to perform the service and the last rites. He started with a prayer, said a few words, and a Bible verse. Then it was Josh's turn to speak. As he walked to the podium, it was my first time getting a real glimpse of him. Joshua was just a few years older than me, maybe 37. He was a lot shorter than Nick, who was about the same height as Jamel and Henry at 6'2". Josh had a full head of dark brown hair, dark brown eyes, and full pink lips. He was handsome, but he also looked tired. Defeated. He took off his hat to speak and put it on the podium, and underneath it, he had a yamaka on.

Josh grabbed both sides of the podium, inhaled and exhaled deeply, looked up, and said, "Nick would have hated this shit." Then he started laughing.

"Shit," Jamel said quietly. But neither he nor Henry moved.

Josh continued. "I mean, really. We all know that Nicky took his job seriously, which was his life by the way. He gave his fucking life to the Army, just like he wanted." He turned to the casket and said, "Just like you wanted, honey. Happy?" He slammed both his hands on the podium loudly and a few people jumped, including me. It reminded me of when my father would slam his fists on the table when he was really upset. Someone's ass whipping was sure to follow. Usually mine.

Josh turned back to the crowd. "He was all about formality and honor and precision and merit and all of that in his job. But for his funeral? Fuck no. Nicky would have wanted a fucking party, with male strip-pers in flag-covered G-strings dancing on straight, male C.O.s, making them pretty fucking uncomfort-able. Nicky would have wanted a cake that said on it, 'Yooooo shit!'"

That was his catch phrase. A lot of people laughed out loud. I laughed too. Henry and Jamel did not laugh.

"Nicky would have wanted fucking chickens run-ning around laying eggs under our feet. Nicky would have wanted us singing and dancing and belting out his favorite songs, anything Jimi Hendrix or Green Day or Linkin Park or fucking Led Zeppelin. Nicky would have wanted me to take a poll: How many of yooooou" he pointed at the crowd, "—fucked my husband before he actually became my husband. Hmmm ....probably a good 67 percent of you. Ha!" Josh laughed hysterically.

There were some oooohs and scattered laughter, someone laughed a really loud belly laugh behind us. I couldn't help but chuckle too. I heard Henry say quietly, "Fuck."

Then Josh abruptly got himself together. "But it's Nicky's fault that this isn't the funeral he wanted. Because Nicky died too soon. He's not here to tell us what he wanted." He sighed and looked down; it got quiet again. "So, we'll go on with tradition because Nicky respected tradition. He loved the Army so much. It gave him purpose and fulfillment after the fucked-up childhood he had."

Yikes. I could see his mother tense up, no longer crying but scowling. Josh took no notice.

"He gave his blood, sweat, and tears to it, because he believed in its core values and missions and everything this country stands for. Freedom. Freedom to worship, or not worship, who they wanted and the way they wanted to worship. Freedom to love who the fuck they wanted to love. Fuck who the fuck they wanted. Marry who the fuck ... they wanted..." He stood there nodding for a while.

"I'm supposed to get up here and tell you about the wonderful accolades of Master Sergeant Nicholas Fedella, who spent years in active service to this great nation. So let me do that. Let me tell you about the countless, young, gay military men and women that my husband counseled and modeled and mentored in an institution that didn't give a shit about them and, in some ways, still doesn't. You should know about the people he met in Kandahar that he listened to their complaints and concerns about how they were treated by military folks that were supposed to be protecting them, and how he took it back to his C.O.s and made real policy changes in training.

"And by far his biggest accomplishment was how he died, shielding a 6-year-old boy that was separated from his mother in the blast. With his entire fucking body. For twelve hours, until they dug them out. Because that was how Nick lived his life: helping others, leading others, protecting others. And that's how he died, leading people out of the rubble by yelling out orders, protecting this kid, helping him stay alive long enough so that they could be found. That was my Nicky. He was deeply devoted to the Army. And I was deeply devoted to him. I've never been prouder to be an American, a soldier, and a husband than I am right now.

"My husband cared about this country. And he cared about people. And now he's gone. So… that's that." Josh looked over at Henry and said, "Now his brother Henry Lane is going to give a real traditional eulogy for Master Sergeant Nicholas Fedella. But this speech right here, this was for my Nicky."

He kissed his two fingers and raised them toward the casket, then walked back to his seat. It dawned on me that Josh had no family there. It was Nick's family, Henry's family, and their military family, but no one was there from Josh's side, who lost his husband and best friend. Which meant Nick was his only family. *Which means he's definitely going to try to off himself.* I reminded myself to tell Mel again.

As Josh was walking toward us, I heard Jamel say quietly to Henry, "You're doing a eulogy too?"

"Guess I fucking am now," Henry said back quietly. "You too. Get ready to get your ass up there, Jay Jones." He stood up and hugged Josh before he sat down, then walked over to the podium. Henry stood up straight and took a moment, probably trying to figure out what to say. Then he began.

"Master Sergeant Nicholas Joseph Fedella was born May 22, 1974, in Atlanta, Georgia. He is survived by his husband, Sergeant First Class Joshua Zimmering; his mother Adelaide Fedella; his sister Monica Hyland and her children and grandchildren; me, his brother, Staff Sergeant Henry Lane; his sister-in-law, Latosha Lane; his nephews Jermaine Lane, Omar Lane, and his niece Katija Lane; as well as countless friends, soldiers, and veterans that loved him. He was an upstanding member of his community and the Armed Forces. His medals of honor include the Army Achievement Medal, Army Superior Unit Award, Army Meritorious Unit Commendation, Distinguished Service Medal, and just recently bestowed postmortem, the Soldier's Medal. He dedicated his life in service to this great country.

"Nicholas's life was not always easy, and he didn't have a lot of people he could rely on, but he had me. He was my best friend and my brother from the moment we met in kindergarten, sitting next to each other and sharing Play-Doh. He had a troubled beginning, but at 15-years-old he told me that he wanted to go into the Army. He said, 'Henry, you are going to have choices when you graduate, but I am not. It's either the Army,

McDonald's, or death for me. And I'm not working at no fucking McDonald's.'" We laughed at that.

"I said, 'Nicky, we promised we were going to do everything together. So, if you're going, I'm going too.' So, in September 1992, one day after my eighteenth birthday, we joined the Army together and vowed to dedicate our lives in service of our great nation. Somewhere along the way, I met my beautiful wife Tosha, an Army Reserves nurse, and had three beautiful children. After fourteen years of serving side by side, I told him I was retiring. He was upset with me because we promised that we would do everything together. But I told him, 'Nick, you've always been a part of my family. So whatever family I have is yours too.' I meant that, and he knew I did. And he became the best uncle and a second father to my children, and an annoying big brother to my wife. He devoted his life and time to his family, which also happened to be mine."

Tosha started silently crying, and I took her hand in mine. She squeezed it and smiled at me, grateful, as we listened to Henry's made-up and perfect eulogy.

"Being a proud, gay man in active military service was not easy for him at all, as many of you here have experienced. But Nick was never afraid to be who he was, so if you did ask him, he would have told you. And thankfully, no one did before 2011." A few people chuckled. "He told me that the day Don't Ask Don't Tell was repealed, he walked into his C.O.'s office and said, 'In case you didn't know, I'm gay.' And his C.O. said, 'Jesus Christ, Nicky, if you think the whole fucking base didn't know by the way you ran through these cadets in your first couple of years, then you're the stupidest gay whore I've ever met.'"

That got a big laugh, applause, and a couple of hooting from the crowd. Even Jamel smiled a bit. When it died down, Henry continued.

"Nicholas stood up to all kinds of discrimination, whether it be racism, homophobia, even Islamophobia, in the military and even in his personal life. He advocated for those that needed a voice. But when Nick met Sergeant First Class Joshua Zimmering, he told me that he finally found it, that one thing in his life that was just for him. He had been living his entire life in service of everyone else, but Josh gave him a reason to care about his own well-being, his own happiness. Josh made Nicky feel alive and loved. From the moment they met, he knew that Josh was the one for him. Maybe everyone else was surprised by their swift wedding, but I was not. I knew that once he made the decision to settle down, he would just do it. And Nicholas loved Joshua. Just like every other decision he was serious about, he dedicated his life to his husband. He loved Josh with all his heart, mind, soul, and spirit, and will continue to do so from beyond the grave.

"Nicky will be missed, tremendously." Henry paused for a long moment and seemed frozen. I thought he was going to break down, but then continued.

"Thank you all for coming out to honor the life of this great man. Thank you for dedicating your time, your effort, and your sweat, literally." That got a laugh out of people. "Thank you for coming to celebrate the life of Master Sergeant Nicholas Joseph Fedella, our Nicky." Henry turned and saluted the casket. He turned back and said, "And now a few words from Sergeant Jamel Jones." He walked back over to hug Josh again and sat in his seat.

Jamel sat there and, for a moment, no one knew if he was going to get up. I reached over and touched the back of his neck with my fingertips, then pulled back. I just wanted him to know I was there for him. He gasped a little, like he did when I kissed the back of his neck the day before. It seemed to be enough, because he got up without looking back at me and walked to the podium. He pulled out his phone and cleared his throat. Then he read a familiar and famous poem, *Do Not Go Gentle Into That Good Night.*

Afterward, Jamel placed his phone on the podium and looked up at everyone. "Nick recited this poem to me from memory when I was 18-years-old, a couple of days before one of his deployments. He told me that he first heard it when he was in the eighth grade, and it had such a profound impression on him that he memorized it. To him, it meant despite what he had been through in his life, he will continue to fight for his own mental and emotional freedom from sadness and despair; to reclaim what was taken from him; to live his life to the fullest with no regrets; to rage against the dying of the light. If we have learned anything from Nicky's life, it is to fight and to rage against the atrocities and trauma and sorrow of this life, reclaiming all the good that this life has to offer. Because there is so much good once you find it. Henry found it. I found it. And Nicky eventually found it too, in Josh. And I'm so glad he did, because he deserved all the love and happiness that this world could ever give him."

Jamel paused, and I could see the emotion on his face. But his voice was steady when he began again. "I'm going to miss my best friend, my mentor, my brother. He gave so much of himself to others, willingly and unequivocally, and always with a smile on his face. He always made everyone around him happy. Joshua is right; Nick would have hated how formal this service is. So, let's make sure we have some fun later on in his honor, the way he would have wanted. Let's all continue to live our lives fully, with no regrets. Let's continue to rage against the dying of the light. For our Nicky."

Jamel also turned and saluted the casket, then walked over. Josh stood up so they could hug, then they both sat down.

Willy asked quietly, "Is it my turn to speak?"

Jamel, Henry, and Josh together said quietly but firmly, "NO."

I bit my bottom lip and resisted the urge to laugh.

♥ ♥ ♥ CHAPTER 5 ♥ ♥ ♥

WHAT'S GOING ON, JOSH?

Jamel

The rest of the funeral went on as normal. The firing party fired the three-rifle volleys. The bugler sounded *Taps*. The six standby honor guards folded and presented the flag to Josh. The priest gave the homily and prayer. Then it was over. We stood up and greeted Nick's mother and sisters, as Josh walked over and watched the casket get lowered, then the dirt put on it. Guests started walking back up the hill to the house, including Tosha and Katija, but the men waited for Josh who stood there for a long time, looking at the dirt. Eventually, he walked over to where we stood.

"Thank you both for saving me out there," he said to Henry and me. After he hugged me again, he looked at Connor in his Marine's uniform and said, "Yooo shit, who let the guy from the women's department in here!?"

Connor smiled at the friendly insult and reached his hand out for a shake. "It's nice to meet you in person, Josh, although in terrible circumstances. I'm so, so sorry for your loss."

Josh slapped his hand away. "Gah! Your husband fucked my husband so we're family!"

Connor's eyes went wide but chuckled, as Josh pulled him into a hug and he hugged him back. Henry and I laughed out loud. Omar asked all confused, "Wait, whaaaat?" Jermaine snickered.

Henry shook his head. "Don't even ask. Just know that Jamel was part of your Uncle Nick's 'mentoring program' when he was still a teen." Henry put "mentoring program" into air quotes, making us all laugh.

"Yeah, exactly what were you doing when he recited that poem, Uncle Jay?" Jermaine asked me amusingly. They all laughed again as I rolled my eyes.

"Alright, alright, let it go." I looked at Connor, who winked at me, making me smile. We started walking back up together toward the house.

"So, what is the plan for tonight?" I asked them. "Going out, getting drunk in Nick's honor?"

"Male strip club, aaaye?" Willy asked.

We all groaned, and Henry said, "Fuck no."

"Actually, y'all can go out," Josh said. "Henry, you need to go do something other than babysit me. I'm going to clean up the house after everything is done and then go to bed, try to get some sleep now that it's all over."

I watched Connor take a small step behind Josh, look at me, and shake his head very slightly.

Henry asked, "Are you sure, Josh? Because I'm worried about you."

"I'm fine. You already took away all the guns, so it's not like I can shoot my brains out." He laughed loudly, but none of us laughed.

"Henry, why don't you go home with your family and get some rest?" I suggested. "Connor and I will stay."

"No, no, you go with Henry; you don't have to stay," Josh insisted.

"We want to," I told him. "I would love to spend some time with you, Josh. Connor too."

"Only if he takes off that fucking suit!" Josh said, looking my husband up and down. "And you too, Omar; what the fuck? Both of you need your heads examined. Fucking Marines." He scoffed. "Only then will you two be allowed to stay." Omar looked affronted, not used to the Army-Marine Corp banter, but Connor smiled at him.

"And Willy!" my flamboyant friend cried. "I'm not liking how you all are forgetting about me. Nicky would never forget about me." He waved his finger and neck at us.

"Will—" Henry started, and I knew it was going to be a barrage of cursing and threats of bodily harm. I tapped Henry's shoulder to stop him.

"We aren't forgetting about you, Willy. I just assumed it was a given that you were staying," I said.

"Well … yes … okay," Will said happily. I saw Connor roll his eyes.

As we made it closer to the house, Connor stepped closer to me and said quietly, "Make sure Henry really did take the guns. That crack about blowing his brains out? He's not okay."

I shook my head and said quietly back to him, "If that speech earlier was any indication, then you're right; he is not okay, not at all."

"Hey." Connor stopped walking and pulled my arm for me to stop walking too. "How are you doing, Sergeant?"

The concern for me etched all on his face made me want to fall into his arms. *But I can't right now. I have to be strong for everyone else: Josh, Henry, Henry's family, Willy definitely, and also him. I know this isn't easy for Connor. I know he is thinking of Vinnie, his life and his death. I'm worried about his emotional well-being too. He uses sex and alcohol to avoid being emotional, and we haven't had sex all week, so if he got drunk tonight, I would understand and wouldn't be upset at all. In fact, I might welcome it, just so he could stop looking at me like I'm a wounded animal. Like he is doing right now.*

I kept my face straight and said simply, "I'm fine."

I tried to turn back around but he gripped my arm tighter. "Mel—"

"I said I'm fine, Connor. What do you want from me?" I spoke harsher than what I intended. He looked hurt, and it made me soften my face.

"I don't want anything from you, Jamel," said Connor. "I just want you to know that I'm here for you. Whatever you need. Whenever you need it."

God, I love him so much. I moved closer and kissed his cheek. "Thank you for earlier."

I got stuck in my head right after Henry's eulogy. *What could I possibly say that would be meaningful enough to honor Nick?* Connor's soft touch did what it always does, rejuvenated and reminded me that I'm not alone and that everything was going to be okay.

He touched my face and said, "Of course. I'm right here. You can lean on me. Okay, baby?"

"Okay." I took his hand from my face and kissed it, then I held his hand the rest of the way up the hill to the house.

❤

The funeral reception ended up on the lawn in front of the house. Most people only went inside to grab a plate and bring it back outside. At least it was shaded there. This part of the land was surrounded by large oak trees, which provided a cool breeze from the hot sun. Monica and Tosha outdid themselves making the food, and all their children served and made sure there was more than enough food to go around. An Atlanta gay bar that Nick frequented donated the drinks and booze, so there was plenty of that too.

I drank a little bit of bourbon, but I did not see Connor drink once, not even tequila, which was his thing. I did see him stay close to Willy for some reason. I could tell he didn't exactly like him, so I wondered about that. And I get it; Willy is hard to swallow sometimes, especially when he is emotional and dramatic, which he was that day. But Connor seemed to keep him occupied and out of the way of Henry and me, which was a good thing.

The funeral was over by 10:30 a.m., so by noon, it had pretty much thinned out from the hundreds of attendees to maybe a good fifty people, including all of us. That's when Josh, who changed into a heather gray t-shirt that had the American flag in rainbow colors on it and a pair of khakis, pulled out a huge speaker and started playing music. The chords of "American Idiot" by Green Day started, and the guys went crazy, running into the center of the lawn jumping around and singing badly. Because what they were doing could not be considered dancing at all, only jumping around.

I was standing on the porch, with a drink in my hand, when Connor and Will came out of the house with the biggest smiles on their faces.

"Oh my gawwwwwd!" Willy exclaimed. He ran and joined them.

I chuckled and took a sip of my drink. Connor moved closer to me and was nodding his head with the beat. I nudged him and said, "You know you want to join them. Take off the jacket first though."

I winked at him. He shoved me playfully, then took off his Marines coat to hand to me and ran to jump around with the other guys.

By the time the next song came on, Henry had come out of the house with Jermaine. "What the fuck is this?"

"'Holiday' by Green Day," I answered.

Henry turned to look at me. "I meant, what the fuck are they doing, not what song this is." He raised his eyebrow at me.

"Oh." I started laughing. "My husband is white."

"Obviously," said Henry amusingly. I shrugged and laughed again.

"Your husband is in the middle of them." Jermaine pointed. I nodded and smiled. Connor was indeed jumping around, belting out the song with the rest of them.

We watched, then Jermaine decided. "I'm getting in there." He started walking toward the impromptu party.

"I'm taking away your black card," Henry said jokingly.

Jermaine shrugged. "If Uncle Nicky was here, he'd be in the middle of them too."

That made Henry smile and his son smiled back at him. He joined the jumping around.

I sat on the steps of the mobile home, and Henry sat with me. We watched song after song play as the men got louder and wilder. Some of the guys took off their shirts. It turned into some kind of alternative rock concert mosh pit, with them trying to hoist each other up. I kept my eyes on Connor, in his white t-shirt and Charlie-blue Marines pants, singing the "Oh oh oh oh ohs" to Coldplay's "Viva La Vida" nice and loud with everyone else. I also saw Willy touch his ass a few times, making me chuckle. *He does have a perfectly round ass.*

"What?" Henry asked.

"Nothing. Just ... them." I pointed at the crowd of no less than twenty men, including both of Henry's sons now. I watched Josh, with his eyes closed and swaying to the beat, while everyone else was moving faster. I turned to Henry seriously.

"Connor thinks Josh is going to try to kill himself."

He sighed. "It crossed my mind, which is why I took all the guns out of the house and put them in my car.

But I told Josh he's my family too. He's Uncle Josh to my kids, and that we need him too."

"Still. Keep an eye on him."

Henry sighed again. "Don't worry, it won't happen. If I have to move him into my basement to keep an eye on him, I will and he knows it."

"Okay."

Henry was quiet for a while, then said, "I can't believe he's gone, man. We've prepared ourselves for this day, you know. We've had several conversations of him dying before me, especially since he was still active. Even if he wasn't doing combat, he was still there, you know? He always knew he was going to go before me." Henry sniffed. "He started ending all our conversations with 'I love you, brother. Never forget that.' That's the last thing he said to me." He sniffed again, and I knew he was holding back tears. "This shit hurts, man." He blew out air, then pinched the corners of his eyes.

I reached over and touched his shoulder, squeezing it tightly. He pulled me into a hug, and I gave him one. In contrast to our heartfelt moment, the guys were screaming a Fall Out Boy song at the top of their lungs, singing about it being a goddamn arms race. I started laughing, then Henry did too. He let me go and wiped his face.

"This is some real white people shit happening. I'm out." I laughed again, as he gave me a dap and stood up. "I'm going to take a nap, then come back later tonight. You got Josh, right?"

"Yeah, we got him."

He nodded. "I love you, brother."

"I love you too, brother," I told him back.

He touched my shoulder, then went to find his wife while I watched my husband, singing and dancing with joy all over his face.

❤

We helped clean up the yard of paper plates and cups, empty beer bottles and cans. There was a lot of food left over so Josh went inside to pack it up while we were outside. Connor came back from the creek with a bag of garbage and looked around.

"Where's Josh?"

"He went inside to clean up."

Connor turned slowly to the house, dropped the bag, and then broke out into a run. By the time I got inside the house, they were arguing in front of the kitchen sink.

Josh saw me and said, "Call your fucking boyfriend off, will ya?"

"Give it to me!" Connor yelled at him.

"Give you WHAT!?" Josh yelled back.

"Okay, you want to play this game?" Connor tried to go around him, but Josh pushed him back forcefully. Connor pushed him again.

"What the FUCK?" Josh yelled at him and pushed him again.

"GIVE IT TO ME!" Connor screamed.

Connor tried to go around him again, but I grabbed his arm. He looked at me angrily and yelled, "What the FUCK, JAMEL!?"

Willy came through the door and asked, confused, "What's … going … on?"

Connor yanked his arm from me and turned to Josh. "What's going on, Josh?" he asked him, angrily. "Tell everyone what's going on with you."

Josh laughed nervously. "Nothing, man. Just … stop. Nothing is going on."

Connor walked slowly over to him, and they stood face to face. Well, forehead to lips since Connor was way taller. Then Connor reached behind him into the sink's garbage disposal and pulled out a small steak knife. He held it up to his face and asked again, "What's going on, Josh?"

Josh gave him a dirty look. "It's a fucking steak knife. For steak. It belongs in the sink." He walked around Connor.

My husband turned around and pleaded, "Don't do it, Josh." Josh turned around and looked at him. "Don't," Connor said again.

Josh ran up on Connor quickly, but Connor did not flinch. He looked up in his face and spatted, "Fuck you, Blue Boy. You don't know shit about me, or my life, or what I'm thinking. Stay the fuck out of my way or I will kill you."

They glared at each other. I was about to intervene, but then Josh turned around and left the house.

I started, "Connor—"

He cut me off. "He's gonna kill himself, Jamel. Either we save his life, or we don't."

He walked past me and Will and left the house as well.

CHAPTER 6

WE'RE HAVING A FAMILY MEETING

Jamel

I kept Josh in my line of sight after that. I believed, like Connor, that Josh would try to do it, but other than watching him at all times, there was nothing I could do. We needed to wait and see if he actually did try something, and then we would stop him. And if that happened, we would get him help. When I told the plan to Connor, he scoffed at me and walked away. And I could tell all this talk of suicide was scaring Willy. His mother was bipolar and ended up killing herself impulsively during one of her manic episodes when he was 11 years old, so this was triggering for him. I figured I needed to keep an eye on him too, making sure he didn't do anything stupid either.

This was turning out to be a bigger shit show than I imagined, and I was counting the minutes until Henry got back, someone more levelheaded like me.

Henry came back to the house around 9 p.m. with our bag. I told him what happened in the kitchen. He shook his head in disbelief. "Okay, I know what Connor is saying has some truth in it. But following him around like he's on suicide watch? Josh isn't the suicidal type. Don't you think he's overreacting just a little?"

I shook my head. "No. Connor is reacting impulsively, yes, but he's not overreacting. Remember what he does for a living. He knows what he's talking about. I don't see Josh having an actual plan just yet, but I believe that if he's hurting enough, he will try it. I just don't know what to do about it."

"Okay. Go get Connor and let's have a sit-down. I'll go get Josh. Where is Will?"

"In the room with Josh."

"Okay. Let me clear off the table, and then I'll go get them."

I went to the room where I was staying with Connor and found him lying on the bed, face up, in the dark. He looked over at me when the door opened, then turned away. I put our bag on the floor, turned on the light, and sat at the end of the bed.

"Connor—"

"Where's Josh?" he interjected. I noticed he was rubbing his wrist tattoo of Vinnie's initials on his right wrist with his left thumb.

"He's in his room. Willy is with him." He didn't say anything else, so I started again. "I'm sorry if you feel like I'm not taking you seriously. I am. I just think there is a better way to go about it than babysitting and yelling at him. Henry is calling a sit-down so we can talk it through with him. Probably like an intervention.

I want you to be there." He didn't respond so I kept going, watching him continue to rub his wrist. "Connor, you're the most empathetic person I know, and you understand more than I or Henry ever could in this situation. If there is anyone that can talk him off the ledge, it's you. Just … don't be so emotional about it—"

He snapped his head toward me and sat up so quickly that I knew I fucked up.

"Which is it, Mel?" Connor said coldly. "You want me to be empathetic or unemotional? Because I can't fucking do both. But if you and Henry don't start getting emotional about this, Josh is going to die. On our watch. You want that blood on your hands?"

"We won't let that happen. We'll—"

But I was cut off by Henry yelling loudly, "WHAT THE ACTUAL FUCK!"

We both jumped up and ran to the bedroom to find Willy on his knees against the wall and Josh in the middle of face-fucking him, letting out one last groan. Apparently, he just finished. *Great.*

"Jesus fucking Christ." Connor scoffed and walked away.

"I'm sorry, I'm sorry!" Willy said from the floor, embarrassed and looking guilty.

Josh, on the other hand, looked nonplussed. He casually zipped back up his khakis and went to lie on the bed. "That's okay; I already came. It's done now," he said.

I visualized myself choking the shit out of Josh for taking advantage of my friend. Instead, I walked over and pulled Willy up by his arm.

Henry said quietly, "Get up, Joshua. We're having a family meeting."

"My family is dead," Josh said plainly.

"No, your husband is dead. Your brothers are right here. And your older brother Henry just told you to get the fuck up, go sit at the table, and let's have a talk. Got it?"

I pulled Willy from the room a bit more forcefully than I intended. Connor was in the hallway, standing against the wall with one foot on it. I pushed Willy toward him.

"Willy, what the fuck are you doing!?" I scolded quietly.

"I'm sorry!" Willy whispered. "We were just talking, and then he was talking about the last time they had sex was a while ago and how he hadn't gotten off in a while, and what would really make him feel better is a blow job, and how Nicky would be okay with it because he's gone now and how I could—"

"Shu ... ugh ... fut ... hmm." I couldn't get out sensible words, so I held out my hand near his face to make him stop talking. "Willy—"

"Will." Connor cut me off, turned around, and faced him. He started talking to Willy like he was a small child. "Joshua is hurting badly. He's on the verge of offing himself any minute now. Him wanting you to blow him was him getting one last orgasm before he does it. You just gave him the last piece of the puzzle. So now he's really ready to die."

Will looked horrified. I resisted the urge to chastise my husband in front of someone else as he continued, putting both his hands on Willy's shoulders.

"But here's the good news: now that it's all out there, we can fix it. You can help fix it, Willy. You are in a unique position to help because you are the one that Josh will let be close to him right now. So be close to him. Don't leave his side all night. Okay?"

Willy nodded profusely. "C'mere," Connor said and pulled him close for a hug.

Henry and Josh came out of the room. We moved aside as they passed us to go into the dining table. Connor nodded at Willy, who nodded back and followed next. As he started walking behind Willy, I grabbed Connor's arm gently. He yanked it from me roughly.

"How's that for unemotional?" Connor said to me nastily.

He stared at me, his blue eyes blazing in anger, his jaw tight. I was at a loss for words, so I just stared back at him. It was rare that I couldn't read him and when it happens, it unsettles me, like now. He wasn't backing down and I probably should have, but my pride got in the way. I wasn't angry at him, but I also didn't understand what he was trying to prove.

We stared at each other for what felt like hours until Henry called out, "The fuck are you doing, Jay? Connor? Get over here."

Connor turned away first and started walking out of the hallway. I stood there, closed my eyes, and inhaled, then exhaled slowly. Then I walked over to the table and sat down with them.

Henry started. "Joshua. We love you. You know that right? We're all hurting from Nicky's passing. But we're going to get through this, together, as a family. You believe that right?"

Josh had a mild expression of amusement. "Yeah, I know," he responded casually.

"Okay, but I really need you to hear me," said Henry. "Things are going to get rough; that's just a given. I lost my brother, but I can't imagine what you are going through. I don't know what I would do if I lost Tosha; maybe I would be thinking crazy stuff like hurting myself too. But I do know that I would have to keep going for my family. I couldn't fall apart. I couldn't be reckless and impulsive. So, all I'm asking is that you don't do anything impulsive and rash. Can you try to resist your urges to be impulsive, and talk to us if you feel like you can't?"

"Well," said Josh, still talking in that casual voice, like we were discussing paint colors. "I did resist the urge to burn the house down earlier. So yeah, I mean, I think I can resist being impulsive. In fact, I'm probably the clearest headed I've been in a long time."

Uh-oh. Henry didn't catch it, but I did, and I know Connor did too. This is not good at all.

"Well, we're here for you," Henry said. "All of us here love you and are here for you."

"Even me," Willy piped up. "I'm here for you—"

"Yes, we know how you're here for him, Willy," Henry snapped at him. "Thanks for that."

"That's not what I mean, *puta*!" Willy said angrily.

Henry looked at him like he wanted to throttle him. I intervened. "We're all here for you, Josh. In a loving, brotherly way, including Willy. You don't need to take advantage of anyone here to prove that."

Josh looked at me amused. "Take advantage of who? Willy?" He scoffed. "I don't have to manipulate Willy for sex; he gives it to me willingly like he always has."

What the fuck?

"What the fuck does that mean?" Henry asked angrily, looking at Willy again.

Fuck a canary, Willy looked like he just swallowed a whole cat as everyone looked at him, with his wide eyes and closed mouth.

"It means," Josh answered for him, "that Willy has pretty much been part of my relationship with Nick since the beginning." He looked around at our shocked faces. "Yeah, your brother kept that part from you because he didn't want the disapproving looks that you're giving me now. The three of us were always doing things together and fucking around."

"Jesus fucking Christ," I said, sounding like Connor. I glanced over at him, and he was quietly watching Josh. Henry was at a loss of words at this new revelation, while Willy looked relieved that it was all out in the open.

Okay, time to take control of this circus. Because apparently, these are my monkeys.

"Okay, Josh, the point is we all want what is best for you, including your mental and emotional health. We want you to talk to us if you're feeling depressed or angry or begin to have suicidal thoughts. And then maybe also talk to a grief counselor at some point. We just don't want you to feel like you're alone because you aren't. We're right here for you. And like Henry said, we're going to get through this. Together."

He looked at me for a moment. Then he said, "He loved you, you know. He said you were the first person he ever really loved."

Shit. I can't feel this right now. "Yes, he loved me, and I loved him. A very, very long time ago. But in the end, he loved you more than anything and he told me that so many times."

"Oh, I know he was in love with me. But there were times I felt like I was competing with you. The great Sergeant Jamel Jones. You were perfect in his eyes: handsome, sexy, intelligent, self- assured, brave. He told me he never felt worthy of you as a partner, so he fucked it up; it was one of his biggest regrets."

"And let me tell you what he told me about you," I said, *because I'm not doing this with him.* "He told me he met this sexy, smart, cool little Jewish boy that 'won't let me fuck him. And now I gotta make him mine.'" Josh smiled at that.

"He talked with me for an hour about you. I teased him that finally he had met his match, someone he couldn't manipulate into a fuck and toss away later. A couple of months after that, I hadn't heard from him for a while so I called him. He said y'all had been spending a lot of time together, and that he found someone that made him feel loved and appreciated for who he was and not what he could do for them. He was falling in love with you and afraid he was going to fuck it up like he did with me. I told him to take it one day at a time.

"When Nick starts thinking of the future, he gets scared and does something stupid. So, I told him, 'Instead, every day, just think about what you are going to do tomorrow with Josh.' He loved you so much and wanted to be a better man for you. And he was. You changed him and made him happy."

"Well, I didn't intimidate him the way you did," he said. "So, it was easier with me to love me, to try to be faithful to me. But I knew if he cheated on you, it was only a matter of time before he fucked it up with me. So, I told him to pick one other person, just one. If you weren't with the leatherneck, he would have picked you. So, instead, he picked Willy. Will was a part of our relationship, but so were you in some way. You would talk on the phone and laugh, talking shit about your husbands together. Outside of Henry, it was the most genuine friendship he's ever had. But I don't think he ever really stopped loving you in that way."

Okay, this conversation was getting way off topic. "And so what if he didn't, Josh? You never really stop loving your first love anyway. It just changes into a different kind of love. But what you had with Nick was real, honest, and devoted love. You understood him better than I ever could in the matters of the heart. Even the fact that you knew him enough to know he would never stop being a free bird. You gave him what he needed, and that's why he loved you."

Josh laughed. "Free bird. I called him my nicator."

"What's a nicator?"

"It's a type of bird found in East Africa," Connor said. I looked at him. *How the hell did he know that?*

"That's right, Blue Boy," Josh said. "How do you know?"

Connor shrugged. "My friend Joe took up bird-watching and studies birds now, specifically birds in Africa."

He didn't look at me as he spoke, and I knew he wouldn't speak to me again for the rest of the night. *Probably for the rest of the trip.* I sighed internally. *I will repair that relationship later, but first...*

"Josh," I started again. "We all loved Nick, and we're here if you need to lean on us. So please, lean on us."

Joshua looked around the table, then he said, "Okay." He stood up. "Right now, all I want to do is sleep." He looked at Willy first, then asked, with a hint of amusement in his voice, "Is Willy allowed to sleep in the bed with me?"

Before Henry could say no, I touched his arm to stop him from talking and said, "Willy is a 39-year-old grown-ass man and can do what he wants. And so are you."

Henry's eyes narrowed at me, but I didn't care. Whatever he needed to make him feel safe and loved tonight, Josh could have it. Josh's head motioned to Will to follow him. Will looked around at us. Connor gave him a slight head nod, then Will left with Josh.

As soon as we heard the bedroom door close, Henry ran both hands over his face and said, "Jeeeeesuuuuus." He looked at me sharply. "Did you know?"

I threw both my hands up. "I swear I didn't. There were times in the last couple of years where I would talk to Nick and he would be like, 'Oh and Willy's here too,' but I just thought that meant Willy was hanging out with them. Not *hanging* out with them."

"But I don't understand," said Henry. "I thought they were in love and committed to each other."

"It's not about love or commitment," Connor spoke up. We both looked at him, but he was looking at Henry. "They were committed to each other, but also real with each other, about their strengths and flaws. Josh's understanding of who Nick was as a person made their love real and honest. Nick is a serial cheater, so Josh opened up the relationship to one other person so that Nick wouldn't feel trapped in it. Willy was the logical choice because he's someone they both trusted. And eventually began to love."

Henry nodded at him, then looked at me and then back at him. "Is there a third party here too?" he asked curiously.

"No," we both said simultaneously, without looking at each other. Henry caught it.

He nodded his head again, though slowly, and then said, "Are y'all okay?" His forehead scrunched up. Connor didn't answer.

"We're fine," I said. *No sense airing out our dirty laundry in front of company.*

"Ah-haaa," Henry said, still nodding slowly, looking back and forth. He knew we were not fine.

"Josh doesn't have a family?" Connor asked, changing the subject.

Henry shook his head. "No. Josh came out when he was 17 and his orthodox Jewish family kicked him out. He slept on the streets of Brooklyn and in homeless shelters until he joined the Army at 18. He hasn't had any contact with anyone in his family since then."

"That's fucking awful," Connor said sadly. "Do you know if he's going back to the base?"

"I don't know. The house was in his name too and the land will be transferred to him as Nicky's legal husband, so he has a home now. It's pretty much the first time he's ever had a home. So maybe he will decide to stay, especially since Nick is buried on the land."

"He wasn't kidding when he said he was thinking about burning it down," Connor told Henry.

Henry waved his hand and said, "He was just talking shit."

Connor scoffed and got up so quickly, the chair fell to the floor with a loud clang. "Okay. You keep thinking that." He walked out of the house without another word, slamming the door behind him.

"What the fuck is his problem?" Henry asked, annoyed. "He acts like we're not doing anything."

"Because he doesn't think we are," I told him.

"Josh is not going to fucking kill himself," Henry said, dismissively again. "I've been with him this whole time. The problem is that he hasn't cried. He just needs to grieve this shit, and then he'll be okay. We'll get him some grief counseling; I will make his ass go. He'll be fine."

"And what about you? Did you grieve this shit yet?" I asked him.

"That's why I went home. I've been with Josh since I found out. So, I needed to be up under my wife for a while, grieving. That's what spouses are for, right?" I nodded. "But I'll be grieving this for the rest of my life. You?"

I thought about that first night and crying on Connor's chest as he held and sang to me. "That's what spouses are for, right?" I said back to my friend.

"Right." He stood up. "I'm going to try to get some sleep. Make sure Connor doesn't get eaten by bears or some shit. It's pitch black out there."

I chuckled as Henry left to go to the room for the night. I sat at the table a bit longer, waiting for Connor but he didn't come back in. So, I went to bed and waited for him there. I must have dozed off because the next thing I heard was Will, screaming at the top of his lungs.

CHAPTER 7

I JUST NEED YOU TO MAKE IT TO THE 17TH

Connor

I used the flashlight on my phone to find my way to the creek. It was so pretty there, with its cedar and oak trees and huge boulders that were naturally placed by the creek for sitting. *I could definitely live in a place like this. I've lived in a small town, in a desert, in a city, and all three were fine but that rural life I could get used to. Maybe Mel and I should think about moving down here. Contracting work is flexible enough, and I can do Vinnie's Vet Buddies from anywhere. He'll be closer to his friends, although I'd be leaving mine behind, along with our siblings. I should talk to him about considering it, weighing out all the pros and cons.*

And then I remembered I wanted to punch him in the face.

The beauty of our relationship is that Jamel and I did not argue. We had disagreements over the years but even then, it was more of a conversation, coming to a mutual understanding, and then moving past it. Arguments that we did have were usually things happening outside of us. In fact, our last major blow-out was when my nephew Freddie ran away from home at 12-years-old, ending up at our house and wanted to stay with us. He had a black eye and confessed that my asshole brother Matty was beating on him the way our asshole father beat on us. I was ready to go to court and get him, but Mel told me I was being irrational and illogical.

We had a huge argument, with me doing a lot of yelling— "I'm not being irrational; I'm trying to save his fucking life!" —and him doing a lot of talking, in a ridiculously calm voice. "No court is going to give him to you on just your word alone about abuse, not when he has two seemingly loving parents with money." After going to bed angry, we talked it out in the morning and came up with a game plan.

We let Freddie stay with us for two weeks until Matty told me to send his son back home. Per Mel's advice, I told him that Freddie is always welcome at my house and that if Freddie ever showed up on my doorstep looking like that again, I was going to take pictures and go to the police. "So, if you don't want to go to jail for domestic violence and lose all your kids to the system, stop beating on your kid. Maybe you forgot what it feels like, but I didn't, and I won't let you continue the cycle of abuse with your own son."

As expected, Matty cursed me out and told me to stay the fuck away from his son and hung up on me, but I told Stephanie, my sister-in-law, the same thing when she came to get him. "Stop letting your husband beat on your son. I will get the police involved, and you will lose your children." She was annoyed at me too for getting involved in their family business, but it had been over a year since the incident and Freddie said he hasn't hit him since. It was also why my nephew had a key to my house and free reign to come and go as he pleased, so he always had a safe place to go, and he could let us know what was happening at his house.

So, Mel and I don't argue. We discuss and listen to each other. But for some reason, he was acting like I was overreacting as I was watching him and Henry underreact about Josh. I told him very simply in several ways that Josh will try to kill himself, and he needed to be watched. So, what did he do? He let him go into the house by himself! By the time I got there, Josh had hidden something either in or around the sink. He looked at me and knew that I knew.

He didn't even deny it; his first words out of his mouth were, "Mind your business, Jarhead."

"Don't do it," I pleaded with him. "Just give me whatever it is first and let's talk about it."

"Fuck off."

"Josh—"

"Leave me the fuck alone!"

"Not until you give me whatever weapon you have to try to end your life."

"Uuuugh why the fuck are you heeeeere?"

"To save your fucking life. Now give it to me!" I yelled at him.

Jamel came into the house, and Josh said to him, "Call your fucking boyfriend off, will ya?"

I ignored him and tried to go around him, but he pushed me and we tussled a bit before Jamel grabbed my arm. Not Josh's arm, mine. *Like, what the fuck!?*

Then later, he tells me I was being emotional. I was trying to save his friend's life and that made me, what, irrational to him? I wanted to punch him in the fucking face. I swear to God if he would have made one false move in that hallway, I would have jabbed him right in his jaw. I'd never been so upset with him.

I already knew something was going on between Josh and Will. I had been watching them all day. Jamel felt he had to be the one to take care of everyone, so I wanted to help out a bit, take care of Willy, and give him one less person to worry about. So, I stayed close to him, and I saw it; Will and Josh had been touchy-feely the whole time. I heard Will whisper loudly to Josh, during the party in Nicky's honor, "I'll stay with you tonight." Josh smiled and touched his face lovingly. It was obvious they were fucking around. I just didn't know if Nick was a part of it or not, but giving Nick's free bird status, I assumed he was. So, catching Willy give Josh a blow job was not shocking, nor was hearing they were more of a throuple than a one-off fuck every once in a while. It made perfect sense to me.

But it wasn't going to be enough to save him. He may care for Will, but Nick was Josh's whole heart. And it was like he was walking around without a heart. I knew what that felt like and how easy it would be for him to end it all; it's the most logical choice to him. We just needed to give him another choice, and I just didn't know him enough to know how to convince him. But Henry and Jamel did know him a lot better than I did, so they would know the right things to say to help him through it. That little powwow at the table was not it. He blew them off and none of them noticed, or if they did, again they underreacted.

So yeah, I'm fucking emotional. It's emotional for me. And I get why Mel doesn't understand me right now. It's because I never told him the whole story. And I will one day, but first, I just want to help him save his friend's life. Tomorrow is August 17th so in my mind, we just need to make it through the first night. I pray to God that I'm right.

I stayed out there a long time and when I went back into the house, all was dark and quiet. I went into the bedroom and looked at Jamel, who was quietly sleeping on his back, a light snore in his chest. He had changed to pajama bottoms and was topless, with nothing but the windows open and the ceiling fan to keep us cool. His hand was at the bottom part of his stomach, and he looked peaceful. I looked at the outline of his long lax penis on his thigh and wondered if he was wearing underwear. I had a fleeting image of waking him up by me riding his cock, which made me smile. Suddenly, I no longer wanted to punch him in the face. But I wasn't ready to forgive him yet. He was closest to the door, so I slid in behind him and rested upside down, my head to his foot.

My sister Mary Kate popped in my head. Her birthday was in a week, and I thought about what I was giving her to cheer her up. Her and her husband Dennis were struggling with infertility, but she wasn't talking to me about it. She used to talk to our sister Angie about their struggles, which I'm not mad about; it made sense for my sisters to talk about those kinds of things together rather than with their big brother. But now that Angie was pregnant with her second, MK just silently cut her off and was not talking to anyone. I knew it was hard watching her younger sister have babies easily while she struggled for just one full-term pregnancy.

Mary Kate and her husband, Dennis Anderson, had been together for seven years and married for six of those years. Dennis was an investment banker and made a shitload of money, and MK quit her job as soon as they married so she could be a stay-at-home mom when the children came. But five years later, it hadn't happened for them yet and I knew it was killing her slowly. MK really hadn't struggled for anything in her life; everything always came easy to her, so it was breaking her down that being a mom wasn't something that had just fallen into her lap. They'd had two miscarriages, the most recent one around Christmas. I planned in my head to see her sometime soon.

Angie was a civil rights attorney, just like she always wanted to be. She worked for a small firm that focused on housing discrimination and tenant's rights in Boston. Eventually she will start her own practice but being a mom happily delayed her plans. She married Chadwick Worthington III, a real-life fucking rich guy named "Chad," who was Lavell's—Jamel's youngest brother—old MIT roommate and best friend. Chad came from money but worked hard as a transportation engineer making decent money, which afforded

Angie the ability to make shit money and do what she loved at the same time. They were also together for seven years and married for three, as they waited until Angie finished law school before they got married, then Angie got pregnant within a year. They had an 18-month-old daughter, Evelyn, and Angie was four months away from giving birth to her son. As they were still deciding on names, I told her if she named him Chad or Blaine, I'm cutting her off.

I actually liked both of my sisters' husbands. Dennis was white but his grandmother on his mother's side is Filipina, so he spoke a bit of Tagalog and felt a strong connection to his culture. They met through work, as MK's marketing firm was contracted to do marketing for Dennis's investment banking firm, and he pursued her hard, in a creepy Mr. Grey from *Fifty Shades*–kinda way if you ask me, but she loved the chase. They also lived in Boston, in Cambridge actually.

Jamel knew who Chad was already because he and Lavell had an off-campus apartment together while attending MIT, but I got to know him over the years. We figured out all those trips Angie was taking to Boston to hang out with her brother-in-law's brother weren't really just about Lavell when she and Chad showed up at our house one Sunday for dinner with Lavell and his girlfriend Kendra, who was now his wife. I made sure I had a relationship with both of these men, mostly because I wanted them to know that their wives had a big brother who was a Marine vet and would put a bullet in their testicles if they hurt my sisters, respectively. Thankfully, they were treating my sisters well.

Mel and I didn't have kids, but we had two dogs and a lot of nieces and nephews around us that fulfilled our lives. My niece Madeline—she refused to be called Maddy anymore—was 19, pregnant with her second, and had a shotgun wedding just like her parents, Matty and Stephanie, did, so that cycle continued. She's a daddy's girl, so we don't talk. My niece Deann would be 17 in a few weeks and starting her senior year of high school, but refused to go the way of her parents. Recently, she had been talking about becoming an Army helicopter pilot so we had been encouraging that. Jamel and I suspected that she was a lesbian, but we were waiting for her to come out to us when she was ready.

We saw Deann and Freddie a lot, despite how much my brother Matty hated me. Hated that I was gay, hated that my husband was black, and hated that I put a bullet in our father Owen seven years ago. The same father who got me arrested for attempted murder hours after he came into my home to threaten us.

Owen is lucky I didn't actually kill him. Fuck him.

I still saw my mom every Thursday for breakfast at a local diner and continued to be worried about her. But she kept reassuring me that everything was fine in the home with him and her. I told her all the time when she was ready to leave his abusive ass, just knock on my door.

Jamel's side of the family had always been my family too, ever since we got together. I thought about Tyrell and Afia, my best friend turned sister-in-law, and their three kids. Ty and I still had this weird relationship where we'd just resolved that I wasn't going anywhere, and neither was he. We were not friends, but we were family. Lavell and I were close, but he's closer to my sister now. He and Kendra had two girls, Vienna, who was six, and Xiomara, who was three. Vee and Zee were what we called them.

He and Donell were like my younger brothers too, and we treated each other as such. Donny and I had always been cool with each other, despite his reservations in the beginning about me being white and dating his brother. Donny was not married but had a seven-year-old son named DJ for Donell Junior and co-parented with his mother Vanessa in Virginia.

Jamel's parents moved to Florida a couple of years back and left the family house in Providence to Ty and Lovie. I missed them a lot, and I know Jamel did too. His father, Major Wendel Jones, gave the company to his two oldest sons and bought the condo in Miami from Xio and Corry, his nieces, as they both moved on to serious relationships. The weather down there was better for Mama Denita's arthritis and for him slowing down and enjoying life. Mama Denita even got The Major taking yoga and Tai Chi, which I would have paid money to see him do. Mama Denita also kept in contact with my mom, who she affectionately called Katie instead of Katherine, the only one to do so. I loved that they were so close.

We had a huge family and that's without mentioning our friends' kids too. Jamel's friends Shawn and Chantel's 13-year-old daughter Kimberly called us her uncles just like Jack and Ethan's kids, 13-year-old EJ, 7-year-old Jackie Chris, 6-year-old Susie, and almost 2-year-old Jamie. EJ, Freddie, Kim, and Imani,

Afia's niece, who was the same age at 13, were the Four Musketeers and always together, usually in my media room. I'm pretty sure EJ and Imani got something going on, which was cute, and I sometimes wondered about Kim and Freddie too. Matty would lose his fucking mind if Freddie ended up with a black wife, so I'm kinda rooting for that to go somewhere when they get older.

They were part of our family. They knew they could knock on our door, drop by unannounced, or spend the night if they needed to, and the Four Musketeers were the main ones that took advantage of that because, you know, teenagers. Our door was always open for any one of our family members.

Except for Matty, with his homophobic, racist, white nationalist ass. Fuck him too.

Now that I'm thinking of all of our family and friends, maybe moving to Georgia is not a good idea. We have people that depend on us in that Rhode Island area. Our relationship and actual home have become a hub and heartbeat of our family. However, if Henry needs Jamel to be closer for the sake of Josh, then I will make that sacrifice for him. He has made so many sacrifices for me and given so much of himself for me. For Jamel, I would do anything.

I flipped up to the top of the bed and laid on the pillow next to him, then I came closer. I kissed his scorpion tattoo on his right shoulder softly, so as not to wake him. *I love him so much*, I thought as I drifted off to sleep.

♥

"STOOOOOOOOOOOOOOP!"

Willy's high-pitched scream tore through the house. Jamel jumped up before I had a chance to and ran out the room. By the time I got to the door, Jamel had already gone to Josh's bedroom and was running in the hallway past me to the living room. I ran behind him, and we stopped cold in the space between the kitchen and the dining room. Henry was already standing in the kitchen, with palms open at his side. Willy was on his knees with his hands folding in front of him, his mouth moving silently as if he was praying. And Josh was standing in front of the kitchen sink with the flag that covered Nick's coffin draped around his shoulders, holding a small .38 to the side of his head.

Holy. Fucking. Shit.

Jamel moved incredibly slow toward Henry who was stone-faced, expression unreadable. They did not look at each other, only at Josh, who was as still as a statue, eyes blank. When Jamel made it to Henry's side, palms also open, Henry began to speak.

"Where did you get the gun, Josh?" he asked calmly.

Josh's eyes slowly glossed over to Henry. "Guess you didn't find them all, brother."

"I guess I didn't, brother," Henry said, palms still out. "So that's what you really want to do right now? Blow your brains out in front of all of us? Because I have a feeling you wanted it to be a private moment."

He looked at Henry surprised. "I did. You were supposed to have gone home by now. I'd fuck Willy, lay on my husband's buried coffin, and be where he is."

"So that was your plan?" Jamel asked quietly.

"It still is. I fucked Willy. Now I just need to get to Nick. So, get out of my way."

"I can't let you do that." Henry shook his head slowly. "I'm not going to pretend that I know what you're going through, Joshua. Just like I told you earlier. If I lost Tosha, I would probably want to blow my brains out too. But do you remember what I said after that?"

Josh looked thoughtful. "I don't, actually."

Jamel answered in an equally calm voice, "He said he would need to be here for his family. His wife. His kids. And you. You're family too."

"You're their Uncle Josh," Henry said. "You want me to have to explain to my kids that they lost their Uncle Nick, and then a week later, they lost their Uncle Josh?"

"And what about Will?" Jamel asked. "Willy doesn't have anyone else; he's just like you. His mother killed herself when he was eleven, did he tell you that? She blew her brains out too, and he found her."

That got Josh's attention. His face softened completely as he looked down at Will, who was still on his knees, eyes closed tightly, hands clasped, mouthing all the prayers he remembered from Catholic school I found out later.

Jamel continued. "Then his dad beat him when he came out at thirteen. And kept beating him. He was on the streets, just like you. Doing what he needed to do to survive, until a cop who was an Army vet took pity on him and introduced him to the service. He doesn't have any other family but us. You and Nick were his family. You're his family."

Josh's hand, with the weapon against his head, started to tremble. He said to Willy, "I'm sorry. I'm so sorry. But ... I can't ... I can't stay. You don't know what this feels like."

Tears started coming down his face, looking at Jamel and Henry. Josh quickly wiped them away with his free hand. "You ... you lost your brother. That's hard. But you have each other. You have your partners. I lost ... the ... only thing ... that mattered to me. I can't stay, I can't stay, I can't stay..."

His words moved to a whisper and his eyes darted around, as if he was convincing himself it was the right thing to do. And I knew what I had to do.

I walked in front of Jamel and Henry at a regular pace. Josh looked up swiftly and turned the gun on me. I immediately raised my hands to my shoulders.

Jamel hissed, "Connor!" I ignored him.

"When I was 22-years-old, I lost the love of my life. So, I tried to kill myself," I told Josh. "A hidden IED took him out, and he died in my arms. And it was my fault. So, I know exactly what it feels like, Joshua. Like you're walking around with a hole in your fucking chest. Like you'll never feel anything again. Like you're already dead. *I* know what it feels like."

Josh's mouth opened slightly, but that was his only reaction. His hands were no longer shaking, as he pointed the gun at my chest. At the very least, my presence got him to take the gun from his temple. I kept going, looking him right in his eyes.

"We had already swept that area two days before, so I thought it was clear. Vinnie made love to me that morning. We had runs to do, but instead I told him,

'Let's sneak out and shoot some shit.' Something we did from time to time. We got dressed and headed out. Joe saw us getting ready and tagged along. We went to the empty street and set up firing posts and were shooting shit. Vinnie missed a bottle, so he went back over to set it up again, skipping like a little kid, making me laugh. He skipped the wrong way, and the blast sent him backward toward us, his whole right leg blown off, the right side of his body burned almost to the bone.

"I ran up and cradled his head in my arms. I kept telling him 'I'm sorry, I'm so sorry, Vinnie.' His eyes were closed, and I thought he was already dead. Then I told him I loved him. It was the first time in the two years of knowing him and the nineteen months we had been together that I told him. He told me all the fucking time that he loved me. It was his idea to get matching tattoos, said that if I couldn't say it, I could at least show him. But I told him with my words when he was dying that I loved him over and over again. And he opened his eyes and said to me, 'You're so fucking stupid. Do you think I didn't know? I know you love me, Connor. I know.'"

I had to pause to catch my breath and keep from crying. I gasped a bit, then I continued, keeping my voice steady. "That was his last words to me, to the world. I can't even tell you what happened after that or how I even got back to the base. I was in a walking dream. I know that Joe went to get help that day while I held his dead body. I know I stayed in Iraq another six weeks to finish out the tour and came back to base. I know that they flew his body back to Houston to his wife and son, and his family. I couldn't ask for leave to attend his funeral. None of them knew he was gay. He had nobody but me. I had a few friends back home that knew about me, but he had no one."

Then I told him, told everyone in that room that was listening. "That first day back on base, I got to my room, and the first thing I saw was Vinnie's pocketknife. He left it on my dresser, like a sign. I didn't even think: I dropped my bag, walked to the dresser, opened the knife, and slit my wrist, right above his initials."

My hands were still up, so I pointed with my left hand to the tattoo on my right wrist. "Then I laid on my bed and waited to join him. Vinnie had no one in this life. I wasn't going to leave him alone in death."

Josh's eyes went from my face to my wrist and back to my face, his mouth still slightly open. I kept going. "Sammie must have sensed it. Apparently, I made way too many jokes about joining him after he died. She convinced Taylor to go with her to check on me. They came into my room and Sammie tried to scream, but Taylor shut her mouth and the door. I had already lost a lot of blood and was too weak to fight them. I told them to let me die, let me be with Vinnie, but they wouldn't let me. They wrapped my arm up in two pillowcases, put a plain jacket on me to hide my wound, and got me off base. They drove me into South Carolina and stopped at the first ER and told them that they had found me on the side of the road with no ID, and I needed medical attention. After the doctors laced me up, my friends snuck me out of the hospital hours later, before psych showed up. Drove me back on base. But instead of going to my room, Taylor took us to the training field.

"We sat in the middle of the grass and Taylor said to me, 'I know you feel like your world has ended. Because it did. But *the* world hasn't ended. And I'm going to show you that. Because the sun is going to rise, and it's going to be a new day. And it's still going to feel like shit. But it's going to hurt a minuscule less because another day has passed. I just need you to make it to the next day, brother.'"

I put my arms down, since I had Josh's full attention. "I don't know how long we laid on the grass in silence. Taylor held one of my hands and Sammie held the other, and eventually the sun started to rise. And nothing really changed; I still felt shitty, still had a hole in my chest, still blamed myself, still felt like I needed to be with Vinnie. Except one thing changed; I realized I wasn't alone. Because the two people on either side of me loved him too and I felt their grief, so I know they felt mine. I was able to share just a bit of my grief with them, and I didn't have to say a word to do it; it just happened. The sun rose, and the trainees came out and a C.O. asked us what the fuck did we think we were doing, kicking us off the field. I put my papers in, trained a Lance Corporal to take my place, and went home months later."

I paused, then said, "Vinnie died September 3, 2006. I tried to take my life on October 16th." I tore my eyes away from Josh and looked over my shoulder to where Jamel was but didn't meet his eyes at first. "I just needed to make it to the 17th."

I looked up and Jamel had a stunned look on his face, his gray eyes wide, his mouth slightly opened again. For once he wasn't stoic, and I knew why. October 17th was our anniversary, for dating and wedding. I never told him any of this.

I turned back to Josh, who was still pointing the gun at me but not really anymore. He was listening to me. "I was 22-years-old and I thought my life was over. First time I laid eyes on Jamel, it was September 4, 2009. Three years later, almost to the day, Jamel walked into my life and showed me it wasn't over. But first, I had to let my boys share their grief with me and show me the new day. I can't do that for you, Josh. I didn't know Nick well enough. I didn't love him like you did. But you have three people, three of his brothers, right here that can. They can take you outside and show you that even though you feel like your world is over, *the* world isn't over. Let them. They loved him too. They are grieving too. Let them take some of the grief from you, just a minuscule. Let them be there for you."

I let a moment pass. "You buried your husband on August 16th. When the sun rises, it will be the 17th. I just need you to make it to the 17th, brother."

It was quiet. Josh looked up at the ceiling, inhaled, and dropped the hand with the gun to his side as he exhaled. Willy got up off the floor and moved quickly toward Josh, throwing his arms around his neck and knocking the flag off his shoulders.

"That's what I've been trying to tell you," Willy wailed on his shoulder. "Nicky told me that if something were to ever happen to him, I had to be here for you.." Willy grabbed Josh's face in both of his hands.

"I'm not leaving you, Joshua. I'm moving down here. Or California. Where you go, I'm going to be there. You need me. And I need you."

He wrapped her arms around Josh again tightly. Josh wrapped his free hand around Will and let the tears drop again and, this time, did not wipe them away. I moved closer to take the gun from his hand. He hesitated when I touched the gun, but then released it to me and I stepped back. Henry came to his other side and hugged him as well. Then Jamel came and hugged him for a long while. Willy and Henry both took his hands on either side of him.

"Let's go watch the sun rise," Henry said.

Josh nodded and allowed them to walk him out. Jamel followed them to the door at first but then turned around and came back to me. I started to say his name, but he grabbed my face and kissed my lips, then peppered my face with more kisses.

"I love you. I love you. I love you," he told me over and over again, in between kisses. Kisses on my cheeks and eyes and nose, my forehead and ears and lips, over and over again.

"I love you," he said. Then he lifted my right wrist and kissed my tattoo. "And I love him too." He kissed it again and looked at me. "Is that weird?" He didn't wait for my response because he said, "I don't care if it is. Vinnie brought you to me. So, I love him too." He kissed my wrist a third time. Then he pulled me into a hug, squeezed me tight, and kissed my neck.

"God, I love you so much, Connor," he said, his voice breaking a bit.

He took my hand and started to walk, but I held back. "Give me a second; I want to grab something first."

"What?"

"Just … Go catch up. I'm right behind you."

"That was…" He looked at me. "Are you okay?"

"Yes," I lied. My chest was getting tighter, the lump in my throat was getting bigger, and I needed him to go. "I'm right behind you. Go be with Joshua. He needs you." I motioned my head toward the door.

He knew, but he let it go because he understood this next part I needed to do alone. "I'm right here. I'm always going to be right here for you," he said, as he touched my face lovingly.

"I know. And I love you too."

He nodded and took the gun from my hand as he kissed me once more. Then he touched my face lovingly again and left.

As soon as the door closed, I crumpled to the floor on the American flag left in front of the sink, raised my knees to my chest, and cried.

CHAPTER 8

STRONG, MANLY, MASCULINE, MACHO, DOMINANT

Connor

After the pain in my chest lessened and I was able to get up, I took the flag off the ground, placed it on the nearest chair and went to change my clothes. I was still wearing my t-shirt and uniform pants from earlier, so I put on a pair of jogging pants instead. I grabbed a t-shirt for Mel, a blanket, and my phone for a flashlight again and went to go look for them. I found them in the same field that held Nick's funeral, about halfway toward the gravesite, lying in the field. There was not a cloud in the sky, and the moon was high and bright so we saw each other clearly. I stood over them and they all looked at me. I looked at the time, 2:42 a.m. *At least three more hours until the sun starts to rise. We can make it.*

I stretched out the blanket on the ground, and we all moved to lay on top of it. I laid next to Jamel, who put on his t-shirt and then instinctively grabbed my hand. We stared at each other, then he reached over to touch my face.

I'm okay, I mouthed to him, then I moved closer, shoulder to shoulder.

He nodded and mouthed back, *Okay*.

I wanted to lay on top of him, but since we were the only ones there with a significant other, I thought it would be insensitive.

We laid quietly for a while, and then Willy spoke. "But do we have to lay here in silence like Connor's story? I mean, *coño*, that's just really hard for me."

We started chuckling. "Sure, Willy, we can talk," Josh said. "What do you want to talk about?"

"I was just thinking, remember when we went to that racist gay bar in Augusta? That came to my head for some reason. I thought we were going to get raped, then hung!"

"Wait, what?" Jamel asked, shocked.

Josh answered, "Nicky took us to this gay bar in Augusta, but we didn't know it was bona fide Klu Klux Klan members until we sat down. Nicky didn't know about the bar ahead of time though. We were always searching for gay bars in the state and this one had good reviews, so we tried it out and got the shock of our lives. If the Confederate Flag wasn't a dead give-away, the dummy of Obama hanging on a noose was."

"Holy shit!" Henry exclaimed.

"Right," Josh agreed. "So, my Jewish ass and Willy's Colombian ass were scared as shit. But when we tried to leave, the patrons wanted us to stay. Nicky put money in the juke box and started a dance party like what we did today and, when they weren't looking, got us the fuck out of there. But not before the bouncer tried to fuck Willy in the bathroom. This bald-headed bear motherfucker."

We all laughed loudly and hysterically. Then Henry said, "Yoooo shit. I just realized I'm the only straight guy here."

"You're always the only straight guy when we're all together," Jamel reminded him.

"Which is why I don't hang out with y'all no more. I got tired of getting hit on by literal cocksuckers. When I go home, I'm going to fuck the shit out of Tosha again. And then again. Just ugh ugh ugh...." Then he started making humping motions, making us laugh again. "Ugh, take that Tosh, ugh ugh, I'm a fucking man. I'm a masculine, heterosexual man, ugh!"

We were still laughing, then Jamel said, "Hey, fuck you, I'm a masculine man."

"That you are, Jay," Henry agreed. "You had me fooled big time. I was ready to introduce you to my sister. That would have ended badly." We laughed. "Nicky told me, 'Jamel is gay.' I'm like nah-uh! Not the big, black dude with the lion paw on his chest. Fuck outta here with that.' He was like, 'I'll show you.' And we all know how that turned out." We laughed again.

"Nicky never tried to sleep with you, Henry?" I asked.

"Maaan listen!" Henry started. "Nicky tried to kiss me one time when we were thirteen, and I punched him in the dick. Told him to never try to kiss me again or he could kiss our friendship goodbye."

"Daaag, why such a strong reaction?" Josh asked.

"Because I'm not gay. And even if I was, I wasn't going to fuck my best friend. There should be a code written somewhere on that."

"Shit, I've never seen it," I said, making everyone else but Henry laugh.

He looked past Mel to me and said, "Would you really fuck your best friend?"

Before I could respond, Mel said, "Ha, Connor *has* fucked *all* of his best friends!"

I feigned a shocked face as Josh yelled, "Holy shit!" And they all laughed at me.

"Not ... *all*!" I tried to say, making them laugh harder.

"Female friends too? Afia who is married to Ty too?" Henry asked incredulously.

"I said *all,* right?" my husband said amusingly and laughed.

"Uuuugh, shut the fuck up, Mel!" I yelled, making us all laugh harder.

"Gaaaaaaah damn!" Joshua yelled, and we continued to laugh at my expense.

"Okay, Connor, you've earned your masculine male card, cuz that's some dickhead shit that only a dude would do. Just like Nicky, sticking your dick in all of your friends, tsk," Henry said, but then quickly added, "Except me," making us all laugh again.

"I'm masculine, *tambien*," Willy said, offended.

"Oh no the fuck you're not, Willy," I said, and we laughed again. "It's not a bad thing. You're still a man; you're just a bit of a queen, that's all. You're still a handsome, sexy man."

"Are you flirting with my fuck toy, Blue Boy?" Joshua asked.

We laughed as Willy said, "Oh, the pretty blond boy with the pretty blue eyes can flirt with me anytime. Anytime you want a third, Jamel, just let me know."

"Fuck outta here with that Willy; that's never going to happen," Jamel said and squeezed my hand, making us laugh too.

When the laughter died down, Josh said, "I consider myself a masculine, gay guy."

Henry scoffed. "Alright, alright, you are all strong, manly, masculine, macho, dominant, cocksucking men, okay!?"

"You're such an asshole, Henry," Jamel said with a laugh.

"Yes and I'm sure you'd all like to see my tight ass hole, and that's not going to happen." It was quiet for a moment, then Henry said, "No homo," making us all laugh loudly again. "Holy shit, I need to go find my lady for real," he said, as we continued in our fit of laughter.

Joshua sat up. "Jamel, I didn't see your tattoo. How did I miss the lion paw on your chest?"

"Ah well, the gun was kind of in the way of your vision, dickhead," Henry said with a bit of edge.

"Oooh. Don't," Jamel said warningly.

"What, too soon?" Henry said amusingly.

It was quiet, then we all busted out laughing again. I don't know why everything was making us laugh so hard, but it was.

Joshua was still sitting up. When the laughter died down again, he looked around and said, "I'm sorry, guys. I didn't mean to scare you all like that. It's just that … without Nicky … I don't know where I belong anymore."

I spoke up first. "You belong right here, with your family."

"I'll show you where you belong, Josh. You're staying with me for a while," Henry said. "When the sun rises, you're going to pack a bag and move into my house, so you can be with your family. And when you decide to put your papers in, you'll have a job in my security company."

"And I already quit my job, *amor*," Willy said, reaching up to touch his arm. "The day I found out Nicky died, I quit my job and put a sixty-day notice on my apartment in Raleigh. I'm moving down here with you."

Jamel added, "And I don't live here but that never stopped Nicky and my friendship. We video chatted all the time, you know that. If he was off base more, we would have seen each other more. But I'll make more of an effort to come down here, to make sure you know you got me too."

"We both will," I told him.

Josh laid back down. Willy took his hand, and Henry grabbed the other. Mel was still holding mine. We were quiet for a long moment, then Josh said quietly. "Thanks. I love you, brothers."

"We love you too, Josh," Henry said.

He was quiet again, then said, "Even the Jarhead." Josh scoffed. We chuckled again.

Then Josh said, "I know who you are, Connor. I know all about Vinnie's Vet Buddies. The moment you started talking, I knew you weren't bullshitting me. I didn't know Vinnie was your lover though, just a friend. I'm sorry you lost him. Fucking IEDs, man. Too many lion of our brothers went out that way." I didn't respond,

of our brothers went out that way." I didn't respond, but Mel squeezed my hand gently.

"You're alright, Corporal," Josh continued. "Keep doing the work you're doing. You're literally saving lives out there."

"Thanks," I said to Josh softly.

We fell quiet again. Then Jamel turned to me. "Hey, Connor? What's that song you were singing to me on Monday night?"

"Oh, 'Leave Out All the Rest'? It's a Linkin Park song. It just seemed fitting for the moment."

"Can you sing it again?" he asked.

I looked at him. *Mel knows I would do anything for him but really, singing?* He saw the hesitation on my face. "You don't have to."

"No, no, it's okay," I told him. "It's still fitting for the moment." I took a moment and closed my eyes as my husband and best friend held my hand. I sang the first verse. Then Joshua started singing with me.

We stopped after the first verse and chorus; it got quiet after that. I heard lots of sniffling, and I knew everyone was crying. I opened my eyes and looked at Jamel, who was looking at me with tears on his own face. I didn't realize I had tears in my eyes until he reached over and wiped them.

Thank you, he mouthed to me.

Fuck it. I moved closer and laid my head on his chest, and he held me until the sun came up.

♥

Jamel

After the sun rose, we waited until Josh was ready and stood up first, then we all stood up, stretched, and hugged. Together, the five of us folded back up the blanket and walked to the house in silence. Henry went with Josh to pack a suitcase of clothes, and we took our rental and Henry's car back to Henry's house. Once at the house, we all went to find rooms to crash, exhausted from all that transpired through the night. Henry told me later that he pulled Tosha and Jermaine aside and told them what happened, and to not let Josh out of their sight.

Connor and I went into our room in the basement and didn't talk as we stripped down to our underwear and got into bed. I laid on my back, and he crawled his whole body on top of me like a small child would, slid his hands under my back and put his head on my chest. I wrapped my arms around him, kissed the top of his head, and held him tight, letting him know he was safe now. He fell asleep almost instantly like that. I said a quick prayer, thanking God for Connor and Vinnie, Nick, Henry, Joshua and Willy, before I fell asleep too.

Connor is still weird with PDA. I knew it made him uncomfortable to be affectionate in public and wouldn't initiate it, and at the same time, I knew he liked it when I did it. But I'm a proud, gay man, and I have never been more in love with my husband than right now.

So, the next day when we got to Hartsfield-Jackson Airport and dropped off the rental, I took his hand, kissed it, entwined my fingers with his, and I didn't let go. He smiled at me shyly as I led him through the airport to Terminal N to head back to Rhode Island. I pulled him to a seat that didn't have armrests between them and when he sat down, I laid across the chairs and put my head in his lap right away, casually holding my book up to read. Connor giggled this silly, little giggle that he does sometimes.

After a minute, I moved my book aside to look at him: his skin a little pink, jeweled blue eyes sparkled, lips curled up into a tight closed-mouth smile looking down at me.

I asked with a straight face, "What?"

"Nothing," Connor said quietly.

We stared at each other for a moment. He hesitated slightly, but then he leaned down as I leaned up, and he kissed my lips softly and rubbed my head. His face was no longer pink. He didn't look around to see who saw us. Connor just put his headphones in his ear, closed his eyes, and sat back as I laid back down to read my book.

I touched his thigh on the plane and held his hand through Philadelphia's airport too. I even returned his kiss right before we got on the connecting flight from Philadelphia to Providence, walking right behind him, licking my lips and planting one on the nape of his neck. Connor gasped loudly, arched his back, and turned around. We stared at each other, and then I gave him a peck kiss. He turned pink again, but he kissed me back more sensually, pulling my bottom lip between his two. I smiled and took his hand again and held it on the plane.

But by the time we got to T.F. Green Airport parking lot, I needed more, and I knew he did too. So, when we got in my truck instead of starting it, I put the key in the ignition, brought the windows down slightly, pulled his face toward mine, and kissed him passionately, which he returned. Then I pushed him back, lifted up his t-shirt, and dragged my tongue across one nipple, then the other.

"Oooooh fuck, Mel. If you don't stop, we're not going to make it home," he panted out.

I lifted my head and looked him right in the eyes. "We're not going to make it home."

Connor stared at me, his lips slightly parted, then said quietly, "Shit."

I lifted his t-shirt all the way off and kissed him again. We reached for each other's belts and zipped down our jeans. Connor got to me first like I knew he would. He pulled my cock out and put all of me in his mouth, making me moan out loud.

This might sound bad, but the fact that Connor has had so many partners made him an expert in many areas sexually. Dick-sucking was one of those areas that I was grateful for. My husband sucks dick like he's going for an Olympic gold medal every time, and every time I gave him one.

Like now. I'm pretty big, and he could take me all in one motion if he wanted to, but he liked to play and tease and drive me crazy instead. He used his tongue and cheeks and jaw bones to create this vice-like suction on my cock as he went up and down, which sent never-ending pleasure from my toes to the top of my spine. He closed his throat and pushed my cock head in there to gag for fun, just so he could leave hot, slimy spittal all over my dick and loudly slurp it back up. That shit was so incredibly sexy, and it made me moan loudly again.

As much as I didn't want him to stop, I wanted to be inside of him more. I sadly lifted his head back up and kissed him. "Get the oil and come ride," I told him.

He smiled and pulled the baby oil out of the glove compartment as I slid my jeans and underwear to my ankles. He handed it to me while he took off his jeans and boxer briefs too, and I lubed my already spit lubricated cock with it. Once he was completely naked, he lifted himself as far as he could go as I slouched just a bit, and he lowered himself backward on my cock, slowly. His body instantly molded around me after almost ten years of lovemaking with me, and only me. He moaned and sighed as he made his way down, and I held his waist gently. He waited a moment, reached out to hold onto the dashboard, and began to move.

Dick-riding is the other area that my husband gets the gold. Connor was like a gymnast with signature moves but changes up his routine every time. Every single time. This time, he slid up squeezing all his rectal muscles until I was almost out, then sent his body downward in a fluid motion until I was to the hilt, circles, then moved upward again. He started out slowly, but then moved faster, making me moan more and the car shake. I closed my eyes and got lost inside of him, moving with him and letting him take me to that orgasmic state that only he could bring me to. He wasn't shit-talking, which only meant he was concentrating on maximizing pleasure for the both of us. And it was working because we were only five minutes in, and I knew I was about to cum.

I reached around and cupped his balls tightly as I told him, "Baby, I'm cumming."

He grabbed my thighs and began to bounce on my dick to directly angle me against his prostate, moaning like he was in pain. His head was hitting the ceiling of the truck, but he didn't care. All he cared about was fucking me harder, bringing me to climax. And he did.

All my nerves rushed through my body to the center of my groin and pushed my sperm from my balls out of my cock, spurting over and over and over inside of him. I groaned and held his waist tighter. Almost simultaneously, his cock that was standing straight up started shooting out ropes of cum high in the air, hitting his face and the ceiling of my car, the dashboard, the steering wheel, and front windowpane. It just kept shooting out, and I couldn't stop cumming either, mostly because of the sight of him cumming, and he was still bouncing on me like he was pumping me dry. I don't know if it was the fact that we hadn't had sex in a week or that we both had such pent-up emotion and sexual energy for each other, but that was the shortest and best fuck we've had in a while. We moaned together and came together, and it was beautiful.

Finally, he stopped and collapsed against my chest. We were sweaty and breathing hard, the t-shirt I never took off was clinging to me. I reached around him, started the car and let the blast of hot, then cool air, hit us both.

"Mmmmmm..." he moaned and leaned over closer to the center vent as it got cooler.

I reached up and traced the phoenix rising tattoo with my fingertips and his sweat. Once again, he showed me and everyone else what a powerful being he was. I could not have made it through this week without him.

I kissed it. *He's my phoenix. My heart. My love. My everything.* I kissed his tattoo again.

Connor reached behind and pulled my hand so that it wrapped around his waist and said, "I love you too, Jamel."

We were quiet for a moment, then I started saying, "Connor. If I go first—"

"I won't," he cut me off. "I know who I am now. With or without you. I know who I am."

Indeed. For the most part, he does.

CHAPTER 9

THAT'S WHAT I'M HERE FOR

Connor

I took the drive over to the Wellington-Harrington section of Cambridge to see my little sister, Mary Kate. I had to trick her though, because she had been getting better at avoiding all of us, so I didn't call her until I was already in the area. She ignored my first two calls but picked up the third time.

"Hey Connor," she said breathlessly. "Sorry I was working out."

Right. "Hey Mini Kat, just checking on you."

"Oh yeah, I'm fine. About to be the big three-one, so I wanna make sure I stay healthy and keep fit."

"Are you working out at the gym or at home?" I asked.

They have this ridiculously expensive 2,000 square foot, four-bedroom colonial home in one of the most expensive parts of the city, and they turned one of the basement rooms into a home gym.

"I'm home," she told me.

"Cool. So, what plans do you have for the day?" I asked, as I crossed the Longfellow Bridge.

"Nothing much. Dennis is working late, some big contract, so I have dinner plans later."

"But nothing right now?" I asked.

"Noooo … Cooooonnor. Where are you?"

"Just going for a drive … in Cambridge."

"Connor!"

"I haven't laid eyes on you in six months, Mini Kat."

"Just because you have a no-knock policy with your house doesn't mean I do!" she said angrily.

"I'm already here, MK," I said calmly. "I will be at your house in less than ten minutes so take a shower and let me take you to brunch." She stayed quiet for a minute, but she knew I wasn't going to back down. "I'll see you soon," I told her and hung up before she could say another word.

I parked in front of her house on the street and by the time I made it up her porch, she had already opened the door and met me outside. She looked thin to me, her flower-printed spaghetti-strapped dress hung a little more loosely off her body than I would have liked to see. But at the risk of sounding like our mom, I didn't say anything. I held my hands out for a hug, which she gave me halfheartedly at first. But then I didn't let her go, and she clung to me a bit tighter.

I knew it. My sister is not okay.

She linked her arm with mine and then looked down at the package I was holding. "What's that?" she asked giddily.

"You'll see," I smiled slyly.

We walked to a local pub, and she did her best to tell me how great everything was as we ate salmon and poached eggs, something I would only do with her. Mary Kate was doing some pro bono marketing for the Women of Cambridge Club that she joined a couple of years ago, and they pick a charity to put on philanthropy events every year. That year, it was raising money for the American Bird Conservancy, so she was learning a lot about the different types of native bird habitats in America. Through this work, she took up bird-watching and started carrying around a bird guidebook. Both of these things kept her busy. I told her about Joe's new bird-watching habit too and what I've been learning from him about birds native to Africa, and she was interested in talking to him about it.

"So, you're only doing the marketing stuff pro bono? You don't want to do it full time again?" I asked.

"Oh, well … It's just not something I'm interested in doing right now. You know Denny makes more than enough to take care of us, so I like to be able to give back to my community in this way."

"And Dennis? How are you and him doing?"

"Oh, we're great," she said a little too happily. "Yeah, everything is great. Just … great!"

I nodded. I didn't want to scare her away. "Okay. Any plans for Thursday?"

"Well…" And then she excitedly told me about her best friend Candice renting a house on Martha's Vineyard, where their friends will be in attendance for a three-day couple's retreat weekend.

I teased her. "Hey, why didn't Candice invite me?"

She rolled her eyes. "Connor, stop. You and Jamel would not want to have to sit around the lake with my stuffy friends, drinking scotch and talking about the stock market with our husbands while dressing up in dinner attire every night, and you know it."

She had a point. I gave her a sour face. "Yeah, that sounds like a nightmare," I said, and she laughed.

"But Denny said we haven't been out your way in a while, so we'll come for Sunday dinner soon."

I already knew that. Dennis and I talked last week about how she had been avoiding everyone since her miscarriage last December. Candice's weekend was really for Mary Kate to feel connected to her friends again.

"Good. Let's plan it." She smiled at me. "So have you spoken to Angie?" I asked.

Her smile faded a bit. "No, not really." She took a gulp of her mimosa. "She's just been so busy lately, and so have I."

"When was the last time y'all talked?"

"I don't know … March? It's fine; we don't need to talk all the time."

"Yeah, but you guys live like twenty minutes away from each other. You should see each other more, or at least talk more."

Mary Kate waved her hand nonchalantly. "Well like I said, she's busy, you know. She has a full life." Another gulp of mimosa.

"She'll never be too busy for you," I told her.

She looked at me sharply. "Is that why you came over here? To talk about Angie?"

"No," I said calmly. "I came over here because I wanted to see you. I haven't seen you since there was still snow on the ground. I wanted to catch up. And I wanted to give you this."

I pulled out two packages: one large and rectangular, and one small square. I handed her the small one first. She opened it, and it was a white gold cuff bracelet with her initials on it, MKA, for Mary Kate Anderson.

She was in awe. "It's so pretty. Tell Jamel thank you!"

I chuckled because she was right; he did pick it out. My sisters were such girly girls. They loved jewelry, and Mel surprisingly loved to shop for them and spoil them.

I handed her the second package. "Ethan made it, but I bought it from him."

She smiled as she ripped the paper off the small canvas, and her mouth dropped. It was a self- portrait, but with her looking like she was in the 1800s. The face was hers, but she wore a powder blue Victorian-style dress with an umbrella to match. Her blue eyes, the same color as mine, sparkled, and her smile looked like she was hiding a secret.

She touched it gently. "God, that man is so talented. I'll never forget how sexy he was cursing out Dad at that dinner. It's a shame he's gay; I would have rocked his world."

I laughed out loud. MK has had a crush on Ethan, my best friend Jack's husband, since he came to town over twelve years ago. The fact that he was gay, married, and had four children had not stopped her crush at all. "I thought you would like it."

She grinned at me. "Thanks, Con. You're the best big brother ever."

"I know," I said and smiled.

"Speaking of brothers..." She trailed off. I raised one eyebrow at her. "Matty's scans came back positive. But it's in its earliest stage so the prognosis is good. Just thought you should know."

I did know. Freddie told Jamel, who told me two weeks before we went to Atlanta, and I gave him the same, unbothered look as I gave Mary Kate. Matty having skin cancer did not concern me, not in the slightest. I looked away and took a gulp of my mimosa. *Must be a family thing.*

"Connor—"

"No."

"He's not that bad anymore, I promise you."

"No MK, he's not that vocal anymore. He's still that bad. He's learned that from Owen, to keep his mouth shut about his far-right wing conservative views in public spaces."

She looked offended. "I'm conservative." I raised my eyebrow at her again. "And so is Denny. We are Republicans," she said proudly.

"Yes, you're fiscal conservatives, believing that 'corporations are people too' bullshit. I can handle that. You're not gay-hating, Bible-thumping, xenophobic, racist assholes like him and Stephanie are. You didn't vote for Trump."

She looked horrified. "Oh God no."

"Exactly. Your husband knows the difference between being a conservative and a bigot."

"Okay, we're getting off topic—"

"No, we are not," I cut her off. "Matty and I don't have anything to say to each other that doesn't involve his kids, whom I love, and our mom. We don't even talk about you and Angie. Well, Angie doesn't talk to him either so that's not even a question. When he stood on the side of his father and denied the abuse we experienced as kids, there was nothing else to talk about. I don't associate with people like him. He's not my brother."

She glared at me. "You're such a fucking hypocrite," she hissed.

I was aghast. "How?"

"You stand there judging people and looking down at people who don't believe the same things or the exact same way you do, but don't like it when your own values are called into question. What happened to the importance of family? So, he couldn't admit the things that Dad did to him in court. You're gonna hold that against him forever? He's. Your. Brother. And yes, he says hurtful and disrespectful shit, but he's still family."

"He hates me, Mary Kate."

"He doesn't hate you. In fact, I happen to know he … *appreciates* how much you care about his children, and how they look up to you and respect you."

I smiled. "Did he use the word 'appreciate'?"

"Something to that effect."

"Get the fuck outta here," I said, sounding like Mel.

"Connor!"

"You're not going to change my mind, MK. I don't hate him, but he does hate me. So, I will wish him the best with his health and life from afar. But he's not my brother. And Angie feels the same way."

She reacted again to Angie's name. "What's up with you two?" I finally just asked. "Did she actually say or do something to make you stop talking to her?"

"Connor, why don't you ask her, okay? You know how Little Miss I'm-Woke-And-Better-Than-You-Are gets. She thinks she knows everything, but she doesn't. And she doesn't get to tell me what to do with my fucking life." She swallowed her entire drink.

Okaaaay. Good thing I'm seeing Angie later, so I can ask her what exactly the conversation was about back in March that it's now August and they still aren't talking.

I reached across the table and touched her hand. "Are you ready? Let's walk back."

We walked through her house, and it was so big and beautiful, with high ceiling chandeliers, white walls, and marbled floors. Nothing was out of place, almost like a museum with the artwork on the walls and sculpture art in random places. We went to the backyard and sat on the three-seater swing that Mel made for her, similar to the one I have in my backyard.

"I'm glad you came," Mary Kate said with a smile.

"Me too. I miss you, you know. Jamel does too."

"I see Jamel. He drops by if he is working out this way or passing by. And he comes with gifts so that's nice."

Did I know that? I don't think I did, but I'm not surprised. He loves my sisters. I responded with, "Well, I miss you."

"Well, you are always so busy, and you're traveling a lot for work."

"Maybe once every couple of months."

She looked at me thoughtfully and asked, "Why don't you and Jamel have children?"

I sighed. "It's just not something I ever wanted. I never saw myself as being a dad. And I am even more afraid of how all the stuff I had been through would affect my child. I didn't exactly have a father figure growing up, so I wouldn't even know what to do with a kid."

She was quiet, then said without looking at me, "I just think that those who can have kids should. For those of us who … can't."

I let her be silent for a moment. Then I asked her, "Do you want to talk about it?"

She shook her head. "Not really. I'm kinda done talking about it."

"Does that mean you aren't trying anymore?"

"No. We're still trying, we're just … giving my body a break. It's been through so much in the last five years—surgery, shots, hormones, and pills and … it's just too much." She sighed and put on a brave face for me. "So, I'm eating right and exercising and hoping that by this time next year, I could join the ranks of womanhood."

I touched her arm. "You're already a woman, sis. Having children doesn't make you a woman any more than driving a car makes you a race car driver. You're still a car driver."

"Yeah, but Connor, I want to be in the Indy 500 with the rest of the drivers." She sniffed and wiped away a tear that was starting to fall. "Also, that was the stupidest analogy ever."

I laughed out loud, and she chuckled as more tears came out. I reached out and took her hand.

We were quietly swinging on her porch. I was about to tell her I was getting up to go when she said, "Denny asked me what I thought about adoption. We could adopt from the Philippines."

"And what do you think about that?"

"I think I want to be pregnant, Connor. And I don't think that makes me selfish or a bad person."

"I don't think it does either."

"Well, tell that to your sister, who's a bitch, by the way."

Ah-ha. Now we're getting to it. Yeah, I'll talk to Angie.

I told her, "I think the question is ultimately, is it more important for you to experience having a biological child or if you are okay skipping all that and moving to the parenting stage? And there is nothing bad or selfish in either decision. Any way that you want to grow your family is going to be perfect, because it's your family and they'll be a part of us. Look at Jack and Ethan's colorful family: Two Irish Catholic men raising a biological kid, a redhead with Scottish roots, a South Korean native, and a biracial child. They're a perfect family. So have your perfect family any way you want it to be."

She nodded. "I just don't think I'm ready to give up trying yet."

"Do you have to give up trying when you are looking to adopt? I mean, what do adoption agencies tell you, you can't fuck your husband until we place a baby in your home?"

She laughed. "I don't know. I've never looked into it."

"Well maybe you should. It doesn't hurt to have the conversation. It doesn't mean you're giving up." I let a moment pass and said, "Let me know if you want me to look into anything with you. I mean, maybe the spirit will move me, and I'll want to adopt too," I joked and rolled my eyes.

She laughed. "Well, Jamel would be happy about that. He'd love to adopt. When we talked about adopting black boys out of the system, I told him I'm really not ready for that, but he would be great at it."

She laughed but I didn't. She saw my face and said, "Oh, I didn't mean it like that! I just meant ... you know. Adoption out of the system in general. Not because they are black boys."

But she had completely misread me. My stunned face had more to do with me no longer listening after she said she and Jamel talked about adoption.

"When did you and Jamel talk about adoption?" I asked her as casually as I could.

But she caught my tone anyway. "We didn't talk about adoption per se; he was just saying that, you know, if he could, that ... that's what he would do."

My face was frozen, but my eyes darted around until they met her face. "When?"

She waved her hand nonchalantly again. "Oh, I don't know. Earlier this year, I think ... I guess..."

I sat back on the swing. *Six months into our relationship, I told Mel I was not having kids and he was fine with it. Now, all of a sudden, he wants to adopt kids? And he tells my sister? What the entire fuck!?*

"Connor? You look mad. Why are you mad? Was it something I said? I'm sorry; I didn't mean to say ... what did I say?"

I shook it off. "Nothing, MK. It's fine. I meant what I said. If you want my help looking into anything, just let me know, okay?" I touched her arm again. "If and when you're ready. If you want to keep trying, I'll support that too."

She reached out to hug me. "Thanks, Connor. You really are the best big brother ever."

Bet you Matty doesn't hear that, I thought smugly. "That's what I'm here for."

♥

I left there and headed to the Brookline section of the Boston suburbs to Angie's Cotswold-style home. She wouldn't be there for another hour or so, but Chad worked from home so he would be with Evelyn. I rang the doorbell, and Chad answered the door happily.

"Heeeey Connor! What are you do—" He pulled me into a big hug as Evie ran between his legs and passed me. "Oh! Evie, no! Wait for Daddy!"

He ran after her and caught her in the middle of the walkway. He lifted her up and she giggled in his arms, as he bounced her along backward on his shoulder, smiling. Chad was an easygoing, happy guy before he had a daughter, and now he was like an extra-ecstatic husband and father. I don't think he's ever been sad a day in his life. He was a bit of a nerd when I first met him and a year with Angie had him going from a big glasses-wearing, messy-haired, geeky

Clark Kent to a contacts-wearing, mousse-using, handsome Superman. He had told me many times he felt like the luckiest guy in the world being with Angie, and it showed in how well he treated her, like he worships the ground she walked on. Sometimes a little too much, as he lets her get away with whatever she wants, but that was their relationship.

He reached in and gave me a hug again. "She's been trying to go outside all day, but I told her we have to wait until her mommy gets home. I'm working on a huge project, and the deadline is midnight. She hasn't taken a nap today so I'm hoping that Angie can either take her to the park or get her to lay down."

"I can take her." The park was around the corner from their house.

Chad looked relieved. "Yeah? You sure? Maybe come in, get a drink or something."

"No, it's okay. I just had lunch with Mary Kate, so I'm hydrated," I told him. I saw him raise both his eyebrows but didn't say anything else.

"Wanna go with Uncle Connor?" he asked my niece. I held my hands out to her, and she jumped in them with glee.

"I'll be back," I told him before he could respond. I started walking away, then realized she didn't have shoes on. I turned back to say, "But I think she needs—"

But Chad had already gone into the house and came back with her stroller, her mini-diaper bag for shorter trips with snacks and a juice box, and a pair of flip flops. *And that's why he's a dad, and I am not. I wouldn't have considered any of those things.*

I strapped her in the stroller, put on her slippers, and the pink Hello Kitty bag on my shoulder, and we took the walk over. Even though I knew the way, she pointed and directed me the whole time, saying words that sounded like, "That way!" *Yep, this is definitely Angie's daughter.*

I brought her to the toddler section of the park that was enclosed and shaded, with smaller equipment and a sand pit. Of course, she dived right into the sandpit with the rest of the kiddies. I sat on the nearest bench and watched her play as I thought about Jamel's admission to Mary Kate.

I'm not even upset. Or maybe a little, but only because I don't understand why he hadn't told me how he felt. I did kinda shut the conversation down early on, but I was in a different place back then. It's not that I don't like kids, I actually love kids. Back then, I didn't want to have kids because I was afraid of becoming like my father, and that's still a reason. But now I don't want to have kids because I like my life and my freedom, and I don't want to change it. I'm not fucking having kids, period. But if Jamel has a desire to have children and it gets stronger, then our relationship is in trouble.

I decided to get out of my head and play with my niece. A couple of moms side-eyed and raised eyebrows at me when I took off my shoes and got in the sandpit with Evie and their kids, but I didn't care. These moments were precious. We played in the sandpit, then on the slide, then the swings and the sandpit again. An hour and half later, when I walked her back, she was passed out in her stroller.

Angie opened the door when I got back. "Hey Connor!" she whispered excitedly. "Thank you for this so so much!"

I came into the front area and was about to unbuckle her from her stroller when both her parents yelled at me in a harsh whisper, "Noooo!"

I stood up confused. Chad said softly, "House rule: we don't wake sleeping babies. If you take her out, she will wake up."

"Yeah, she'll be fine in the stroller; just roll her to the living room. She needs this nap," Angie said. *And that's why they are parents, and I am not.*

I rolled and parked her near the armchair. Chad handed me a glass of fruit punch. "Thanks, man. Really." He turned to his wife. "I'm headed back to my office. Let me know if you need me."

They kissed and he left. Angie stretched out on the couch, and I sat in the armchair next to my sleeping niece. Her round belly protruded through her lime green sundress, and she laid her hand across it. I looked around their house, which ironically was about the same two-million-dollar price tag as Mary Kate's, but it just felt homier. Maybe it was the bright colors they had all around, or the fact that it was a complete mess, with kid toys everywhere. It was going to look like a preschool play area when they had two little ones.

"It's good to see you," she said in a low voice. "This is a nice surprise. Are you off today?"

I also spoke in a low voice. "I just moved around my schedule so I could have a day off. I wanted to see my sisters." I watched her response, which was a hesitation before a smile.

"Well, it's always good to see you. I saw Mel, and we spoke last week when he stopped by. I gave him my condolences about his friend. How is he doing?"

"He's okay. We haven't really talked about it since we got back, except to make plans to head to Atlanta for New Year's to check on Josh, Nick's husband. But you know Mel; he's going to keep busy and not talk about his feelings."

"Yeah, that's true." She sighed. "And how are you? That couldn't have been easy for you, going to a military funeral."

"No, it wasn't easy for me. But you know, it wasn't about me; it was about Jamel. So, I had to put my feelings aside and be there for him," I said proudly.

"How very mature of you," she said, mocking me.

"Shut up." She laughed. "And how are you?" I asked her.

"I'm good," Angie said happily. "Work is good. I'm in the middle of a settlement with a woman whose stove was broken so she stopped paying rent until they fixed it and they tried to evict her. Come to find out they have a history of doing this to longstanding tenants just so they can kick them out, fix up old apartments, and raise the rent. Such assholes." She talked about it a bit as I listened.

Then she asked, "Are you staying for dinner? I could call Lavell and Kendra over."

"No, I was going to head back home soon."

"Oh, you can have lunch with Mary Kate but not dinner with me?" she said testily.

Well, that escalated quickly. I said to her very calmly, "I went to take Mary Kate to lunch because she's been going through a hard time. I didn't plan on having dinner here, but I can, no biggie. I came to see you and spend time with you too. I love you both the same."

She looked at me, then turned away. "Okay well, do what you want."

"What's up with the two of you?" I asked her.

"Did you ask her that?"

"I did, and now I'm asking you."

Angie took a moment before she answered. "She told me that Dennis wants her to consider adoption and I told her it would be a great idea, and I was talking to her about all the positives of it. Apparently, I was way too pro-adoption for her, and she snapped at me. Now she's not talking to me."

"Yeah, okay." I knew my sister could be pushy. "So, what exactly did you say to her?"

She gave me a hard look, but I didn't back down and gave her a look back. She sighed loudly. "Okay, I might have taken it too far. I told her that with all the resources they have, they should be jumping at the chance to adopt. That being pregnant isn't all it's cracked up to be. That maybe she should try to be a little less ... self-centered."

"So you did call her selfish for wanting to have children of her own?"

"Well, she kinda is!"

"Angela." I tried to keep my voice calm. "You can't tell someone that doesn't have children that they are selfish for wanting children, especially if they just had a fucking miscarriage. What the fuck?"

She got louder. "I didn't say she was selfish for wanting to have children. She can have all the children she wants; there are plenty of orphans right here in the United States that need her. Statistically—"

"Shut the fuck up, Ang," I told her. She narrowed her eyes at me. "She's your sister. And she needed you to support her. And instead, you give her statistics? Here you are, pregnant with your second child, telling your sister with fertility issues that being pregnant isn't that big a deal, and she should just go find a child instead of giving birth to one. Do you know how completely insensitive you sound?"

When my friend Benjin and his wife were going through infertility, I learned the do's and don'ts to say to families struggling to conceive. This was a huge fucking Don't.

"I wasn't trying to be insensitive; I was trying to help her."

"She didn't ask for your help; she wanted her sister to be a sounding board. And instead, you hit her with the board. I wouldn't be surprised if she never talked to you again."

Angie didn't say anything, just stared at me. And then the waterworks started. And then I felt like shit because I made my pregnant sister cry. *Fucking great.*

I got up to sit next to her, and she moved her legs so I could. I started, "Angie—"

"No, it's okay," she said between sniffles. "You're right; I'm a horrible, fucking sister and I did a horrible thing, and she's never going to talk to me again and it's my fault."

I hugged her and let her weep on me. "I didn't say you were a horrible sister. But our family is already split. You and I don't talk to Matty. Matty only talks to MK. I don't talk to Owen but the rest of you still do. The last thing I need is for you and MK to stop talking. Can we please come together again?"

"I didn't stop talking to her; she stopped talking to meeee!" Angie wailed. "I don't know how to make it right. She won't pick up my calls, and she slammed the door in my face last month. She didn't even come to my birthday dinner! I don't know what to do."

"Okay, let me fix it. It's been too long, so let me bring y'all back together," I said. "I'm going to plan a dinner at my house in a couple of weeks. You and Chad need to be there. MK and Dennis will be there too. The three of us need to stick together."

She nodded. "Okay." She sniffed. "Stay for dinner, please? Chad is making steak salad."

I turned up my nose. "What the fuck is steak salad?"

She laughed. "It's a kinda Greek salad with steak strips on it. You'll like it."

"First of all, that sounds like some rich people, health-kick shit." She punched my arm playfully. "Okay, I'll stay. Let me call Mel and let him know."

"Yay! I'll call Kendra now. Thanks, Connor. You're the best big brother ever," she said.

I hugged her again and smiled. "That's what I'm here for."

CHAPTER 10

HOT, SWEATY, NAKED

Jamel

I parked my car in the garage and went into the media room instead of upstairs, laying down on the large sectional. The Four Musketeers had taken over my house in the last two years, and I felt like I rarely hung out there anymore. Freddie had a key to the house, so they all just rode their bikes over and crashed at my place whenever they felt like it. I would have loved to set some ground rules, but Connor had this *mi casa es su casa* attitude, so I picked and chose my battles and got down there when I could. We finally finished the Attleboro project, and my father would be proud of the work we did there. I had three days before we started the next project and a housing inspection in Worcester in two days, so tomorrow was my only day off. Connor had already called me to say he was having dinner with Angie's and Lavell's family, so I was on my own. The media room was all mine.

After I took a shower, I decided to order chicken pasta primavera and a salad from a local restaurant, open a new bottle of Pinot, and listen to music. I considered watching porn but opted not to because I figured Connor would probably want sex when he got home. We still had an active sex life but between our dueling schedules, sometimes it was hit or miss. Tonight might be a missed night. But porn was not something I did on the regular anymore. I used to watch it all the time: exercise after work, cook dinner, and beat-off to porn to sleep. That was my life before Connor. Now Connor and I watched it together, and rarely did I watch it by myself. I was pretty much addicted to PornHub before I met him, with a very active account.

Nick used to laugh at me, telling me, "Just go get some strange and stop torturing yourself, dude." And when I'd give into that, he would say, "Now isn't cumming on someone else so much better than cumming on yourself?" I smiled at that thought.

Nick. This shit still hurts. I can't just pick up the phone and find out what he was into today like I normally would. I would call Josh but that wouldn't have been fair. I only call when I can be there for him and listen to him, not to unload my shit and grief on him. I'll call him tomorrow. I can keep my shit inside until it dissolves. I'll be fine, I told myself.

I put on an old Zhane album after I ate and dimmed the lights. I sat back in the corner of the sectional, with my eyes closed and my third glass of wine, listening to

"Groove Thang." I really did have a great life. Great job where I felt like I was giving back to my community by only hiring ex-convicts, something my father started when he had the company that I continued. A great home and my two great dogs that finally discovered I was home and came to lay in the basement with me.

And, of course, Connor, the center of my happiness. He loved me with every inch of his soul, and I was still irrevocably in love with him. I think I fell in love with him on the boat during our second date. Or that same night when his cute, drunk ass told me to stay with him forever. I held him as he clung to me like he never wanted to let me go. So, I never let him go, and here we were ten years later.

I started missing him, wanting to feel his hard body and soft skin curled up on me. I didn't know if it was the fine hairs all over his body or just the way his skin was naturally, but it always felt like silk, especially when he was sweaty. Thinking of a hot, sweaty, naked Connor started making my dick hard. *Fuck it.*

I turned the music off and opened up my phone first, then casted PornHub to the 60-inch screen. The first thing that always comes up is skinny white girls sucking dick. I immediately logged into my account, BBC-OnDuty, and gay porn came up instead. My cock immediately twitched. I went to one of my favorites on my playlist, an interracial couple poolside. They remind me of us; the one guy was blond-haired and the other guy was dark-skinned. They fucked like a real couple, touching, kissing, staring into each other's eyes. I pulled down my sweatpants and pulled out my cock to watch. A minute in, my eyes wandered to one of the videos underneath. I moved my cursor down to it and played that video instead. Two brown-skinned men getting ready. I slouched down and watched them kiss, then eat ass, then one entered the other.

My dick was stiff as a board, watching those two black men fuck. For some reason, it brought me back to my ex-lover D'wayne. That man knew how to submit and get fucked. Not better than my husband, just good in a different way. A fleeting memory of he and I fucking in my old apartment popped in my head, and my cock involuntarily oozed out pre-cum. I grabbed my phone and paused it, feeling guilty. I love my husband and our sex life was phenomenal, but every once in a while, I missed fucking a black man, that brown skin-on-brown skin action.

I would never cheat on him, but in my mind, sometimes I allowed myself to envision fucking someone else, someone with melanin: the Starbucks barista near Ty's house who openly propositioned me more than a few times; the new sanitation man who smiles at me every time he sees me; the owner of Crunch Fitness who had been trying to give me free personal training sessions … I got hit on all the time, which gave me more than enough mental images, and I didn't feel guilty about it. *But jerking-off to a past fuck? That just feels disrespectful.*

My cock felt otherwise. It was begging me to stroke it, pulsating and twitching in my hand. The wine wasn't helping either; my inhibitions were low, and I needed a release. I started the video again and watched it, stroking myself and using my pre-cum as lube. They were not sensual like my favorite couple. This was a hard-hitting fuck. Strong, muscled thighs hitting a strong, muscled ass over and over again, that clap clap clap sound like my favorite song on repeat. When they did a close-up to a big, black cock going into a strong, dark brown ass, that was enough for me. I closed my eyes and stroked myself ferociously and grunted out loud. I thought about D'wayne again, then made my mind switch to Ishmael the barista, who was about the same complexion. I pictured taking him right on the Starbucks counter, flipping his green apron over to reveal no underwear and an open hole. I fucked him hard on that counter; the clap clap clap sound from the TV was now me fucking the barista. The moaning that I heard was now his moaning for my dick to cum inside him.

"Fuck, I'm coming," I said breathlessly to no one. I grunted and streams of cum flew out of my cock all over the carpet.

The men were still at it as I used my foot to mix my semen into the brown, white, and cream carpet threads. I used the remote to turn it off, forgetting that it was casting from my phone and not on the TV. I took off my tank top, cleaned myself up, pulled back up my sweats, and fell asleep on the couch.

"Jamel." Connor was tapping me awake. "Why are you down here?" he asked quietly.

I looked up groggily, somehow laying on my stomach. I lifted myself to my elbows and said, "Oh, I was watching something, and I fell asleep."

He looked at me amusingly. "Yeah, I can see that."

He pointed to the TV he had turned on and it still had porn on it, black men giving each other blow jobs compilation. It had no sound so he must have seen my phone first, realized it was casting, and then turned down the volume to watch it on the big screen. I stared at the screen lost for a moment, and my dick twitched. I jerked off around 7 p.m., and it was close to midnight. *I just might have one more in me tonight.*

I pulled him by his shirt so his face was closer to mine and pulled his thin bottom lip in between my full thick ones. "Mmmmm," he moaned. "Somebody missed me."

"Shut up and come here," I told him as I kissed him again.

Connor laughed. "Okay wait, I'll be right back."

He kissed my lips a few times, then went to the bathroom. I knew he was going to clean himself and grab the lube. I took that time to strip my sweatpants all the way off again, so I was naked and continued to watch cock after cock get sucked until someone got sprayed in the face. I started to stroke myself. *Connor better hurry the fuck up before I start and finish without him.*

When he came out, he was also completely naked and the lube we keep in the bathroom down there was in his hands. He walked over and straddled my legs first, his cock against mine, and wrapped his arms around me. I held him by the side of his butt cheeks as we kissed. I ran my hands up his back, feeling the curve of his body. He kissed my neck and my ears from one side to the next, then put his tongue in my mouth again. I lifted him up and flipped him down on the couch, and kissed his neck and ears too, grinded my body onto his. He shivered underneath me. I loved that I had that effect on him, even after all this time.

I made my way down his body, kissing every inch of him and putting his cock in my mouth. We both turned our heads slightly to watch other people give head while I gave him one. Connor started moaning, holding me down there for a while, but I let him fall from my mouth as I moved further down. He instinctively lifted up his long legs for me to lick his balls, then his hole. He waxes there so his balls and inside of his thighs are just as soft as his arms. Even the inside of his crack is soft. He smelled fresh and tasted clean with a hint of his natural musk, just like I knew he would. His body gave into me as I used my tongue to worship his genital area. I stayed down there for a while too, listening to him moan, feeling the softness of his skin on my tongue and him shudder underneath me.

Eventually, I lifted up to grab the lube off the floor, fingered his insides first, then coated my dick, and entered him. He held onto my arms while I fucked him, slowly at first, then with a little more speed. I loved watching his face when I was over him like that. His mouth opened as he moaned, his eyes squeezed closed, his forehead scrunched up, and his cheeks getting red. I put my tongue in his mouth, and he instantly wrapped his lips around it and sucked my tongue hard. I moved my face just inches from his, and he called my name softly, "Jamel," melting my heart. Suddenly I wanted to change up.

I stopped moving as I kissed him and said to him softly, "I want you to cum inside of me."

Connor's eyes opened slightly. Even in the dim light, his blue eyes sparkled. "Yes, please," he said and then smiled, making me laugh.

I slid out and he gasped, as if I'd taken something precious from him. We moved together. I slowly laid backward, and he slowly moved over me, kissing along the way. Neither of us were paying attention to the porn anymore; they might as well have been watching us. He grabbed the lube and pulled both our cocks together, then glistened and stroked us at the same time, making me moan out loud. Then he reached down and put two lube-coated fingers inside of me, making me moan more.

When he felt we were good and ready, I lifted one leg over the back of the couch and held the other up. Connor slid inside of me, pressing in without stopping, grazing against my prostate, and making me gasp. We switched once every other week, not because of me but because Connor almost always wanted me to do him. Truthfully, I would rather be on top; it's kind of in my nature to do so, but I wouldn't mind getting fucked more. Because it was Connor, the only person in the world that made me feel secure when I gave my all to him. Only he could touch that part of me. Not just physically but emotionally too.

He bottomed out, then looked at me. "You're so beautiful. Even in the dim light, your eyes still sparkle," he said softly.

I grinned. "I just thought the exact same thing about you, baby," I told him.

He smiled, and we kissed. Then he pulled back slowly to the head, then pushed in hard and with speed, making my body jolt and my eyes roll back, and I hissed. He saw that reaction and laughed.

"Fuck you, Connor," I said jokingly.

"No sir, I'm fucking *you*," he said jokingly back.

We laughed and kissed. He took my leg from me and continued to fuck me in this way, grazing his big dick against my walls slowly, then sliding past my prostate forcefully. I knew what he wanted, for me to be more vocal, and I gave it to him. I moaned louder and held onto him tighter, letting him fuck me harder and letting my inhibitions go. We were going to be there a while, and I was okay with that.

He slammed into me repeatedly and told me, "I know you love this dick, don't you? You fucking love this cock. Look at you, begging for this cock. Fuck, this hole is tight. Keeping this hole nice and tight for me, don't you? Cuz you love when your man is fucking you like this. I know you love this dick. Take it, take all of this cock. This is my ass, you hear me? This ass belongs to my dick. Take this cock all in you, fuck!"

Connor's shit-talking was funny and erotic, like he was in a 1970s porn flick. Good thing he didn't need a response from me, except my loud moaning, to keep him going. Dirty talk wasn't my thing, but I'd gotten used to his. It's adorable. It also amazed me that he didn't initiate this more. He obviously enjoyed fucking me more than he let on.

He began to move faster and more erratically so I knew he was close, less shit-talking and more cursing. He was about to make me cum too when he slammed into me one last time, moaning out his orgasm and ejaculation. I felt his sperm pool up inside of me and warm me up from the inside. This was still the most amazing feeling ever, him cumming inside of me. And because he was the only one that had ever done it, it truly made me feel one with him.

But I was ready to switch back. I let Connor catch his breath, then lifted him off me and pushed him onto his back. He laughed as I pulled him closer by his ass cheeks and laid all the way down on him.

"Big Daddy didn't cum yet," I said on his lips. "My turn." His eyes went wide, and he gasped in mock fear, which I loved.

I quickly added more lube to me, pushed his legs up, and thrusted inside of him all the way to the hilt in one motion. "Fuuuuck!" he screamed.

With his legs on my shoulders and his knees in his chest, I fucked him mercilessly. His moans became high-pitched sounds of pain and pleasure. He dug his nails into me, leaving scratches on the back of my neck. His body was completely lax and malleable as I buried myself as far as I could go, pulled out halfway and buried myself again. He called upon Jesus and God and someone named Ahh Fuck as I pounded him, mimicking that clap clap clap that I heard earlier. My midsection was on fire as my orgasm rose. I couldn't stop; I pounded right through it, losing my fucking mind as I climaxed, growled, and came inside of him like a volcano eruption, like I hadn't just came a few hours ago. I slowed down with a bunch of "ughs" and "ahs" escaping my mouth, as the last strands of cum spurted out of me into him. Then I moved his legs to the sides of me so I could lay against his chest, my face against his. Only then, feeling the wetness on his chest, did I realize he came a second time.

We laid there for a long moment, our heartbeats against each other slowing down together, me still buried deep inside of him. He rubbed my sweaty back with his fingertips softly, still sending chills through my body. Connor told me a long time ago this was the best part of our sex life, the coming down from our high and holding each other, and I couldn't agree more. I could have fallen asleep like that, and almost did, when he started talking.

"Can I ask you something, Jamel?" he said softly.

"Yeah?"

He let a moment pass, then asked, "Did you tell my sister that you wanted to adopt children?"

Fuck.

Mary Kate and I had the conversation around Easter and afterward, my fleeting thought was that Connor was going to act up if he heard that I had said this. Since he never brought it up, I assumed she never mentioned it to him, and I relaxed. But it sounded like she had that day, which meant I had to placate my husband, who I was certain was on the verge of losing his shit, no matter how calm he appeared to be.

I tried to slide out of him, but he grabbed my ass and held me there. I looked up at him and his face was composed, but I knew him.

I admitted. "We were talking about adoption months ago and yes, I told her that I had envisioned myself adopting children of color out of the system at one point."

"Well, that's news to me. You never mentioned it." Connor had a bit of edge to his voice. I tried to slide out of him again, and he again held me there by the bottom of my cheeks. "Was this dream of yours before you met me or during our entire relationship? Or a new dream?" He raised his eyebrow.

"You gonna let me go?" I asked him, my eyebrow also raised.

I was kind of annoyed that Connor was ruining the moment with this bullshit, and that I had to manage the emotional explosion that was about to happen. He sighed and removed his hand from my ass. I slid out but I didn't move off his chest.

"It was before," I told him. "And no, not during our entire relationship, but yes, I do think about it some-times. I don't mention it to you because I already know how you feel. So, there's no point in bringing it up."

"But now I feel like our whole relationship is a lie," he said.

I kept my face straight, but inside I was groaning and rolling my eyes. *Dude, really?*

He continued, "Because when I told you that I didn't want to have kids, you said you were cool with it. You said it wasn't a deal-breaker, that you could take them or leave them."

"I know what I said, Connor."

"But that wasn't the truth. The truth was that you wanted to be in a relationship with children. So now I feel like I've taken that from you. How do you think that makes me feel?"

I inhaled and exhaled through my nose. "I told you I was fine with not having kids and I meant that. I still mean that. I don't feel an emptiness or incomplete because we don't have children, Connor. We have more than enough children around us. But as far as our own, I was good with not having kids then. And I'm good with not having kids now."

"But see, I don't believe that, Mel. I believe you did want to adopt kids out of the system and raise them as your own. And when I told you that I didn't want kids, you told me what I wanted to hear so that you could keep me in your life. But here we are ten years later, and you still want kids. You may not feel an emptiness right now, but you might in another five or ten years, and then where does that leave us? This is the fucking nightmare that I never wanted!"

Okay, I'm done. He wants a fight, and I'm not giving it to him. And really, who needs kids when your husband acts like a moody-ass teenager?

Connor was under the impression that our relationship was one where we didn't argue. That we have disagreements that we talk it through like well-functioning adults. But the truth was Connor can be completely sensitive on one hand or a complete asshole on the other. He's an emotional ass Cancer, but I could never say that to him. The only reason we didn't have blowouts was because I stay calm and rational, and I don't let arguments escalate. This was one of those times.

I came off his chest and stood up, putting on my sweatpants as I talked. "Connor, here are a couple of things you need to know. First, yes, I did see myself adopting children out of the system before we got together. There are too many African-American children, especially boys, that are in foster care and age out of the system without homes or families. I wanted to stand in the gap for that."

"Jam—"

"Let me talk," I said sternly, cutting him off. "I let you say how you feel, now let me tell you what it is." I let a moment pass, then I continued.

"When I had this vision, I did not consider a partner; it was my own, personal goal. When we met and fell in love, you made it clear that was not your goal. I told you I could take them or leave them. That wasn't a lie; that was me shifting my personal goals to make room for you and your goals in my life. Because that's what people do for each other. Compromise. But understand that me saying I could take them or leave them meant if you wanted to have children, we would have children. If you didn't. then we wouldn't. I don't have a hard and fast rule on this either way. Ten years later, you still don't want to have children so we don't have them, and guess what, I am still fine with that."

Connor had sat up, so I knelt in front of his naked body and touched his thighs. "When I told you it wasn't a deal-breaker for me, that wasn't a lie either. I am not going to wake up one day and all of a sudden decide we need to get a divorce just so I can have children. That's not how real life works. That's not how real relationships work. You and I, we have a real relationship that works."

I pulled his face close to mine and stroked my nose against his, then kissed his lips. He asked me, "Jamel, do you want to adopt kids?"

Fuck, I knew he wasn't going to just let this go. I told him calmly, "Only if you do." I kissed his lips again.

"That's not an answer."

"That's the only answer you're getting." I kissed his lips again. *Let it go, man.*

"I don't want kids of my own," he said plainly. "I like my life. Our life."

"Then we won't have kids." I kissed him again. "We're pretty much feeding, clothing, and raising the Four Musketeers with their parents, so they are kind of our kids anyway." He laughed at that. *Good. He was letting it go.*

"Are we okay, baby?" I asked him sweetly.

He kissed me back. "We're okay." Connor pulled me in for a hug and said, "I'm so glad we can have these conversations and always come to an understanding without fighting."

I rolled my eyes in his neck. "Same, baby. Me too."

"But you do want kids, Jamel," Ethan said, as he raised his eyebrows at me. We were sitting in the Red Rock Bar and Grill having lunch the next day, and I told him about the conversation with Connor. "You told me that when we adopted Susie from South Korea. That was four years ago."

I sighed. *Why does he remember such things?* "I said I would have liked to adopt too. Not a baby like when you adopted JC, but a toddler, sure. Definitely school-aged."

"So why didn't you tell him that?"

142

I gave him a look. "You know why."

"This is like the one subject y'all completely ignore any time it's brought up," he said, shaking his head.

"We don't ignore it; we addressed it like we did yesterday. I told him like I always tell him, I could take them or leave them."

"But you would *prefer* to take them."

"Not at the expense of my relationship. It's not that important to me," I told him.

"Okay, I get that," Ethan said. "But just don't make it sound like you never wanted to have kids. Or that you wouldn't be really happy to have them now."

"I didn't. I was honest with him and told him it was a goal of mine. But I was okay with not having children of our own if that's not what he wants. Because I am."

"Hmmm ... alright," Ethan said, unconvinced. "Jack and I talked about it early, maybe because we were pretty much raising EJ together before we actually got together. He always wanted a house full of children and I wasn't sure if I did want more, but his enthu-siasm for us having kids together got me excited too."

"Well, you got four. Are you planning on more?"

"Hell no!" he said, making me laugh. "EJ is a pain in my ass as a teenager. I'm apologizing and thanking my parents profusely for not beating the shit out of me daily, if I was even a small amount of disrespectful to them as he is to me. Most of the time I just leave him to Jack. And you too; thank you for taking that one off my hands. When he turns 14 in a couple of months, he's going to be a full-fledged asshole."

I laughed as he lamented about being a parent. "And the girls, holy shit! They're only six and a half months apart, but they might as well be twins. All they do is fight and cry, fight and cry. Half the time I don't even know what they're fighting and crying about! 'She took my hairbrush,' 'she threw my doll,' blah blah blah. When they start getting their periods, I already told Jack I'm going to take week-long monthly trips somewhere. Jeeeesus." He slapped his hand on his forehead.

I laughed and asked, "And Jamie?"

"He's the only one I still like," he said with amusement. "The one I didn't even know I wanted but now I can't live without. He completes my family."

Ethan's ex-wife Patricia pulled a fast one on him. She showed up nine months pregnant, actually at our house during our Halloween party, looking for Ethan. She asked him to be her labor partner because she didn't have one, refusing to tell anyone who the father was. Then she gave birth and snuck out of the hospital on day three, leaving him alone with the baby after putting his name on the birth certificate and telling everyone at the hospital that the baby was his, knowing full well Ethan hadn't touched her since Ethan Junior was born. Ethan was pissed and, at first, considered dropping the baby off with her family but by the time they found out and came for him, he had changed his mind, already naming the baby Jamison. A nasty family court hearing happened between them and her parents, but eventually the judge decided it was in the best interest for the baby to stay with Ethan and Jack, where he already had a half-brother and had been in a loving two-parent home for almost a year, rather than his older maternal grandparents. It had been almost two years, and no one had heard from Patricia to this day.

"He's a great kid. All your kids are really great, you know. Even EJ." I smiled at him.

He smiled back. "See that twinkle in your eye when I talk about my kids? You want kids, Jamel."

I sighed again. "Let it go, Ethan."

I looked around and saw Winter coming from the back room of the bar. I was about to call her name, but then I saw BJ pull her back and kiss her, passionately. My mouth dropped.

Ethan saw it too. "Whoa. When the fuck did that happen?"

We looked at each other and snickered. This pair was definitely unexpected. Husky, reddish brown-haired, bearded BJ with sexy Winter, whose perfectly shaped breasts and hips with a small waist in between made it impossible not to stare at her, even as the gay men Ethan and I were. It was literally a beauty and the beast situation happening.

"Well, she probably hangs around them a lot since Mina and his brother Sam started a family," I said.

"Yeah, but that looked a lot like a 'we just had hot, sweaty, naked sex' kiss rather than a 'let's babysit our niece together' peck," Ethan said. He turned back to me. "You think Connor knows?"

"Probably," I said. "Connor knows everything that goes on with his friends, even the stuff they don't tell each other. He's the keeper of all their secrets. And they still have their so-called tribe meetings every other week or so."

Ethan rolled his eyes. "Thank God Jack was never a part of that."

"Well, I think you had to be of a certain level of promiscuity to be included in the tribe." I laughed and Ethan laughed with me. "I don't know if Jack ever reached that caliber."

"Naaah. Jack was 23 when we met and had less partners than he could count on his hands. He was pretty much a novice when I got a hold of him."

"And I assume you showed him the ropes?" I winked at Ethan. He laughed and shrugged, making me laugh.

"I don't know how it would have been if Connor was less experienced than me," I said. "I don't know if I'm the teaching kind."

"Son, I'm pretty sure Connor was teaching *you*. I'm pretty sure he's more experienced than the both of us." Ethan laughed.

"Ay yo, don't talk about my husband's whoring past," I said seriously, then laughed. Ethan snorted in laughter.

"What's so funny?" a female voice asked.

We had been laughing so hard we didn't see Winter make her way over. She squeezed herself on the bench next to me, her hips with nowhere else to go but touching mine. She smiled at me with her bright hazel eyes, then at Ethan, who she reached across the table to touch his hand.

Ethan smiled and cleared his throat. "Nice to see you, Winter. You're not working today?"

He did not move his hand from underneath her, and she took that opportunity to begin to stroke it with her perfectly manicured fingers. "Yes. I had a break and wanted to grab lunch. Glad I got a chance to see you here," she said to him seductively.

Then she turned to me and leaned in real close. "And you too, handsome."

I grinned and said, "Winter, sweetheart, whatever man gets a hold of you won't know what to do with you."

She smiled and kissed my cheek, then turned back to Ethan. "So, what were you laughing about?" she asked, still stroking his hand and he let her. Winter had been shamelessly flirting with him since he moved to town twelve years ago, and he allowed it to happen all the time.

"You came all the way over here from Providence just for lunch? That's a helluva drive, hun," he said amusingly, ignoring her question.

Winter gave no indication of her indiscretion. "Yes. I like the food here."

"Hmmm ... and the company," he said with a smile. I grinned again.

She moved in closer to him over the table. "The only company I have right now is you, Ethan. Do you want to keep spending time with me? My next hair appointment is in two hours, so I have time. We can call Jack over if that makes you comfortable. Maybe I can finally see what you both are working with."

Ethan shifted close to her and said in her face, "Winter, love, I haven't touched a woman in fourteen years. I am not about to start now." He leaned in closer and kissed her cheek. "But if I did, it would be you," he said sweetly.

Surprisingly, Winter blushed and sat back. She fanned herself dramatically. "Whew, Ethan, you are one sexy-ass man."

She looked over at me and winked. "You too, handsome." I laughed out loud.

❤

The sound of the garbage truck in the distance woke me up. It was Connor's turn to take it out, and he typically forgets the recycling bin. Connor had to leave early to let the exterminator in The Residence, so I begrudgingly got out of bed and made my way downstairs, and lo and behold, the blue bin filled with cans, boxes, and bottles was still there. I grabbed it and made it outside just in time, as the truck was passing my house.

I was still holding it when the cocoa-skinned sanitation man came up to me and grabbed it from my arms.

"Thank you," I said, trying not to stare at his full lips.

"You're welcome." He paused holding the bin and asked, "What's your name?"

"Jamel," I said, then internally kicked myself. *Why did I tell him my name? And don't do it, Mel. Don't do it, don't—*

"What's yours?"

He smiled widely. "Jonathan. I'm new on this route."

I know, I thought slyly. But I kept my face straight. He went to take the recycling bin to his truck and came over to hand it back to me. He looked up at my house, then looked back at me and smiled again.

"Hey Jamel?" he said, as he walked backward.

"Yeah?"

"I think you're missing a flag." He winked and turned around to cross the street and continue his work.

I turned and looked up at the three flags on my porch: the Army, American, and Marine Corps flags, side by side. I laughed out loud and turned to him as he watched me, then he laughed. I turned around and went back into the house.

CHAPTER 11

HIDDEN AFFECTION

Connor

Three days after her 17th birthday, Deann knocked on our door and brought her best friend Mackenzie with her, a raven-haired, cute girl that was always happy and smiling. Or maybe she was just always happy and smiling with Deann. *Maybe Deann makes her happy.*

"Can I stay here with you for a few days, Uncle Con?" my niece asked me. "I did a thing, and I don't want my parents to know."

I thought the "thing" was her coming out, but then she lifted up her shirt and showed me her small phoenix tattoo below her right breast. It was shaped differently than mine but just as beautiful. Where the one on my back has wings spread out and is colorful, hers was black and sideways, where the wings were behind it. It was actually pretty good.

"Mackenzie got one too, so we just need a place to crash so it can heal," she said. Then Mackenzie pulled up her shirt and showed her phoenix tattoo in the same place. I also caught that this conversation started in a "Can I stay" and ended up being a "We need a place to crash" kinda situation.

I smiled at them. "You girls got matching tattoos?"

"Yeah, cool right?" Mackenzie said with a smile.

I looked over at Jamel lying on the couch, who said, "Connor and I have matching tattoos too. On our forearms and our ring fingers. Funny, huh?" He had a straight face, but amusement was all in his eyes.

Deann caught on and did not like it. "So what?" she said with an attitude. "Lots of friends get matching tattoos. What are you tryna say?" she challenged him.

But he stayed cool and said, "I'm not trying to say anything. I was just pointing out that people get matching tattoos all the time, especially when they are so close, right?"

Deann was about to retort, but Mackenzie touched her arm. "Right," her friend said and smiled. "So, can we stay, please? Three days, tops. Just until it heals."

"Sure," he answered for us. "You girls can take the basement."

I looked over and gave him a warning look. He glanced at me but then turned back to them. "But we have a barbecue to go to tomorrow at my brother's house, and you're coming with us."

"Only if there will be cute boys there," Deann said confidently.

Mel and I exchanged looks of amusement, but then he turned back to her and said, "Well it's Providence and some neighbors will be there too, so maybe."

The girls smiled at each other. I asked them, "Did you eat yet? We already had dinner but there's stuff to make fish tacos left on the stove, if you want to make you some."

"Thanks, Uncle Con!" Deann said happily.

"You're so cool, Uncle Con. You're like the coolest uncle ever. I wish you were my uncle," Mackenzie flattered me. "You too, Uncle Mel," she added, as they made their way into the kitchen.

We watched them lightly touch each other as they piled on the food, made popcorn, and grab our two-liter coke, then headed down the basement stairs.

"Okay, see you in the morning. And thanks again," Deann called out.

As soon as we heard the door closed, I sat back down next to Jamel, who was watching a *Grey's Anatomy* rerun. I put his feet in my lap and rubbed them as I stated, "You do know they're going to munch each other in our house, right?"

He smiled without turning away from the TV. "They were going to have sex somewhere. Might as well be here and not in some shitty motel."

My mouth opened in shock. "So, you would allow your kids to fuck in your house?"

"If they were safe, yes. Because I know where they are and who they're doing it with."

"You are the worst fucking parent ever," I teased him.

Jamel chucked, then looked at me. "It was kind of an unspoken rule in my house. You know, with four boys, my parents were no fools. I didn't take advantage of it, but Ty and Donny definitely did. Instead of sneaking girls in, they brought them in to greet my parents and respectfully asked if she could stay the night. As long as they did that, the answer was yes. How do you think Afia was always over there? Did you think my parents didn't know they were sleeping together?"

"Wow," I replied, shocked. "I couldn't imagine being that open. In my house, it was kinda an unspoken rule to sneak around. I'm sure they knew I had girls in there, but they pretended they didn't. And if I was out all night, they never said a thing. And forget it for my sisters bringing home boys; that shit would never happen. Unless the guy wanted to wake up with a bullet in his ass."

He laughed. "Want me to tell your queer niece who hasn't come out yet not to fuck her pretend best friend?"

"No, it's fine. You're right, better here than some back alley. Besides, lesbians don't fuck. They just..." I rubbed my hands together, making him laugh out loud.

"You must not know many lesbians," he deduced. "Don't ever say that to a lesbian. They will beat the shit out of you."

My unit and I didn't meet annually anymore, as our lives ended up being so busy between our regular work, Vinnie's Vet Buddies work, and growing our individual families. The last one we did was in 2016 at my house, but six months before that, we were all in

California for a board meeting with DefaultShare and the August right before our retreat, Joe, Taylor, and I were in Texas to meet with another investor, so we really didn't need to meet up again. We started it as a way to honor Vinnie, but since we do it every day in our work, we decided to forgo these annual trips. So, for Labor Day weekend, we would do barbecues at Ty's house, Jamel's family home.

There were a ton of people there, including EJ hanging out with Imani before we got there. We brought Freddie with us because we knew Kim was going to be there, and as usual, the Four Musketeers huddled. Deann and Mackenzie did find some guys to hang around and flirt with, so they were enjoying themselves. *Maybe she's bi and not a full-blown lesbian.*

Afia and I sat together on the back porch steps. Her hair was natural, thicker, and longer with all the breastfeeding and vitamins she was taking. We still talk all the time, but we rarely hang out, just her and I like it used to be. *It's so crazy how many things have changed for us. She was still my best friend in the whole world, and still my Lovie. But we have other people we love now and other responsibilities. We're all grown up.*

I was thinking about it, so I said it. "You've been my best friend for twenty years, Lovie."

"And I'm going to be your best friend for the next twenty. But no more after that. That's all you get, forty years, tops. After that, you're gonna have to find yourself a new best friend," she joked and we giggled like we do.

She reached over and held my hand. "How's Mel?"

I sighed. "You know Mel. He's 'fine.'" I put "fine" in air quotes with one hand. "He's not gonna talk about it. I'm sure he wrote it all down and burned it by now."

She nodded. "It must be really hard losing your best friend. I don't know what I would do if I lost you. Even twenty years from now."

I squeezed her hand. "We'll just meet again. In another life."

She put her head on my shoulder and said, "Okay. But for now, I really like this one. Really, really like this one."

I smiled too. "Me too, Lovie. Me too."

We sat comfortably in silence until Tenille came running up in tears. "Mommy! I have a bruise; it's bleeding."

Her 4-year-old showed us the barely notice-able cut with the invisible blood on it. Lovie became overly dramatic. "Oh noooo! I'm so sorry, baby! Want mommy kisses?"

"Uh-huuuuh," her daughter bemoaned.

Afia kissed the area with three loud kisses, then rubbed it twice. "It's okay now, right?"

Tenille grinned with all her teeth. "Yes." She turned to walk away but then turned back like she remem-bered to thank her mother with a hug and kiss. Then she ran off.

I smiled. "Motherhood looks good on you."

"Thanks. You should try it." She smiled knowingly.

"Motherhood? Nah, I don't have the childbearing hips for it," I joked. She bumped her shoulder against mine and then leaned back on my shoulder.

"How's work?" she asked after a while.

"Good. I actually don't have anything scheduled for the rest of the year. I wanted to make sure I wasn't wearing myself thin with our trip to Aruba in October, Thanksgiving in Florida with our in-laws, and New Year's Eve in Atlanta."

"I saw your talk on YouTube. You did really well. You have a gift for motivational speaking," she told me.

"But not for property management?" I asked amusingly.

She laughed. "I'm just saying. I think you've found it. That thing you are passionate about, that also pays the bills."

"Sort of," I admitted. "Jamel still makes a shit-load more money than me. He pays the mortgage and I pay the rest of the bills, but I know his slice of the pie is a lot more than what I'm contributing to the savings account."

"There's nothing wrong with that, Connor. Because regardless, you're doing it together."

She was right, so I nodded. Then I asked her, "When are you going back to the pharmacy?"

"After Lil Ty turns one next month. Just part-time though, so I can feel productive. I need adult human contact during the day."

"Yeah, no more watching *Doc McStuffins* and *Elana of Avalor?*"

She looked up at me. "No, but you can come over and watch it any time."

I laughed. "I think I'd stick with watching *Property Brothers.*"

"You do know that neither of them is gay, right?"

I looked at her skeptically. "I keep telling you Jonathan is gay."

She laughed at my celebrity crush. "Stick to David Bromstad. He's more of your type."

"He sure fucking is," I agreed and stared out dreamily, making her laugh. "I'd lick every tattoo on his body. That's one sexy bottom."

"Hey, married man. You're not supposed to be fantasizing about anyone but your husband."

"Says who!?" I said shockingly. "Jamel probably pretends I'm Jussie Smollett when he's fucking me."

"No, he doesn't!" she laughed again.

I shrugged. "Maybe. Maybe not."

"No. Jamel is still so much in love with you. It's you and only you he wants."

I looked over at him in conversation with Dante. He was listening to his childhood friend that he rarely saw tell him a story. But he must have sensed me because he glanced at me too. We stared at each other, then he switched hands to hold his beer in his left and discreetly put his right wrist over his heart, then he winked at me. Even though he didn't have to do it anymore, since everyone there knew we're together, it still made me smile.

Lovie broke my focus on Mel by saying, "You should watch those four when they're at your house."

"Huh?"

She lifted up her head and pointed her chin at the Four Musketeers. "They are coupling up."

I laughed. "They're thirteen."

"Didn't stop you at thirteen. And they are all turning fourteen in the next couple of months. Starting high school next year. Kim is the only one that won't be at Rockville High but that won't stop Freddie from getting in a cab or bussing it to see her like EJ did to get to Imani. But it will be easier for them to just meet at your house … to fuck."

My eyes went wide. "Freddie is not ready for that. Shit, I'm not ready for that."

She shrugged. "Well, get ready. Look at them."

I saw what she saw. Usually, I see them just sitting together hanging out as they have done since they were five years old. But Kim had her hand on Freddie's knee. And Imani was sitting so close to EJ, their thighs were touching. There was definitely some not so hidden affection there. I wondered when that started officially.

"Hmmm…"

I looked back over at Jamel, who was laughing at whatever Dante was saying. *His unbelievably sexy best friend, who probably has an unbelievably big dick the way he fucks around.* I internally slapped myself. *Stop it, Connor.*

I told Lovie, "I'm still in love with him too, you know. I mean, I still think about fucking other people. I can't help that. But after all this time, it's still only him that I want."

"And that's a good thing." She sighed.

"And how are you and Ty?" I asked.

"We're good." Her voice went up an octave with that.

"Uh-oh. What's going on?"

She laughed. "Nothing. We're good, really. We're just … finding our way back from the sexual rut we put ourselves in. Having kids puts a real damper on your love life."

"Well, you're done, right? So start doing date nights again."

"Well..." she trailed off.

I turned all the way around and looked at her wide-eyed. "You better not be fucking pregnant! I cannot take you and Mina pregnant at the same time again, and I know she's trying."

Afia giggled. "No. I'm not. But you know ... One more in a year or two. Maybe one more after that."

"Fucking hell," I scoffed, and she laughed again. "Your vagina's going to look like the latest giant Balenciaga bag when you're done."

She laughed loudly at that, so loud others turned around to see where the sound was coming from. I giggled into my fist.

"Fuck you!" she eventually said. "He'll still eat it." We giggled hysterically.

"What are you two hens cackling about?" Ty said, coming over. He leaned in and gave his wife a kiss, then a few more. He ignored me like I knew he would.

I resisted the urge to roll my eyes and stood up. "We'll talk later, Lovie."

She turned her head briefly to grab my hand, squeeze it, and then let go before turning back to her husband.

A couple of weeks later, my Vinnie's Vet Buddies phone went off at about 5 a.m. Although I don't take hotline calls anymore, I still put myself in the rotation for emergency calls. Taylor was on call and for whatever reason he couldn't pick it up, so it automatically forwarded it to me. I grabbed it and went to the other bedroom to answer.

"Hello, this is Connor. How are you feeling right now?"

There was a brief silence. "Shitty," the man eventually said.

"Well, I'm glad you called. What's your name?"

He hesitated again, then said, "Call me L."

"Okay, L. Do you want to tell me why you're feeling shitty right now?" I asked.

"Are you a homosexual?" he asked.

Well, this is a first. But it made sense because Simon identifies himself as part of the LGBTQ community on our site. He was born Samantha, transitioned about eight years ago, and lives with his partner Mason. They have been together as long as Jamel and me. I made an internal note to ask Simon if he got this question regularly and how he responded to it.

But for now, I decided to avoid it. "Are you asking me because it's relevant to what you're going through? Are you homosexual?"

He laughed harshly. "Well, I just fucked a man about an hour ago so I'm not sure anymore."

Ah-ha. "Do you want to talk about how that came about?"

He paused, then started talking. "I just … I don't know … I've been married for sixteen years and we're going through a divorce. Lately, I've been hanging out with … a friend from my military days. And it just happened. I could blame it on the alcohol, but the truth is I wanted to. I've been dreaming about fucking him for months. Maybe years. I don't know..."

He stopped talking. I asked him, "Is this the first time you've had these feelings for a man?"

"I don't have *feelings* for him; I just wanted to fuck him," he said angrily.

"Okay," I said calmly. "Did you want to sleep with him or any men while you were in the service?"

"Did you?" he asked.

I didn't know why he kept turning the question around, but I was getting increasingly annoyed. I asked, "What branch of the military were you in?" I needed to get him talking about him.

"Marine Corps," he told me.

"When did you come home?" I asked.

"Five years ago."

"And how long have you been going through a divorce?"

"The last year. It's almost finalized."

"That's tough. The last five years sound like it has been rough for your relationship. For both of you." He didn't respond. "What do you think contributed to the divorce?"

"Well, my wife is a whore and has been fucking someone else for the last six years, so there is that."

"I'm sorry. That must have really hurt for you to find out," I responded with compassion.

"Honestly, not really. We didn't have a lot of sex to begin with. And we fell out of love a long time ago. We were still together for the children."

"So why are you getting divorced now?"

"Because her lover wants to marry her and be a family. Not with my goddamn kids though. I'll kill that motherfucker first," he said coldly. And I believed him.

"So, what is it that you want? For yourself that is?" *Not from me. Stop asking questions about me.*

"I want to know why I did it. What makes a man want to fuck another man? It's ... unnatural."

Not like I haven't heard that my whole life. "How did you feel when it was over?" I asked him.

"Fucked up. Dirty. Ashamed."

"What else did you feel?" He didn't answer. "It's just you and me here. I can't help you if you can't be completely honest with me."

He let a few moments pass, then said, "Satisfied." I didn't respond to let him keep talking if he wanted to. After a couple more moments, he said in a low voice, "I wanted to do it again. And again. It was awesome." Then he yelled, "FUCK!"

"L, I think—" I started, but he cut me off.

"I can't be a fag," he said. "I can't give into this ... shit. What the fuck do I look like? I'm a fucking man! I fuck women! I. Don't. Fuck. Men!"

"But you did," I challenged him. Typically, I don't challenge people too much on these calls, but L had some serious issues he needed to face. "You had sex with a man. And you enjoyed it. And by your own admission, you want to do it again. I'm not saying you're gay; only you can answer that for yourself. I'm saying after the things people like us have been through while in the service, it is not uncommon, or unnatural, for you to want something different for yourself, to go for the things that make you happy."

He was quiet for a moment. Then asked, "Is that what happened to you? Or were you always a fag?"

I inhaled and exhaled. *The word "fag" is getting old really fast. That was the last time I'm going to ignore it.*

"No, that's not what happened to me. But I've spoken to people who have come home and find themselves wanting to experiment with same-sex relations. Some found themselves to be gay and some bisexual. And all of this is normal."

He was quiet again, then said, "I know who you are, Corporal Connor McIntyre. I know you live in Rhode Island. And I know you fuck men."

Okay, that shit rattled me. And it's been a long time since I've been rattled.

I kept calm and said, "I'm sure you do. My name and information are on the website. So, you should also know I'm not bullshitting you. I've spoken to and counseled countless men and women. What you're experiencing is not unique. Maybe talking to others that have had similar experiences may help you. I can connect you with a few if you would like."

"Why, so you can make me a fag?" he said nastily.

"L, I'm going to ask you not to use that word. Not in reference to yourself or to me. You used the word homosexual earlier. Keep using that. But to answer your question, I'm not trying to make you into any-thing. I just want you to understand yourself better. Isn't that what you want?"

L ignored me and said, "I went to hear you speak a couple of years ago in New York. You were talking about the effects of secondhand trauma, how we experience it watching and hearing about the deaths of our comrades, and how our families experience it through us. You were great."

"Thank you. But L—"

"But you didn't mention that you were a fag. You didn't mention that you were married to one."

"I've asked you not to use that word."

He ignored me again. "I dreamed about you that same night. It made me wonder about you. Wondered if you were a top, because you seemed like a top."

What. The. Fuck.

"I'm not going to respond to that, L," I said staying calm, despite how I was feeling on the inside. "Did you call to talk about me, or did you call because you needed my help?"

He ignored me a third time. "But then I saw a picture of you and your partner at a past event. And I'm like, this black guy is definitely a top, so Connor is a bottom. That surprised me."

I chuckled despite my anger. "So, you looked me up. Great. So, what is it that you want, L?"

"I had been calling for about a month now, trying to get you on the phone, Connor. I wanted to talk to you," he said.

Okay, now this is getting really unsettling. He's stalking me? No bueno. "Why did you want to talk to me?"

"I just told you. I saw you speak, and I dreamed about you. I was curious about who you are, your life, your relationship. Curious about you."

"So, is everything you said on this call a lie, just to get me talking?"

"None of it was a lie. I'm a Marine vet. I'm getting divorced. I had sex with a man last night. And this morning. And I don't know what to do."

"You need to talk to someone that can understand what you are going through. Let me help you do that."

"No, because you're just going to connect me to other fags that are going to tell me that being a faggot is okay when it's not. It's not okay. It's sick and depraved, and I'm not a fucking faggot!"

I inhaled and exhaled again. "Actually, I was going to connect you with a counselor that talks to vets. Where are you from?"

He hesitated, then said, "Connecticut."

"Okay, would you like me to give you the information of a counselor in your area that can help you process this? He does video therapy sessions, so you don't have to go anywhere."

"No, I don't want to talk to him," he said dismissively.

"Then what then!?" I gritted through my teeth, losing my cool. This had never happened before. I'm usually patient and understanding, but the fact that he knew too much about me was making me freak out a bit. "What is it that you want from me?"

"I want to know if you're a top or a bottom. Do you fuck or do you get fucked, like a good, little fag?" Then he laughed.

Aaaaand now I'm fucking done with this conversation.

"That's not relevant. It's more important to know if you did the fucking or got fucked last night. Because I think you did both, especially the getting fucked part. And having a dick in your ass would make you very gay, just so you know," I said conversationally. *Because fuck this guy.*

And, apparently, he felt the same about me. "Fuck you, you fucking faggot. Go suck a dick because that's all you're good for, right? Sucking dick you—"

I hung up.

A part of me expected him to call back and continue to curse me out, but he didn't. I realized I was breathing really fast, so I stood up and left the room. Maje met me happily in the hallway, and we walked downstairs together. Diesel was on the couch and just looked at me when I came down. He was only twelve years old but had a lot of health problems, so he rarely slept in our bed, as the stairs bother him. I tried not to think about my dog dying, not while I was already keyed up and anxious. I went to the kitchen sink and threw water on my face first. Then I went to fill their food bowls, started the coffee pot, and watched it prepare as I became lost in thought.

After I came out to my friends and eventually my family, I experienced very little homophobia, save for my father and my brother. Almost everyone showed me love and support, and it made me feel great to know that I could be me and no one would stop loving me or change their relationship with me. But when I started becoming more of a public face for the organization, I kinda left out the stuff about my personal life. On the website, my CEO blurb had my full name, which state I live in, about my time in the Marines, and my "friendship" with Vinnie that led us as a unit to start this organization. I did that on purpose.

Jack said that when he met Ethan, Ethan said he considered his bedroom private, that he wouldn't volunteer the information. But if someone asked him if he was gay, he wouldn't deny it. So, I wanted to be more like that. My sexuality was not the forefront of what I'm doing with VVB so it shouldn't take center stage, and that was how I looked at it. I'm the Anderson Cooper of veterans: a gay man who was also a reporter in his line of work, and that is what he focuses on. So I was good being the Ethan Starling or Anderson Cooper of the LBGTQ community.

Ethan, like Jamel, had no qualms about holding hands in public and some level of PDA, and neither did Jack. But all of them had been out since they were in their teens and I was late to the game, having only come out officially seven years ago. My eyes still dart around when Jamel holds my hand in public, so I noticed when people gave us dirty looks and he clearly did not give a shit. I was still afraid to put rainbow flags in my home or wear them like Josh proudly did with his t-shirt of the American flag with the rainbow colors on it. I thought it was such a cool shirt, but I wouldn't dare. And the small rainbow sticker Ethan put on the leasing door of my office still made me nervous. I knew it was his way of saying gay applicants are welcomed, but I always think, *If someone comes in here, they would automatically assume I'm gay.* And then I laugh at myself, because, *fuck, I AM gay!*

Ugh, this double mind that I have about acknowledging my sexuality and showing gay pride is kinda awful.

My old therapist told me it will take time to feel comfortable being gay and not to worry so much about being loud and proud but just being comfortable in my own skin. To keep doing the things that made me feel happy, regardless of how anyone else felt about it. And I have tried to do that. The trip back from Atlanta was everything I needed from Jamel; because he had been so distant from me for so many days, I was eager for his touch. So when he took my hand and held it throughout the airport, I held his back tightly, trying not to care who saw us. It made me so happy when he became overly affectionate with me, even if it was in public. And he continued to be affectionate with me, laying his head in my lap at the terminal, leaning on me on the plane, kissing me with soft kisses here and there, and that very public, broad daylight, awesome car fuck. So, I was getting better at not caring about the negativity from strangers of who I am and who I loved.

L rattled me because he was everything I was worried about: someone finding out about my private life and using it to try to hurt me mentally, emotionally, and even professionally. The military had changed some, but there was still a lot of prejudice out there. And I didn't want vets to not want to use our services just because their CEO happened to be gay. I would love to say that we didn't care about those homophobic vets, but even fucktwat vets needed help too. L was a fucktwat, and I hoped one day he came to terms with his sexual fluidity. But I also hoped he never used our hotline again. I reminded myself again to call Simon today to give him a head's up. And a warning.

Jamel came downstairs as I poured a cup of coffee. I handed him the one in my hand and made another one for myself. He was already dressed for work so he must have gotten up shortly after I left him in bed.

"Good morning." He kissed my lips before he took a sip.

"Morning," I said without looking at him.

He cocked his head to get a better look at my face. "You okay? Was it a bad call?"

I sighed and told him. As his face became more stoic, I knew that meant he was becoming increasingly angry. I could read his unreadable faces now.

"I'm sorry that happened." Jamel pulled me into a gentle hug, and I put my head on his shoulder. Then he said, "I think you should stop taking calls from the field. You don't need to do that anymore; you have more than enough volunteers all over the country. Simon doesn't take calls, and neither should you."

I pulled back from him. "He does though. He covers emergency calls more than I do. I only cover when they need me to cover. Taylor needed me to cover this week, so I did."

"Someone else can do it," he said, with concern all in his gray eyes.

I shook my head. "It's my unit. You know I have to."

He shook his head too, but he understood. "If you ever get a call from him again and I'm next to you, put me on the phone," he said seriously.

I chuckled. "Yes, because having my big, black husband threaten someone is exactly how I want to be portrayed, like a damsel in distress."

"Well…" He nuzzled his nose with mine. "You're more like my don in distress." I giggled as he kissed me softly. "And I'm your black knight in shining armor.

I will defend your honor, sir." I touched his face, and he kissed me softly again. "Are you okay, really? I know that rattled you."

He also could read me well. "I'm fine. Thank you." I put my head on his shoulder again.

Jamel kissed my head and said, "I gotta go."

"Okay." We kissed one more time, then I walked him to the door, reminding him, "Don't forget the family dinner with my sisters is tonight. I'm cooking. Just be home before six o'clock, okay?"

"Okay, baby," he said, as he made his way down the outside steps to his car.

I saw the garbage truck turn on our block and ran back to the kitchen to see if I remembered the recycling bin, because I typically forget. But it wasn't there so Mel must have brought it out last night. I went back out to the porch to thank him, and I heard the man before I saw him say, "Hey, Meeel."

I stepped closer to the rail, my coffee cup still in my hand, to look down and see my husband greet the garbage man in a very friendly voice. "Hey, Jon. How's your day going?"

"Better now that I see you," Jon said and smiled at him, as he pulled the bin to his truck. Jamel laughed.

For the second time that morning, I thought, *What. The. Fuck.*

The thing is, everyone flirts with Jamel. Men, women, even kids stare and admire him. I was used to it. But something about that guy, same race and arguably a little handsome, flirting with my husband made all my Spidey senses start to tingle. Jamel thought I didn't know that he specifically seeks out black male porn, but I had his PornHub account info. It used to make me insecure, but I let it go a long time ago. Fantasy was just fantasy.

But this was too close to reality because this man obviously wants to fuck my husband. And Jamel is obviously encouraging the attention. And I obviously ain't having it.

I bent over the porch rail right next to my Marines flag to make my presence known. Jon the fuckface garbage man looked up at me, as he dropped the empty bin off, and smiled. I did not smile back. Jamel didn't look up as he dragged the bin back to the house, but I knew he knew that I was there.

I stared at Fuckface with a hard look. He looked back at Jamel with an all-too-familiar face, one that said, *Really? A white guy?* And Jamel laughed, again.

I'm going to kick his ass.

Fuckface Jon moved on, and Jamel was about to get into his truck when I started coming down the stairs, leaving my cup on the rail. He had this goofy smile on his face, like he expected me to flip the fuck out, which honestly his assessment was correct.

"Hey Meeel," I said, mocking his new friend as I walked up to him. He still had one foot in the car and one foot on the ground. "Who was that?" I asked casually.

"That was Jon. He introduced himself to me about a month ago."

"Yeah?" I cocked my head to the side.

He chuckled and said, "Don't start, Connor."

I threw my hands up in a shrug and said, "Start what? I'm just interested in why I'm just now finding out about your new best friend Jon. Why hasn't

Jon introduced himself to me since, you know, he wants to greet all the neighbors on his route?" My eyes narrowed.

"Because you don't get up this early when the trucks come," he said factually.

"Well, I think I am from now on," I told him seriously. He laughed; I didn't.

"I'm not fucking kidding. What the fuck was that!?" I said angrily.

"What was what?" he said calmly, making my blood boil.

"That—" I pointed down the street at the fading truck, "dickhead was flirting with you."

"A lot of people flirt with me, Connor," he said, still being factual. "I can't stop it when people decide to flirt with me."

"But you were flirting back, asshole!"

"How was I flirting back?"

"By..." *Fuck, he got me.* But I wasn't letting up. "It wasn't what you said; it was how you said it. And your body language and shit. Laughing with him and shit … Don't play like I didn't just see what I saw!" I yelled at him loudly.

Jamel inhaled and exhaled through his nose. He pulled me roughly by my t-shirt toward him and kissed my lips. I tried to pull back, saying, "Get the fuck off me!" But he used both hands to pull me closer, wrapping them around me and pressing me tightly against him. I kept my arms at my side and turned my face away, looking upward.

"Coooooonooooor." He drew out my name in a sing-songy way. He kissed my open neck with two soft wet kisses, which I hated and loved. Then he kissed the back of my ear, which cooled my anger down just a bit. He knew that was my spot.

"Look at me," he said softly.

I did, letting him see how upset I was. We stared at each other for a moment, his gray eyes into my blue ones. Then I said, very seriously, "You know I will kill him, right?"

Jamel laughed his big laugh and kissed my face. "Yes. I know. And you know I never would. So, stop it."

"Just as long as you know, motherfucker."

I wrapped my arm around his neck, forgetting we were outside our home on the street and kissed his lips roughly, then put my tongue in his mouth. Our neighbors knew we were gay, but they hadn't actually seen us affectionate like that. I wondered for a brief second how many were looking at us from their windows. Then I didn't give a shit.

He moved his face into my neck and said in my ear, "Love you."

Then he kissed my neck again, trailed his fingers from the back of my neck down to my ass to make me shiver, patted it twice, and let me go. I watched him get in his car, and he smiled at me as he drove off. I pulled the last empty trash can back to the house, making it my sworn mission to be the only person in this house to take out the garbage from this moment on. *Fuck that guy too.*

❤ ❤ ❤ CHAPTER 12 ❤ ❤ ❤

MARRIED WITH CHILDREN

Jamel

Apparently, Connor did not tell Mary Kate that Angie was coming to dinner too. When I got home, I met Mary Kate and Dennis on the couch, having a glass of wine and looking comfortable, and that was my first clue.

Connor came over to me, handed me my own glass of chardonnay with a kiss on my lips and said, "Go freshen up." Then he lowered his voice more and said, "Angie will be here soon."

"She doesn't know," I said instead of asked. He shook his head. "Connor..." I said warningly.

"It will be fine," he said dismissively. "I got this."

I shook my head, but I was going to let it go because he was going to play ringmaster tonight. *This is not my circus and not my monkeys.*

I went upstairs to shower and change. By the time I came back down, the table had been set for four, and we sat down for dinner. Connor baked some chicken breasts in a light garlic and herb seasoning, mixed veggies, and warmed up bread rolls. He had gotten to be a pretty good cook over the years.

"So, how's business?" Dennis asked me.

"Going well. We're making a name for ourselves in Massachusetts, just like I wanted, and I'm still individually inspecting homes but not so much electrical work. You? Still making the rich richer?"

I invested in some stock with him over the years for savings but mostly as a retirement plan, and he had been making me pretty good money. It was how I paid for our anniversary trip to Aruba next month. Dennis laughed and dived into telling us about the last huge acquisition his firm made until the doorbell rang. They both looked at the door, and I looked at Connor. He smiled at me, then got up to answer it.

"Hi Connor!" Angie's voice rang out.

Mary Kate snapped her neck around to me and gave me a dirty look. I shook my head to say to her, *Not me.* Her nostrils flared. She started to get up, but Dennis held her arm, a little more tightly than I cared for, then let her go just as quickly as she sat back down.

Angie, Chad, and Evelyn came in. Angie looked at her sister and said meekly, "Hi MK."

MK did not respond, just glared at her. But sweet Evie walked right up to her aunt and raised her hands to be picked up. That melted Mary Kate's heart and she smiled at her, then lifted her into her lap, giving her a tight hug.

"I missed you too, sweetie," she told her.

Angie came over to her sister, as Chad and Dennis greeted each other with handshakes. "I missed you too, MK," she said softly.

MK looked at her, then looked away with her eyes upward. It reminded me of Connor earlier that day when he wouldn't look at me, upset when he caught Jon flirting with me and me allowing it. I knew I would have to find a way to nip it in the bud. The way he looked was the same anger, annoyance, and frustration that MK had on her face right now. They were more similar in their features and mannerisms than Connor would like to admit.

Angie took the seat across from MK next to me and Connor sat at the head of the table, with Chad at the other end. Connor smiled widely. "I love when we all can get together like this." He clapped his hands gleefully, as everyone glared at him. He pretended he didn't notice. "Dennis, you were talking about work."

"Yes, I was," he said and delved into his story again. Chad helped, and soon it became a conversation between Connor, Dennis, and Chad, while Mary Kate spoke softly and cut up little pieces of her food to feed her niece, and Angie and I were silently eating.

Toward the end of the meal, Connor said, "Oh, I got dessert. Guess what kind?"

He didn't wait for a response; he jumped up and went into the freezer, bringing out a half sheet of tiramisu. Both of his sisters' faces lit up. "Good, right? I got it at a local Italian restaurant in Providence. Mel, remember our first date? That one, I went all the way over there just to pick this up." I smiled at him for that.

He put the tray between the two of them and went to grab a couple of spoons and said, "We're going to play a game though." Angie and MK groaned simultaneously. When the six of us come together, usually eight with Lavell and Kendra there too, we typically end up playing some kind of game: charades, Pictionary, even drunken games like Never Have I.

"C'mon, it's a fun one. More like an ice-breaker than a game. We take a bite and say one thing you like or love about someone else at the table, who's not your spouse."

"Connor," Mary Kate said his name threateningly.

"It'll be fine; here, you go first," he said, handing her a spoon.

She took a bite, and it melted in her mouth, making her smile. "Hmmm … I think the only person I like at this table right now is Jamel. And you too, Chad, I guess." He smiled at that, happy that Mary Kate did not hate him by extension.

"Pick one, Jamel or Chad," Connor said.

She looked at me and said, "I love how loving and loyal you are, Jamel, even to backstabbing traitors that happen to be your husband."

I laughed loudly at that. Connor smiled, not taking any offense, and handed me the next spoon. I decided to play along with this circus. I took a bite of the delicious cake and said, "Angie, I love how much you love your family, and you would do anything for them."

Angie smiled at me. Connor handed her a spoon. She took a bite and said, "Mary Kate, I love how strong and beautiful you are. Resilient. Confident. I have always admired and even kinda envied my big sister a bit. And I could learn a thing or two from you, like how to keep my big mouth shut and just listen more."

No one spoke until Connor said, "Mary Kate, you go again."

She swallowed and dipped her spoon in to take another bite, then said, "Evie, I love how sweet and precious you are." Then she kissed her face, making her giggle. She handed Evelyn her spoon, who excitedly took a big chuck off of the cake, making us all laugh.

Connor said, "Evie, who do you love?"

Evie mimicked Connor in her toddler voice, "Hodouvoov." We all laughed.

"Mommy or Daddy, pick one, Eves," Connor said.

"Mommy!" she squealed.

Angie took a bite and said, "Dennis, I love how well you take care of my sister. How much you love her. I would say that she is lucky to have you, but I think you're the lucky one, because she is perfect."

Mary Kate scoffed. "Perfect but defected, right?"

"I never said that," Angie denied.

"You all but said it. You implied it."

"No, that's—"

"You think because I lose babies and you get to keep them that somehow makes me less than you. But it doesn't."

"I don't think that at all!" Angie yelled

"Yes, you do; yes, you fucking do!" MK yelled back.

Poor Evie, who was sitting on her lap, was confused at all the yelling. She jumped off Mary Kate and ran into her dad's lap, holding onto him tightly.

MK stood up and started yelling at Angie about how she made her feel when she told her to just go adopt a child when she was still mourning her miscarriage: hurt, uncared for, unheard. That she didn't give a fucK, with a hard K, how Angie felt about her trying again and again and again, that she will have her baby, whether Angie supports her or not. And Angie tried to defend herself at first, saying that wasn't what she felt or said, but after a while, she just shut down and let Mary Kate go off and cried in her hands. I put my arm around her shoulder and let her weep.

Then Mary Kate started crying too. "You know damn well that you've always been the perfect female McIntyre, not me. And this just goes to prove it once and for all. You can have it all. The family, the house, the career. And I can't." Then she sat down and cried as Dennis held her.

Connor let it all happen and didn't say anything. When it was nothing but sniffles left at the table, he stood up and took his bite.

He said, "The reason I was so afraid to come out is because I thought you would never accept me. I knew Owen and Matt wouldn't, so you know, fuck them. But my greatest fear was that I wouldn't have a family anymore. And by family, I mean the three women of my own flesh and blood wouldn't love me anymore if they knew I was gay. My mom and my two amazing sisters." He pointed his spoon at both of them.

"It meant everything to me to finally be able to show you all who I really am, and to introduce you to who I really love. My family was still my family, you know? Now we all have our faults, but the one thing that the three of us have in common is that we all get emotional and impulsive. And sometimes we say what we want without regard to how the other person feels until it's too late. But you know the beauty of family? We can forgive each other; we can take it back; we can have do-overs; and we can make it right.

"Now I need you two to forgive each other and make it right. Because this right here at this table, this is my family. But you two are my flesh and blood. Our family is already split up, so you two are all I really have. I need the three of us to stick together, because … then I have no one if you don't. And it will be my worst fear coming true."

He sat back down. I looked at him, but he wouldn't look at me, not at anyone. He wasn't crying, but I know he was on the verge of it.

Angie let go of me and reached for her hand across the table. "I am so, so sorry, Mary Kate. I love you, and I just want you to be okay. And I will shut up and support whatever you want to do from now on, I promise. I need you, MK. Please don't shut me out anymore."

MK took her hand. "I'm sorry too. I know you were just trying to help me see the other side of it. And I forgive you." She squeezed her hand.

Angie stood up and walked over to her sister, and they hugged and cried again. Dennis looked over at Connor and said softly, "Thank you."

He nodded. Chad spoke up and said, "Yeah, thanks, man."

"That's what I'm here for," Connor said smugly and took another bite of his tiramisu. I smiled at him, and he winked at me.

After dinner, we left the women upstairs to talk and went downstairs to the media room. Connor and Dennis started a game of pool while Chad went through the Amazon music collection on the Smart TV. I started the Keurig in the small kitchenette.

Connor asked Dennis, "So, how are you holding up, man?"

He shrugged. "I just want to make sure she's okay. Because she's the one going through it, right?"

Connor shook his head. "No, not by herself. You're going through it too."

Dennis gave Connor a skeptical look. "We know it's always about the women here. The one that's carrying and miscarrying. So, I just have to be present for her. I'm fine."

Connor let a few moments pass, then said, "I remember when my friend Benjin was going through this with his wife. He also always felt he needed to be strong for her. But one day he just broke down with me, you know, confessed that it was taking a toll on him. Losing hope. He felt like the only person he could do that with is me, because you know, men are supposed to be strong, and he couldn't fall apart in front of her. But he didn't feel so strong at that moment. After our talk though, he felt like he could be there for her."

Dennis shook his head. "Connor, what are you trying to do here?"

"Nothing," Connor said innocently. "Just giving you an outlet. It's just us men here. We're all family here, right? If you want to talk is all."

He nodded, and they played pool silently until Chad found what he wanted to listen to, an old 3 Doors Down album. Then Dennis started talking and moving his hands around like he was explaining a business deal.

"So, the problem is twofold; the blame is not all on her or on me. I have oligospermia, which is, you know, the boys aren't as strong as they should be, and she has a tilted uterus and endometriosis. These things make it almost impossible to meet conception on our own. So, the use of a reproductive endocrinologist was to greatly improve our chances of fertilization and maturation. The shots, the pills, the surgeries, all suggestions by a highly recommended physician that still gave us a 35 percent chance of success rate. And to me, 35 percent is still good; I gamble with people's money with less odds than that, you know what I mean?" He laughed at his own joke. "But after all these years, 35 percent started feeling more like 5 percent or 3 percent. That last one, three months in … that was hard … on both of us, you know." He coughed and wouldn't look at any of us.

"We thought we'd beaten the odds. But I guess not … So, after that last one I'm like, okay, next chapter, adoption. I said something one time, and she snapped at me, so I didn't say it again. But you know maybe it was selfish of me because I kind of sent Angie in there to get her warmed up to the idea. And when it backfired, I just thought, *Well shit.* Now we won't have kids, and she lost her sister. I'm just fucking up all the way round this husband shit, you know." He sniffed and coughed again.

"So, you know, I'm ready to be a dad. I just want to be married with children. I don't give a fuck what they look like or where they come from. I got all this fucking money piling up and no one to give it to, you know?" He laughed a hollow laugh and coughed again. I realized the veiled coughing was his way of keeping from crying.

"But if she wants to keep trying, then what the fuck am I to do, you know? I'm watching her pretty much kill herself physically and mentally and emotionally, and there isn't shit I can do about it because she's so fucking stubborn!"

He leaned on the pool stick, as we all looked at him, and asked, "What the fuck do I do, fellas?"

Connor was about to talk, but I interjected first. "I know how you feel. It's hard when you want something, and your partner doesn't."

My husband tried to catch my eye with a warning look, but I ignored him. *Connor tells anyone who will listen that he doesn't want to have children. I've always been silent about it. But fuck it, now it's my turn to talk. Because one, I'm not afraid to have this conversation despite what Ethan may think, and two, we're all family here, right?*

"When Connor and I talk about having kids, we're kind of on different sides of it. Obviously, he doesn't want kids. I wouldn't mind being married with children too, one, maybe two. But one thing I've always said to myself is what you want worth losing what you have? Will having kids together make your relationship better because it's something you both want, or will it tear you apart because you weren't in agreement with it in the first place? In our family, my desire is not something I'm willing to gamble for the sake of my relationship. Now in your case, you both want kids;

it's just a matter of coming to an agreement on how to get there. But you don't want to push the issue and she just agrees, because then it might just tear you apart."

"But I can't let her keep trying, Mel," Dennis said exasperatedly. "She is wasting away on me. She's twenty pounds smaller this year than she was last year. I convinced her to give her body a rest from everything before we try again but the truth is, I don't want us to try again. The amount of time and money and emotional energy it's taking without results can be put to an adoption that will be a guaranteed baby. I don't know how to get her to see that."

"You gotta give it time," I told him. "And it's not a complete no for her. I know because we talked about it earlier this year. She is considering it, but she is also grieving. She just needs time. She'll come around when she's ready to talk about it. And it may not be this year, or next year and that's okay because y'all are still young. But she will talk to you about it. And when she does, be ready to give her all the benefits of it, but in doses. She doesn't like to be hit in the face, which is what Angie did. She needs gentle drops of stones in a pond, making small ripples in her brain." I used my hand to mimic dropping stones in water, and they laughed, even Connor.

"And you can't come from it from the 'time and money wasted,' angle," Connor said. "You have to appeal to her emotions around it, the whole being a mom thing. Because that's what she wants. We grew up with a stay-at-home mom, and she wants to be one too. Listen, I told her I'm going to look up some stuff for her, but I'm going to look up some stuff for you too and give you some pointers. You're good at talking points. You can sell this idea to her. Just let it be her choice."

"Thanks, guys." Dennis looked at Chad and asked, "Anything to add?"

"Nope. I'm just glad we're one, big, happy family again. I love her to pieces, but Angie's a bitch when she's pregnant and she needs somewhere to go again, like her sister's house. No offense, Connor," he said, with a bit of fear in his voice.

"You don't have to tell me; both my sisters are pains in the asses when they want to be," he said nonchalantly.

Then he walked over and hugged Dennis unexpectedly. Dennis tried to back out, but Connor would not let him go. Eventually, he wrapped his arms around his brother-in-law. Chad and I smiled at each other.

I thought I had avoided catastrophe but as soon as the door closed behind our guests, Connor turned to me, as I was sitting on the couch in the living room. "Yeah, Mel? So we're on different sides of this having kids shit?" he asked, clearly annoyed with me.

And here. We. Go.

I stayed calm and said, "Is that the only thing you heard me say?"

"No, I heard what you said. You said you want us to have kids. It's a *desire* of yours to be married with children. I just find it crazy that we went ten years and this wasn't an issue, and now all of a sudden it's an issue."

"And what did I say after that?"

"I heard what you said, Mel."

"Obviously you didn't if you're all upset about it."

"I'm not upset," he said nastily.

I smiled at him. "Okay, baby." I got up and started going upstairs. "You coming to bed?"

"Nope." He glared at me.

Halfway up the stairs, I looked at him. *He wants to fight and again, I'm not giving it to him.* "Okay. Want me to wait up for you?"

"Nope."

Oh, we don't want sex either? I wanted to laugh, but I knew he must have been really mad if he was refusing to come to bed with me. I nodded. "Connor—"

"Why the fuck did you tell them all that!?" he exploded on me.

I inhaled and exhaled. "Is that what you're upset about? That I aired our dirty laundry out to our family members?"

He started yelling. "You're the one upset; that's why you keep bringing it up! You think if you tell people what you want, I'm going to change my mind but I'm fucking not; this conversation is a non-starter, and it ain't gonna happen so if this is going to be our constant fight, then just fuck this whole thing because I'm not doing this for the rest of my fucking life! Get over this shit!"

Fuck this whole thing? Get over this shit? Who needs kids when you deal with this immature bullshit?

"You know what would be really nice?" I said calmly. "It would be really nice if you would address your own feelings on the issue instead of focusing on mine. Because I didn't bring this up last month; you did. I didn't bring this up today either. I was trying to help your brother-in-law, which, by the way, worked."

"No, you brought it up months ago, to my sister!"

"No. I had a conversation with your sister who started talking to *me* about adoption. I didn't start that conversation either."

"Jamel—"

"Connor," I cut him off louder than what I intended. "I need you not to get emotional and impulsive right now." The look he gave me for throwing his own words back at him was like he wanted to stab me, but I didn't give a fuck because he was really pissing me off.

"I need you to think before you say anything else that you may regret later. Because this is the last conversation I'm having with you about this. The. Last. One."

"Then stop mentioning to people how you feel about it," he said coldly. "Because it changes nothing, and frankly, I don't give a shit how you feel. Suck that shit up."

So, I'm supposed to suppress my feelings and words around this issue because it makes him uncomfortable? Got it.

There were few moments that I wanted to flip out on him the way he flips out on me. This was one of those moments. Instead, I said quietly, "Goodnight, Connor."

I went upstairs and closed the bedroom door. I took a couple of deep breaths, stripped down to my underwear, and turned off the light. I laid on my stomach facing away from the door, trying to calm myself down. It wasn't so much the subject matter; it was how he was acting about it, like a complete asshole, unnecessarily. *And soon he's going to come in feeling guilty and apologize about him being an asshole and, frankly, I don't give a shit how he feels either.*

He came in about fifteen minutes later, left the light off, and stripped to nothing. I knew because I felt his skin as he moved next to me, which I hated and loved at the same time. His body was like a drug to me, but I was still wounded from the conversation earlier, so I didn't reach out to touch him.

He hesitated to touch me, as he should have because he knew I was mad. But then he gently touched my back and said softly, "Okay, I handled that really, really badly. I'm sorry." I didn't respond. "It just … it drives me crazy that we're on the same page about everything else except this. And it's a huge thing. And it's scary to think that … you know … you might leave me over this." I heard the fear in his voice, and it melted my anger for him.

I said to him, without looking at him, "Connor, I love you. And I need you. I'm not going to leave you over this or anything. We're going on ten years together next month so I don't understand how you could still feel this way. I thought we were done being scared shitless?"

He put his head on my shoulder blade and rubbed my lower back. "We are. But lately I've just been feeling like … something is going to happen to pull us apart. When Nicky died, you pulled away from me. And that scared me. Now all this talk about you wanting something different than what we have right now? It's scary. It's my own insecurities, I know. I'm still working through a lot of things internally."

The thing I discovered about Connor early on was that he puts up a really good facade as a strong, confident, put-together guy. But he had a lot of insecurities and when it came to relationships, his biggest fear was being left behind. His first love, Jack, left him by ending the relationship because Connor wasn't ready to come out. Vinnie, his second and greatest love, left him by dying. He spent years avoiding relationships and ending any real connections so he would never be left behind again. So almost from day one, I felt a sense of responsibility to reassure him that I will always be by his side, no matter what. And even on the rough days, like tonight, it was easy to do so, because I really did love him that much.

I said to him, "I'm sorry I pulled away. I wasn't trying to; I just didn't know how to handle what I was feeling. I've never really been great at expressing my emotions, not after I've been taught my whole life to keep my emotions in check. I've learned to keep silent on issues, and maybe I do that too much. So, it's not just you; it's me too, working through my stuff. But you need to know this...."

I turned my body around, and he lifted his head up so we could face each other. I put my hand on his waist and said, "I am deeply devoted to you. Nothing you could ever do or say is going to make me leave you. Or not love you. You have to know this in your heart no matter what happens between us. No matter if I pull away for a moment because I'm in a bad place emotionally. No matter if I disagree with you on huge topics like having kids. Even when you yell at me and become a complete fucking asshole, like you did just now. It's not going to happen. You get me?"

He sniffed. I couldn't see him fully in the dark, but I knew he was holding back tears. I pulled him close to me and we held each other, his head right below my neck on my chest.

Eventually, he said, "Same, Mel. Same."

♥

I came in from work through the garage and heard them in the media room, yelling over gunfire. When I walked in, Freddie and EJ were stretched out on the large sectional playing Fortnite on the big screen using the surround sound. They wore pajama bottoms and sweatshirts like they had been there all day, with empty cereal bowls, three different types of cereal all opened, an empty milk carton, snacks, and candy wrappers all around. It smelled like armpits and farts. They both greeted me together without taking their eyes off the screen, "Hey, Uncle Mel!"

"Hey. Why aren't y'all in school?" I asked.

"I don't know ... some Jewish holiday," Freddie responded.

I walked over and grabbed the remote, turning it down. "It sounds like a war zone in here. Keep the volume down."

"Okay," Freddie said. I started to walk away when he called, "Hey Uncle Mel, I have a question."

But EJ hushed him. "Shhh. He's not going to know the answer."

"Why not?"

"You know why. He's… You know why," EJ said, and Freddie laughed.

"Answer to what?" I asked.

Freddie paused the game, which made EJ groan. "Is it true that a girl can get pregnant while on her period?"

My eyebrows went up, as I looked at both of them. "Is this for research purposes or for your own personal knowledge? Something you want to tell me, boys?" They giggled like little kids, and I shook my head.

"We were watching *Maury*, and the girl said this guy was the father but the guy said she was on her period when they did it, but it turned out that the baby was his, so somebody's lying," EJ said.

I came over to sit at the back edge of the sofa. "So, if you paid attention in health class, you would know that a female can get pregnant at any time. Because while it is a twenty-eight-day cycle, ovulation occurs right before her menses and sperm can live inside of a woman for up to three days … why are y'all laughing?"

Halfway through me explaining to them basic biology, they started giggling. Freddie said, "It's just funny, Uncle Mel. Ovulation and sperm talk. It's funny!" They start laughing again.

"I really hope neither of you are having sex because your maturity level is one step above the ground right now." They both started laughing again as I shook my head.

"How do you know this stuff, Uncle Mel?" EJ asked.

"Because I paid attention in school, knucklehead!" I told him, lightly popping him on the head.

"Yeah, but you've never been with a girl before. Right?" EJ asked.

"No, I haven't. But that doesn't mean you shouldn't know basic things like how babies are made. Even gay men should know this."

"Well, I'm not gay so..." EJ said, defensively.

"No one said you were, EJ." He was always sensitive about this, and it drove his father crazy.

"Craig and Mark did," Freddie teased.

"Shut the fuck up!" EJ yelled at him angrily.

"Yo! What's up with that reaction?" Neither answered. "You wanna tell me what happened?"

EJ shrugged. Freddie answered. "What always happens. People find out EJ has two dads, and they become assholes. But don't worry; I got EJ's back, always." He flexed his knuckles, saying smugly, "I punched Craig in the mouth, and Mark ran away. Pussies."

Freddie looked so much like a young Connor, he could be his son. They have the same blond hair, icy blue eyes, and shaped face. But his attitude and his short fuse were different from Connor's, a little more reckless and always ready for a fight, which scared me a little. He was kind of an instigator like his father; his mouth was always getting him into trouble. But at least he was using his powers for good, standing up to bullies for his friend.

EJ definitely looked like a young Ethan, same sandy brown hair and light brown eyes, but ironically was more like Jack than his biological dad. He avoided trouble if he could and didn't snap out so easily. But when he did, he exploded, like he had all this pent-up anger inside of him. Their friendship made sense because they balanced each other out, despite how much their parents hated each other.

"Did you tell either your dad or your pops?" I asked EJ.

"No, they just gonna make a big deal out of it. Then people are really gonna think I am gay," he said sheepishly.

He was right. Ethan would go down to the school and call a meeting and such. I made a note internally to mention it in passing to Jack, just to make sure someone knew so it didn't turn into outright bullying at school.

"So what?" Freddie said. "Ain't nothing wrong with being gay, right, Uncle Mel?" I smiled at him. Then he said, "I wouldn't mind being gay."

"Are you gay, Freddie?" I asked with my eyebrow raised.

"I don't know." He laughed. "I doubt it though, because when I jack-off, I visualize Zendaya's face with Cardi B's ass." Then he fell out laughing, and EJ laughed with him.

I laughed too at how crude he can be. "So black women?" I asked him amusingly.

My nephew shrugged, then said, "You know what they say. The blacker the berry, the sweeter the juice, amirite?"

He raised his hand to me for a dap, smiling widely. I slapped it away and lightly popped him on the head.

"Boy, no one says that, especially you. Don't say that ever again." The boys fell over laughing again. When it died down, I asked them seriously, "Are you having sex, boys?"

"NO!" they both yelled simultaneously.

I nodded. "What about the girls? Are they?"

"No, Imani is saving herself for marriage," EJ said.

"Yeah, your marriage!" Freddie joked.

"Shut up!" EJ shoved him. Freddie shoved him back, and then they continued to shove each other playfully.

"And Kim?" I asked.

Freddie said, "Kim is just waiting for the right one to come along." He smiled at me knowingly.

I put my face in his and said, "Freddie, if I catch you with my niece, I'm going to hang you upside down by your baby balls."

Freddie's eyes went wide, and EJ fell over cackling. "I didn't say me! Honest!" he cried.

I gave him a stern look and sat back. Then I asked, "Where are the girls today? They didn't come over with you?"

"Imani is working on a school project, and Kim is with her two moms." EJ said, turning back on the game and unpausing it.

I stood up. "Y'all staying for dinner?"

Freddie answered, "Yeah, Uncle Con said he was bringing Chinese food on his way home."

"Okay." I looked around. "Make sure you clean up before you come upstairs."

"Yes, Uncle Mel," they sounded off together again.

I glanced at them and looked around again. They were both growing up so fast, with Freddie turning fourteen in December and EJ right behind him in January. I watched them both grow up in the last eight years, having their birthday parties, barbecues, and Halloween parties right there at our house. I complained a little about not having my media room to myself, but the truth is if Connor and I had kids, that was pretty much what it would look like anyway. And I wouldn't want to change a thing about it.

Maybe my desire to be a parent has been met all these years, and I'm just now realizing it.

CHAPTER 13

THIS ONE MIGHT BE DIFFERENT

Connor

In early October, I met my tribe at Billy Beez, the indoor play yard in Kingston, Massachusetts, to celebrate Tyriq turning one, my treat. Mina had her daughter, Mary Elizabeth, and I borrowed Ethan's girls, JC and Susie. Together, we had six children between one and seven years old. Winter did not bother bringing a kid; she just brought herself, late and looking like death warmed over.

"I'm sorry, guys," she said, her nose completely stuffed. "I think I'm coming down with the flu or something. I feel awful."

She sat next to me on the bench and put her head on my shoulder, as we watched the kids disappear in the nets and tunnels above us.

"At least yours is short-term," Mina said sitting next to her, rubbing her belly. She just found out she was eight weeks pregnant. "But I haven't felt any of the symptoms I felt the last time so this one might be different. A boy."

"I'm sure that will make Sam very happy," I said to her.

"What are we talking about?" Afia said, as she came over holding Tyriq's hand. Despite knowing how to walk, he didn't want to walk on his own, only if someone was holding his hand. I held my hand out as she sat down, and Lil Ty climbed into my lap. She put her head on my other shoulder and yawned.

"How Winter feels like shit, and Mina does not," I said.

"I'm just glad I'm not pregnant too. We were pretty awful together, weren't we?" She started giggling, and so did Mina.

Winter rolled her eyes. "Awful wasn't even the word. Y'all were either crying or snapping on each other. Or on me."

"And me," I pipped in. "We couldn't wait for it to be over."

Afia sat up and clicked her tongue at me. "Yeah, you as a man couldn't wait for *our* pregnancies to be over? Imagine how I felt! If I wasn't throwing up, I couldn't eat anything. I was tired, hungry, and moody. Until you grow a tiny human, don't talk to me about wanting it to be over."

"Exactly!" Mina said. "Men have no idea; their bodies have never gone through this change."

"Didn't Sam put on sympathy weight?" I asked, smiling at her.

She laughed. "Okay yeah, he did do that." We all giggled again.

"The best part was not having a period though," said Afia.

"Oh God no!" I groaned.

"So true!" Mina talked across Winter and me to Afia. "It's what I'm looking forward to. No cramping, no bloating—"

I jumped up, still holding onto Ty. "Stop it!"

Our tribe meeting conversations had completely changed, and I was okay with that but not this. *Hell no.*

Winter said, "Well, my period was always irregular so—"

"GAAAH!" I covered one of Ty's ears. "This is the problem with having female best friends. I don't want to talk about this!" They all laughed at me. "Talk about something else. Winter, how are things going with Kevin?"

She had been trying to be in a relationship with one guy for the last year. She had a couple of slip-ups however, because Winter, like I was, found it hard to stay with one partner. She gets bored easily, but I figured he was still around.

"Fuck him. He told me I was fat the other day, so I haven't spoken to him since," she said. *I guess he's not around anymore.*

My eyes went wide. "What an asshole."

"I mean … you have been gaining … a little, Winter," Mina said cautiously.

She snapped her head at her. "I'm 36 years old. I'm allowed to gain some fucking weight!"

"I didn't say you weren't; I'm just saying. You can't eat like you were in your twenties and think your belly is going to stay flat," Mina said matter-of-factly. "You still have the best body of all of us."

Afia nodded. "Even though I have officially moved into a C cup, thank you, my babies," she said, happily grabbing her full breasts. We giggled again.

"It's this stupid cold I have that won't go away," Winter said. "It has me feeling nauseated, then when I feel better, all I want to do is eat."

"Well, maybe you should go to the doctor," Afia said.

"Maybe you're pregnant," I joked.

"Shut up before I kick you in the balls, Connor," she said nastily to me, and I laughed.

"Hmmm ... are you and Kevin using condoms?" Mina asked.

"Of course, we're using condoms! We're—"

My friend's face froze in complete shock, then she stood up. Her eyes darted around, as if she was thinking really fast.

"Oh shit oh shit oh shit oh shit oh no no no no no no no no no...." She started spinning around in place, saying "shit" and "no" in a repetitive fashion.

My mouth dropped. "You can't be serious, Winter."

Afia stood up and made her stand still. "When?" Winter's mouth moved but no words came out. "When did you slip up?"

"I've been slipping for months," she said quietly. "But I'm on the ring."

Mina came and stood next to her. "Okay. So, we take a test. Then we decide. Okay?"

Winter nodded, then shockingly started crying. *I don't think I have ever seen her cry. She must be terrified. And hormonal. Christ.*

She grabbed Afia's neck and sobbed. Mina held her too, rubbing her back. I walked over and wrapped one arm around her, still holding Lil Ty.

Three hours later, we were all at Afia's house, with the kids playing downstairs in the living room and us upstairs waiting for Winter to come out of the bathroom. We stopped at a Rite Aid on the way down and bought four different tests, and she was in the bathroom doing them all at the same time. She was in there longer than the one to two minutes allotted and after three minutes, Afia started banging on the door.

"Winter! Open the door or I swear to God I'm going to kick this shit down!" she yelled.

Winter opened it and looked at the three of us standing there. Her eyes were bloodshot from crying.

"I'm pregnant," she said, plainly and unemotional, then walked past us to go downstairs.

The three of us looked at each other with wide eyes. Mina went into the bathroom and looked at all four sticks on the sink counter. She came back out and nodded. "Very pregnant."

"She's not going to keep it," I said. Winter had been pregnant at least twice before in her life and, like me, did not want children.

"This one might be different," Afia said.

"Why?" Mina asked.

She looked like she was going to answer, then decided not to, and went downstairs too. Mina looked at me as confused as I felt. "Because it's Kevin?" she asked me.

"I don't think so. Kevin is to her what Sam was to you eight years ago. She's not ready to settle down with him."

"Well, maybe this will force her to," Mina said, and she started walking down the stairs. I followed her.

Winter was laying on the couch, face up, and Afia was sitting by her head, talking to her in hushed tones. We both sat on the floor with her. Afia told the girls to go upstairs and play dress-up, and Lil Ty followed them, crawling up the stairs with his big sister Takeya behind him to protect him from falling.

Mina said, "Whatever you want to do, we're here for you, you know that. Even if you don't want to tell Kevin—"

"It's not Kevin's," she said plainly.

"Do you know who?" I asked her. Considering Winter sleeps around, that was a legitimate question.

"Yes."

"Someone you can get in contact with, or someone you want to leave in the dark?" Mina asked. "Because either way, it's fine. We got your back."

She was quiet for a moment, then sat up. "I need to tell him. Because if I don't ... that would be fucked up."

Okay. Must be someone she actually cares about. But other than Kevin, I hadn't heard her specify any randos that just might be potential.

"Whose is it?" I asked. She looked at me like she expected me to know. "Shit, it ain't me!" I said incredulously.

That only made her laugh harder, which made Afia and Mina laugh as well. She stood up. "I have to tell him first. Before I tell you. And you," she said to Mina. She gave Afia a small smile, who smiled back at her knowingly.

"I'll see you guys later." We gave her hugs individually, and she walked out.

Mina turned to Afia as soon as the door closed. "Out with it, bitch. Who is it?" Afia smiled with a closed mouth and shook her head. "Ugh, I hate you!" Mina scoffed and I laughed.

I didn't even bother asking. My Lovie, who spent a lifetime keeping my secrets, was not going to break Winter's trust for anything. *She'll tell us herself soon enough.*

♥

Jamel and I flew to Aruba for our ten-year anniversary of being together and our two-year wedding anniversary. After the wedding ceremony last year, we didn't have a honeymoon but agreed to plan a real trip somewhere this year. We picked Aruba for their progressive nature toward LGBTQ folks and great reviews for a gay-friendly, all-inclusive resort. Neither of us had been on an island before so it was going to be a real treat for both of us. I was excited about this vacation. Ten years was a milestone in any relationship. We'd been away together several times, but I just knew this one was going to be different, in the best way.

As we sat on the plane, heading toward paradise, I thought about the last decade of my life and how much had changed for me. I wondered if I would still be sucking and fucking my way through New England. Now that I knew a bit more about Nick, I'm pretty sure I would have been, just like he did for the first forty years of his life. Maybe Jamel and I would have randomly found each other, but I doubt it. There isn't anywhere that we would have crossed paths, except through Ty and Afia. But even then, I wouldn't have pursued him out of respect for her. Maybe Vinnie really did lead us together.

For some reason, Lex popped in my mind. I hadn't thought about him in years, not since I ran into him at a restaurant one night when Mel and I were out to dinner. I just happened to glance over and saw him there with another Latino guy, also having dinner. He caught my eye, smiled, then looked away. When I saw him get up to go to the bathroom, he looked my way, purposely catching my eye again. I excused myself and went as well. When I got there, he was pretending to wash his hands and smiled at me through the mirror.

Xavier "Lex" Lemos was still a beautiful man. His locks had gotten much longer, tips still golden brown. His face was still smooth, but he looked older; He had to be about thirty.

"How you been, Lex?" I asked him first, as I leaned on the wall behind him.

"Can't complain," he said through the mirror. "You?"

"Can't complain. You look good. Happy."

He smiled at the glass and said, "I am. Eduardo is good to me. We're getting married so no more Grindr dates." We both laughed. Then he said, "You look happy too."

"I am. Very happy."

I held up my finger with the ring tattoo. It was after we legally got married in 2017 but before our wedding ceremony.

Lex eyes went wide. "Whoa. That's … surprising."

"Trust me, I'm still shocked myself." We chuckled again.

"It's good though. I'm glad that you found someone to settle down with. How long you've been together?" he asked.

I hesitated, then was honest. "Eight years."

His mouth opened slightly, then he nodded. "He's hot. I would have broken up with me for him too." He chuckled.

I chuckled back. Then I said seriously, "I'm sorry if I hurt you."

Lex shrugged. "I'm a big boy; I handled it. And it was for the best. Now we're both happy."

Then he turned around, walked up to me quickly, and put his arms around my neck. I held him back around his waist. "Bye Connor," he whispered in my ear.

Then he let me go just as quickly and left the bathroom. I waited a couple of minutes, then went back to my table. Lex did not glance my way again. I told Mel that night in bed, and he didn't say anything about me meeting him in private, except that he understood. But we made love that night like the first time, all with passion and love between us. It was his way of reminding me who I belonged to; I knew that about him.

All these years I had been feeling a bit guilty about when I ended things with Lex, so it was no time like the present to fess up.

I looked over at Mel, who was reading the third part of the apocalyptic trilogy, *City of Mirrors*. "Hey Jamel?"

He looked at me. "Sup?"

"So I love that we got married on the 17th, so that it can really be our anniversary. But as far as dating, our anniversary should have been on the 18th."

He looked at me curiously. "Why? October 17th is when we decided we were going to be exclusive, no?"

"Yes." I inhaled and exhaled. "But I didn't exactly … start my exclusivity with you until the next day." His eyes went up in confusion as he was thinking, then started grinning knowingly at me.

"Tell me more about that," he said amusingly.

I groaned. "Ugh, Jameeelll…"

My hubby started laughing. "Connor, if you think that I didn't know that you were going to fuck him that night when you left my house—"

My mouth dropped, and I cut him off waving my hands back and forth. "Whoa whoa whoa! I did not leave your house with that intention. Not at all!"

"Oh, okay." He turned all the way around to face me. "How did you accidentally sleep with your fuck toy hours after I had told you to stop fucking him? I'm listening."

He had this shit-eating grin on his face that I hated and loved at the same time. *He thinks he knows me so well.*

"Okay," I started. "When Lovie drove us home, I did text him to tell him it was over. He asked why; I just said it's for the best. He asked me to come over so we can talk about it. I told him there was nothing to talk about; it was over. But then he said that we started it face to face, and it's only fair that we end it face to face too, and that we should meet up the next day. But I said no, if we're going to meet up, it needed to be tonight. So, he told me again to come over. And I did. But not with the intention of doing anything. He was a cool dude, and I knew he really liked me so I didn't want him to think it was something that he did or anything, I wanted to explain to him it was my decision because—why are you laughing at me!?" Jamel was nodding mockingly as I was talking, then started laughing, the asshole.

"Because Connor, I knew who you were back then, and I kind of expected you to give him a goodbye fuck, especially because I left you wanting that night," Jamel said, again knowingly.

I thought about it. "Yeah, why the fuck did you do that?"

I never asked him about why he jerked me off but wouldn't let me touch him. It honestly didn't help me resist Lex because I was already keyed up with sexual frustration.

Jamel leaned back, then looked at me. "The truth? If you would have touched me, we would have never made it upstairs for dinner. I wanted you so bad, but I had just asked you if sex was all you wanted from me, so then I couldn't turn around and just take what I wanted from you. I needed to know that you really wanted to be with me."

I smiled at him. "You were already falling in love with me," I teased him.

"Ahhh, I wouldn't go that far," he said and laughed. "But I knew I wanted to be with you."

"I would go that far," I said smugly. "You were already in luuuuuuve!"

"Shut up." He laughed. "You were already in love on day three, asking me to stay with you forever."

"Nuh-uh, I was drunk as a skunk; you can't hold me to anything I said."

Jamel was quiet for a moment, then said, with all seriousness, "Okay. So, what if I was falling in love with you by then?"

As usual, my husband left me speechless. We had only known each other for two weeks and been on two dates by then. I just stared at him wide-eyed, and my mouth slightly opened. Then he shook his head and said, "Nah, I'm just fucking with you."

He started laughing again, and I playfully punched his arm. "Fuck you, Mel."

He pulled me close and said, "Maybe later." Then he kissed my neck and said, "Definitely later."

♥

Jamel pretended like he didn't care about his appearance but he did. He took great pride in his 2 percent body fat, his hard chest, his muscles, and the shape of his thick thighs. And if there was ever an opportunity to show it all off, it was on the beaches of Aruba.

I was putting a bit of mousse in my hair to keep my quiff up when I saw him come out of the bathroom from the mirror. He was wearing all white, a beautiful contrast to his dark brown skin. A simple white ribbed tank top and white linen beach pants that were so light you could see the boxer-type swim trunks underneath. It was cut so low at the waist it stopped right before the bulge of his lax penis, and his white wave cap was on his head. He had a thin but full beard that accentuated his perfect full lips, and those amazing silver eyes to top it off.

He's still so gorgeous, he takes my breath away. Sometimes I still can't believe he's all mine.

I turned around to face him fully, and he looked at me with the same expression of love and lust that I have for him. I had on dark blue boxers-type swim-shorts that were also tight and hugged my package, and a tank top to match. Sure, I'm cute and sexy but standing next to Jamel, no one was going to look at me.

He walked right up on me and said, "Your tank top is so tight, I see the outline of your nipples." Then he pinched one.

"Ow!" I feigned being in pain. "Well, I see the out-line of your dick!" I grabbed him hard, and I felt him twitch in my hands.

He moved closer. "Maybe we should stay inside instead of going to the beach," he said.

I laughed and caressed his groin area. "Don't test me, Jamel. We don't need to leave the room for the next four days as far as I'm concerned." And I meant that shit.

He laughed and kissed my lips. "One hour on the beach; I want to see the sunset. Then we come back and make love. All night. Yes?"

"Yes." I pulled him closer and kissed him, then sniffed him. "Fuck, you even smell good." He used the coconut oil again.

Jamel pulled back and lifted my tank top off. I smiled at him, but then he grabbed the suntan lotion and I groaned. "This is not my idea of foreplay."

He turned me around and started lathering my back and the parts of my legs that were exposed. "Neither is melanoma," he said. When he was done, he kissed my lips again. "Let's go."

As usual, he took my hand and led me outside and on the white sand. We walked slowly, watching other people sleep, read books, play volleyball, and jump around in the ocean. I watched heads turn as we walked past, but mostly it was Jamel turning heads. We walked by a group of five or six drunk women, who started catcalling him.

"Sexy chocolate! Come play with us! Bring your boy toy too!"

That made us both laugh. "He's all mine, ladies!" I called back at them, and they started cackling.

He kissed my face, and they called out, "Awwwwww!"
Yeah, we like Aruba.

We moved closer to the water to walk along the gentle laps as the sun dipped lower. A man was coming toward us with a shirt with the same logo as our hotel. As we came closer, his mouth opened slightly as he drooled over my man. I saw how handsome he was. He was light brown-skinned, like if Mel and I had a baby, that would be the child's skin color, right in the middle of us. His arms were thin but defined, and he was shorter than us. He was slightly bowlegged in a sexy way, and I wondered how flexible he was. Nice full lips and smooth skin. He had to be in his twenties, younger than us, but none of that mattered to him.

Jamel pretended not to notice as usual, but I knew he did. The guy was obvious in his attraction to him. I smiled absentmindedly, and the man turned his attention to me. He caught my eyes and held my gaze, which surprised me, because I didn't expect him to. His lips were still opened slightly, and he licked the bottom one. My body reacted, and my cock began to swell. I turned away from his gaze out of embarrassment of my sexual reaction toward another man to look at Mel, but Mel was watching him too, so I knew he saw our exchange. I looked back at the man as he got closer, and I got to see his handsome features, his skin looking golden in the setting sunlight. He had a diamond stud in each ear and the top part jutted out, like they were begging to be sucked.

When he was just a few feet away, he spoke. "Hello, gentleman." He had a nice, deep island accent.

"Hey," Jamel said at the same time I said, "Hi."

He smiled at both of us with perfect white teeth but kept walking. I wanted to turn around and look at him again so badly, but that would have been completely disrespectful.

Neither Jamel nor I spoke for another few steps, then he started laughing. "I think he wants to fuck you, Connor."

I scoffed. "It wasn't my body he was gawking at from a mile away."

"Yeah, it was your eyes that mesmerized him," Jamel teased. He let go of my hand and wrapped his arm around my waist.

I did the same and said, "Well, it's a good thing I only have eyes for you."

I kissed his cheek. He stopped walking, turned all the way around, and kissed my lips, simply at first, then he licked my lips before he pushed his tongue inside. I locked my hands around his neck, and at no point did I look around to see who saw us. I felt how hard he was, and I was too. I wondered if he was hard because of the man or because of me. But seeing how I started getting an erection while I was getting eye-fucked, I wouldn't be mad at him if he did too.

We kissed for a while, my sexual appetite getting hungrier. He pulled back and looked me in the eyes, and I saw his appetite for me. There was just a slither of sunlight left. He stepped back and dropped his linen pants right there on the beach, then took off his tank top. He reached over and lifted my tank top over my head too. There was hardly anyone on the beach or in the water, as people who had been out all day were headed back inside to their prospective hotel rooms or to dinner.

"C'mere," he said.

Jamel pulled me into the ocean, which was still warm, as it was baked by the sun all day. We walked into the water until it was up to our nipples. Then he turned me around and kissed the back of my neck. He continued to kiss my neck as he rubbed my torso, then moved his hands down to my swollen cock. He loosened the draw string and put his hand down there, pulling it out and stroking it in the water. I moaned as he stroked me and continued to suck my neck harder, leaving a mark. Jamel let go of my penis and moved his hands to the back of my swim trunks, then pulled them down, so that they were on my upper thighs.

I closed my eyes and waited for him, the knocking of his cock on my back entrance. He entered me slowly but in one motion, and I gasped and moaned. He must have only pulled his cock over the swim trunks because I could feel the nylon on my ass instead of the pubic hair I normally felt. He was still sucking my neck hard, one hand guiding his cock in me, the other hand across my chest to hold me up. When he bottomed out, he let my neck go and sucked and bit my ear instead. He reached up and held me by the front of my neck, slowly moving in and out of me. He barely pulled back, just about one third of the way out, only to push back in. His mushroom head was pressed against my internal nub, rubbing it back and forth.

I started moaning louder. Jamel put his fingers in my mouth. I immediately sucked them, bit them, and moaned on them. Then Jamel started talking in my ear, something he rarely did. He sucked on my earlobe as he talked, while he continued to love me with his dick from behind, stroking me from the front.

"You're my reason for waking up every day and all of my happiness. I've never loved anyone as much as I love you. Me being inside of you, being one with you, pressed against you like this—"

He pushed inside me harder. I moaned out loud again, tears falling out of my eyes from his words and his sex.

"I'm never going to let you go. Ten years isn't enough. I want an eternity of being inside of you just—" Jamel pulled back almost all the way out, "like—" He pushed in all the way, "...this." He circled his waist grinding against me and came inside of me. I came over and

over again, my seeds floating up and away with the
Caribbean Ocean.

He pulled out, and more tears fell out of my eyes.
The sun had completely set, and the lights from the
hotels along the beach were the only thing showing
the path back. I turned around, threw my arms around
his neck, and he held my waist tightly. I sniffed and let
more tears flow freely.

"Don't ever leave me, okay?" I said softly on his neck.

"Never, baby," he told me back. "I told you. Nothing
you could ever do or say could make me leave you or
stop loving you. I'm deeply devoted to you."

We did indeed make love all night, forgetting about
dinner. When we got back to the room, we didn't even
bother showering, only rinsed our feet off but left the
saltiness of the ocean still on our skin. Jamel kissed
and licked me from my ears to my toes, his beard
leaving tickles all along my most sensitive areas. He
inserted himself inside of me from the front, then on
my stomach, making me cum two more times but
refusing to cum himself. Not until I returned the favor,
licked and sucked every inch of him, then rode his
cock until he emptied out inside of me. Then I turned
him on his stomach and entered him, fucked him nice
and slow, like he did to me, and made him putty in my
hands. His body molded and melted underneath me.
I kept him there for a while, and when I came, I didn't
pull out. I just stayed inside of him, laid on top of
him. As I got soft, he got hard again, and we started

over, with him inside of me. When he came again, we were face to face, and he stayed inside of me as we kissed softly, lovingly until he had no choice but to pull his soft penis out. We hadn't been that passionate with each other for a long time, and bodies craved the closeness and intimacy we gave to ourselves. We barely spoke words the entire time.

He laid on his side, taking me with him, holding me tightly against his chest. I wrapped my free arm around him and my legs in between his. There we slept, my body sore and his body exhausted, more in love then than we were when we first started this journey together.

♥ ♥ ♥ CHAPTER 14 ♥ ♥ ♥

LOSE INHIBITIONS. FIND YOURSELF.

Connor

I opened my eyes, and he was already awake watching me, his gray eyes piercing my soul. We were still on our sides, my head on his arm, our legs still wrapped around each other. In his arms was the most loving and safest place on earth to me.

"I love you," Jamel said as his morning greeting.

"I love you too," I greeted him back. "What time is it?"

"A quarter to noon." He kissed my lips softly. "Let's stay in today. We can check out the rest of the resort and go to the beach tomorrow."

"Okay," I agreed. I closed my eyes again, still feeling the heaviness of my body that needed more rest.

When I opened my eyes again, Jamel was sleeping beside me. I kissed his bare skin before I slid away and off the bed, ordered a feast of room service with breakfast and lunch combined, and started a hot bubble bath in the huge Jacuzzi tub. As I was soaking, I heard the knock on the door, but I also heard Jamel move off the bed to open it, so I didn't bother leaving the bathroom. After a couple of minutes, he came with the bowl of fruit. He put it on the ledge of the tub, unwrapped the sheet from around his waist, and joined me, putting his body between my legs and his head against my shoulder.

I started feeding us: one grape for him, one strawberry for me, one pineapple for him, one melon for me. We sat in silence and enjoyed the closeness of our bodies, until the fruit was gone, and our hands turned wrinkled, mine more than his because I was in there longer. I took the washcloth and rubbed it all over him under the water, then moved from behind him to kneel between his legs and clean his face, neck, and ears. I had already done so for myself before he joined me. Then I stood up, grabbed a towel, and held it out for him to walk into. He stood up and smiled, stepped into my towel as I dried him off, then wrapped it around his waist before I put on my own towel.

We sat on the bed and ate our eggs, sausage, and bacon with jerk chicken, curried meat, wild rice, and plantains with our hands, feeding each other and licking each other's fingers until there was nothing left. He got up to move the plates off the bed and when he came back, I sat in his lap facing him, my legs on either side of him, arms around his neck. He broke the silence that we had for the last couple of hours.

"How are you feeling?" Jamel asked, as he kissed the red-and-purple marks he left all along my neck from the night before.

"Amazing. Loved. Sore."

"Okay," he said. "We'll just hold each other tonight." I nodded, loving his concern for me. He nuzzled his nose with mine, then looked at me.

"So, since you confessed something, I feel like I should confess something too," he said.

I looked at him amused. "Go on."

He rubbed his nose against mine again and said softly, "I know how much you love when I do this."

I really do. He's about to ruin this for me, isn't he?

"Okay, I don't want to know." He laughed. But then I said, "Okay, tell me. Which one of your ex-boyfriend's did you do this with?" I rolled my eyes.

"Only one. Nicky did it to me the first time we made love when I was 18. He used to do it to me all the time when we were together. I never did it with anyone else. The first time you and I made love, I couldn't help myself. Maybe it was the contrast of our skin colors, because you know he was the only other white guy I had been with. I found myself giving you a nose kiss and watched your eyes light up when you looked at me. I knew I would never stop doing it." He rubbed his nose against mine again.

"Don't ever stop doing it," I told him softly. Knowing it was Nick didn't bother me at all. I kissed the tip of his nose, then his lips. "What do you want to do now?"

"I could go for something sweet."

I resisted the urge to have a sexual response and said, "There is a bakery near the bar. Let's bring up a pitcher of whatever the drink of the day is, grab some dessert, and watch a movie."

"That sounds like a great plan," he said.

We got dressed and made our way to the large vestibule where all the shops and restaurants were. Jamel went toward the bar, and I went to the bakery. On the way back, I passed by a small ice cream shop. I glanced inside and I saw him, the guy from the beach yesterday. He was working, changing out the empty mint chocolate tray for another full one. He happened to look up and caught my eye.

I turned my face to keep walking and heard him call out, "Hey! Blondie!"

He came running out of the shop and stopped in front of me. He smiled his perfect white teeth at me and slid his tongue over his bottom lip, making my dick twitch.

"Hey," I responded, keeping my face neutral.

He reached into his back pocket to pull out what looked like a postcard and handed it to me. "Come out to the Underground tonight. Bring your boyfriend," he said in his thick island accent.

"Husband," I corrected him, as I took the card from him.

He smiled. "Even better. I want to see you both there. It's only for us." Us meaning gay men, I caught that right away. "When you get there, show them the card and tell them Romulus sent you. Or say you're here with Romy. That's the only way you're getting in." He smiled slyly, then went back into the store.

I met Jamel at the elevator and told him what had just happened. He looked at the card and smiled. It read, *Club Underground. Lose Inhibitions. Find Yourself.* It had pictures of men dancing together.

"So, some kind of gay club?" he asked.

"Looks like it."

"Do you want to go?"

I shook my head. "No, we already planned to stay in today. I'm good with staying in if you are." But I kinda hoped he pushed for us to go.

Instead, he shrugged. "Okay." Then he held up his full hands. "I got a pitcher of Arubian Sunrise, and they gave us two champagne bottles because of our anniversary. Apparently, they give us a bottle a day while here, just give them your room number at the bar. We missed yesterday so they gave us two."

"Niiiiiiiice!" I grinned. "I got two slices of chocolate cake, a big slice of cherry pie, twenty soft-baked chocolate chip cookies, a cup of apple crisp, and four strawberry cupcakes."

"Niiiiiiiice!" he said mimicking me, making me laugh. We went upstairs together.

♥

Jamel

After we ordered room service for dinner, we settled in to watch a movie on TV, with Connor snuggled on my chest. Because we made love all night and slept most of the day away, we were both wide awake at 10 p.m. For some reason, the card that Romulus gave Connor came to mind. It would be nice to go out clubbing. We didn't go out to gay bars in Providence, mostly because Connor didn't want to run into anyone he used to fuck. When we were in Miami, we did. And I already told Josh when we go down to Atlanta for New Year's Eve that we'll be hitting up a club there too. But I didn't want to push Connor to go out, especially since we already said we were staying in.

Connor rolled off me onto his back and sighed. "You okay?" I asked.

"Yeah," he said. He got off the bed to make himself a cup of Aruban Sunrise, the last few ounces from the pitcher. He leaned on the counter and looked down at the card, then casually turned toward the TV and took a sip.

Connor wants to go, I thought happily. "You wanna go?" I asked him.

"Go where?" he answered innocently.

I started laughing. "Cut your shit and just say you want to go."

He laughed too. "No, no, you said you wanted us to stay in so we're staying in. Maybe tomorrow night."

Oh, so this is for my benefit? I decided to help him out. "I want to go," I told him as I sat up on the bed.

Connor looked at me skeptically. "No, you don't. You're just saying that because you think I want to."

"Actually, I *know* you want to go. But I do too. I was just thinking about it right before you got out of bed. I want to go too. So, let's go."

He smiled. "Really, Mel?"

"Yep," I said, as I stood up. "Shower first." I pulled him with me toward the bathroom.

♥

An hour later, we were in a cab going fifteen minutes inland. We didn't know how to dress so we chose regular blue jeans and shirts, him in a short-sleeved button down plaid shirt and me with a tight crew neck mauve t-shirt.

I looked out the window on the ride over. "This is not the resort area at all. It looks a bit seedy. All eyes. We need to be careful; make sure this isn't some kind of prey on foreigners," I said seriously.

Connor touched my thigh. "Don't worry, baby; I'll protect you."

I smiled at him. "I'm sure you will, Corporal."

The cab stopped us in front of a two-story building with no lights on top, but music coming from inside. There were a few men standing around, but one was standing in front of a big black door, and the other at a desk, casually talking to each other. When we got out of the cab, they straightened themselves up, all business-like.

Connor walked up to the one in front of the door and handed him the card. "Romulus sent us," he said.

The guy nodded and handed the card to the other guy at the desk, who said, "$30 American dollars. Each. Or $50 per couple."

My cute husband looked at me with wide eyes, as if he didn't expect us to have to pay. I, on the other hand, pulled out my wallet to hand him three twenty-dollar bills. The guy at the desk took it and stamped our hands with a Mickey Mouse stamp that could only be seen under a UV light. The doorman patted us down and opened the door.

There were two doors, but only one was open with loud reggae and dancehall music coming from it. I reached out to grab Connor's hand, and he immediately laced his fingers with mine. We smelled the weed before we started walking downstairs into the large, dim-lighted basement.

It was filled with men. Men dancing in the middle of the floor, men lining up the walls grinding against each other and making out, men at the bar at the far end of the room. Men of all colors, shapes and sizes, guys bigger and blacker than me, guys scrawnier and paler than Connor. There was barely any seating, but a couple of old couches here and there that were again filled with men kissing and touching all over each other. Some were fully clothed like we were in jeans and shirts; others in nothing but underwear, like the guy that just walked past in a silver bikini bottom with silver nipple rings to match. This was a gay man's wet dream. I also noticed there were about six doors along the other side of the room, which opened and closed quickly. I wondered what was behind those doors but considering the sexual tension in the room, it wasn't hard to figure it out.

I glanced at Connor, who surveyed the room just like I did. But when the music changed to "Murder She Wrote" by Chaka Demus, he turned around to face me and grinned. Then he took both my hands and danced backward toward the middle of the dance floor, taking me with him. I allowed him to drag me and when we were squeezed into the crowd, I pulled him closer as he put his arms around my neck. He moved his right leg between me and straddled my leg, then swayed his groin against me from side to side and I moved with him. Connor was a pretty good dancer, which I had discovered years ago when we first started dating. Just like his love-making, it was fluid and easy; his body was malleable and changed with the music. Someone came up and pointed at his tray that had little white pills and little white joints on it. Connor shook his head and hand at the guy who politely moved on. It didn't matter because there was so much marijuana in the air, we were definitely getting a contact high, whether we wanted to or not.

Another someone came by selling little sealed bottles of tequila, and we bought four. Connor downed the first one quickly and drank half of the second one while I nursed the first one. We danced for a while. Connor turned around and put his ass right up against my hard-on and rotated his hips. I moaned in my throat as he continued to push against me, getting me excited. He reached down and grabbed my jeans at the thigh, then reached his other hand up to wrap his fingers around the back of my neck. He exposed his purple splotchy neck to me, and I started sucking it. He closed his eyes, and I felt him humming erotically in his throat. I reached one hand and rubbed the front part of his jeans, and he moaned again. We had been drinking since the afternoon, and he was in that place beyond tipsy but not quite wasted, right where I like him to be: happy, sensual, and enjoying himself.

I was trying to be good to him and give his body a rest, but I really want to fuck him senseless again.

His movement against me was making it harder for me to show restraint. The people around us had less restraint, kissing and touching each other, hands down their dance partner's pants and exposed underwear, and stroking each other's genitals right in front of us. Watching everyone around us get frisky made me want to get frisky. It was hot as shit, and just getting hotter, both of us sweating through our shirts. I opened up a couple of Connor's buttons and played with his nipples, making him moan again. We were there for over an hour on the dance floor, and I was ready to tell Connor let's go back when someone touched my arm. I turned my head, and Connor lifted his head up too at the feel of me no longer kissing on his neck.

The guy looked indigenous. He said, in my ear, "Come with me. Bring your boyfriend."

He didn't give me a chance to say no; he just took my arm and started walking. I don't know why I let him, but I did. Connor had a look on his face that was a cross between confusion and annoyance. I took his hand and together we walked toward one of the doors in the back. The guy knocked, and another indigenous-looking guy opened the door, eyed him and us, then opened it just enough for the three of us to slide through.

We heard them moaning before we saw them and smelled the sex in the air. The man pulled us to the closest wall and left us there. The room was less crowded, quieter, and had an air conditioner on. Men were lining up the walls all around watching the show but seemed to be mostly in pairs. In the center of the room was a king-size circular bed, and there were four people on it, two white men and two black men, in the middle of an intense orgy. I was still holding my husband's hand, and he was squeezing me tightly. I looked at his face, but his eyes were glued to the live porno happening in front of us. Currently one white guy was getting fucked from behind by one black guy while he sucked another big black cock. The second white guy was rimming the guy doing the fucking. My dick was hard and tight in my jeans.

Eventually, Connor spoke. "It's a sex club," he said quietly.

I nodded. "You want to leave?" Knowing the answer but I wanted him to tell me.

"No," he said automatically. "Do you?"

"Fuck no." I told him quietly.

He smiled at me widely, then let go of my hands to wrap both arms around my waist from the side of me, his hard dick against my thigh, his head on my shoulder. I wrapped one arm around his neck while I finished my bottle of tequila, and together we watched the four men fuck and suck their way into oblivion. Again, other couples around us had less restraint. On one side of me a white couple two paces down from us were actively jerking each other off, while the black couple right next to us on the other side were grinding against each with their clothes still on. Connor and I were probably the only ones not touching each other in some way.

I didn't notice him until he started walking toward us, the gorgeous golden-skinned man with the perfect lips and bowed legs that went by the name Romulus. When he locked eyes with me yesterday on the beach, the stirring in my loins was unavoidable. But I pretended like I didn't really notice or cared. But when he locked eyes with Connor, that completely got my attention. A rush of jealousy hit me, but also intrigue at their blatant attraction to each other. Me pulling my husband into the ocean and making love to him like that was me reminding him that he was mine. Not that I needed to; he knew. Especially when he turned around, I saw his tear-streaked face and my heart melted. I didn't know why a brief encounter with the man stirred up so much sexual emotion between us, but we gave into it, all night in fact. And there he was again, stirring up my loins. My thoughts were all over the place. I didn't know if I wanted to fuck him or fuck Connor, or let Connor fuck him while I watched. Maybe all three.

The man was nursing a beer as he walked across the room past the bed, as if it was normal to have four strangers engage in coitus in a room of about twenty couples. Connor stood up straighter but kept one arm around my back.

He looked at me and smiled lustfully, then turned to Connor and said, "I'm Romulus. Romy. I didn't catch your names."

Romy's accent was thicker than the ones around us, and I assumed he originated from a different Caribbean island. He held his free hand out for a shake.

"Connor," my husband told him as he shook his hand.

Romy turned to me. "Jamel," I said and shook his hand as well. It was strong and manly.

"How long have you been married?" Romulus asked me.

"Two years," Connor answered him. "But we've been together for ten. That's why we're here. Celebrating both anniversaries."

He turned back to Connor and nodded. "Ten years, you say? That's quite an accomplishment. You must really love each other." He gazed into my husband's icy blue eyes.

"We do," I told him.

He turned his attention back to me. "Good. This room is for real couples only, looking for a good time. Anyone can join the bed. We change the plastic covering after every session and provide protection and lubrication for those that want it. Only a few of us are here in case they want company. For a price."

I nodded, understanding his meaning. He looked at Connor to make sure he understood his meaning too. Romulus turned around right in front of us to watch the show. He put his bottle on the floor, then stepped backward so that he was right in the middle of us, even though Connor and I still had our arms around each other's lower backs. He slowly extended his hand until he touched my genitals. I was about to slap his hand away when I saw he was doing the exact same thing to my husband. Connor did not slap his hand away, instead gasped and looked at me with wide eyes as this stranger rubbed us both.

Romulus's hands ran the length of both our cocks as he said, "I hope you enjoy your anniversary and vacation. If you are looking to spice things up, don't hesitate to reach out." He let us both go and turned around again. I didn't give him a reaction, but Connor's face told it all: surprise, lust, even a bit of fear.

Romy reached into his back pocket and handed me a different card than the one that gave us access in there. "My private number is on here. Call me if you want company."

I took the card from him, and I saw through my peripheral vision Connor's eyes go wide with surprise that I did so. Romy picked his beer off the ground and walked back to his spot on the other side of the room. I put the card in my pocket.

Connor resumed holding onto me with both hands on my waist and his head on my shoulder. He said quietly, "Yeah, Jamel?"

I chuckled. "I think we just got propositioned. For a price of course. Probably a high one."

"I don't know; he might give you a discount," he teased me.

"It's you he wants to fuck," I reminded him.

"I'm pretty sure he wants to fuck us both. At the same time. Right here on this bed."

I laughed quietly again, as we watched the quartet finish and move off the bed. A group of guys, including the guy that brought us in here, pulled the plastic covering off the bed and put a fresh one on. A young white couple moved quickly toward the bed and hurriedly took off their clothes, making Connor and I both giggle. Once they were completely naked, they started touching and kissing. They weren't physically attractive, both young and geeky-looking; one was a skinny twink, and the other had a bit of a pot belly and a hairy body, like a baby bear. But there was so much love they had for each other in the way they touched and held each other, whispered softly to each other in between kisses, it made them attractive. I knew the whole room felt what they felt and wanted a love like that. *Like what Connor and I have.*

They started out 69ing each other, the baby bear flat on his back rimming his lover while the other deep-throated his favorite anatomy. They moaned in sync and continued to worship the other's body with their hands. It was incredibly romantic and erotic. Connor felt it too. I could hear him breathing with his mouth open, panting. His cock was so hard, it was pressed tightly against me, and I could feel the pre-cum sliding out my cock, one drip at a time.

I don't know what made me ask him, maybe because I felt his energy, his desire, his restlessness. Maybe because I knew my husband well enough to know he needed to express himself sexually. But either way I asked the question, and I wasn't ready for what came next.

"What do you want to do, Connor?" I quietly asked him.

"I want you to fuck my mouth," he said without hesitation, as if it was the most naturally thing to say in a back room full of strangers. He let me go and stood in front of me. We held each other's gaze for a long moment.

Then he said, "Make me."

And I didn't hesitate either. "Suck my big, black dick," I ordered.

He immediately got on his knees and undid my belt buckle, unzipped me, and pulled my jeans down to my ankles. Suddenly I was the self-conscious one. My eyes quickly looked around to see who had noticed that my lover was rubbing his face across my black boxer briefs over and over again, kissing my penis through the fabric, rubbing his hands along my thighs, massaging me near the groin area. And quite a few people had noticed, including Romulus from across the room. I looked back down when I felt the air on my genitals, as Connor pulled my underwear all the way down, my cock popping out and pointing straight ahead. It hit me like a ton of bricks that this man, who was nervous about holding my hand through a crowded airport, had absolutely no qualms about blowing me in a crowd of strangers. It was fascinating seeing that side of him.

And I had another epiphany: that he had done this before. *Several times probably. I will have to ask him about that,* I thought. And then I had no more thoughts, as Connor began to lick me from base to tip, repeatedly.

He took his time and put on a show, wrapping one hand around my cock as he licked me up and down and all around, catching my pre-cum with the tip of his tongue, pulling back to elongate the string of cum. The couple next to me gasped as he lapped it up and licked around my head over and over again, making me moan loudly. Then he sucked my testicles and made loud popping and slurping sounds. Those who weren't paying attention before were definitely paying attention now. Connor put my cock head in his mouth and slid down, pulled up, then slid further down, inching me down his throat. I gently put my hands on his head, guiding him all the way down to my pubes. He was concentrating on getting me off.

One of the black guys next to me said, in a British accent, "Bloody hell, mate, he's going to take your entire cock down his throat."

And indeed he did. Connor's lips touched my groin, and I moaned as I felt him swallow and suck me. He pulled all the way off, took a deep breath, and plunged back down, taking me down in one motion, pulled off with a loud POP noise, and then took all of me down his throat again.

I moaned a loud "UGH," as others around us exclaimed, "Whoa!" "Holy shit!" and "What a good, little cocksucker!"

He stayed longer and gagged, then pulled back coughing up phlegmy spit. He looked up at me as he stroked my sloppy wet dick and grinned, spit dripping off his chin. I smiled at him too, touched his face lovingly. He continued to suck me off, taking me all the way in at times, halfway at other times, while stroking me with two hands in between. At one point, he stroked me upwards, put one of my testicles in his mouth again, then the other one, and then he juggled both in his mouth. Others came closer to watch, including Romulus, forgetting about the couple on the bed who didn't notice or care as they made love to each other.

After he engaged my balls the second time in this mission of public sex, I lost all inhibition as well. I grabbed his head and gave him what he wanted. I fucked my good, little cocksucker's mouth, slowly at first, picking up speed, then slamming into him. I locked eyes with Romulus as I did, saw him touch himself through his jeans, and that made me smirk at him. Others around us started pulling out their dicks and stroking it as they watched us. I looked at my husband, red-faced, drooling spit, bright blue eyes looking up at me, him holding onto my thighs, and I fell in love with him all over again.

I continued thrusting into his face over and over again until I was close. "Fuck! Yeah, suck this dick, baby!" I exclaimed, a small part of me asking myself, *When did I become this person who talked dirty?* I must have been way drunker than what I thought, and probably a little high from the weed in the air.

"I'm about to cum," I told him, still fucking his face. "Where do you want it, huh? Where do you want your Big Daddy to cum? On your face or down your throat?"

I started moving faster, almost ready. Connor looked up at me with those piercing blue eyes and I knew where I was going to cum.

"Here it comes, ugh!"

I slipped my dick out of his mouth, and he kept his head up and stuck his tongue out. I stroked and came. Streams of thick white cum painted his hair, eyes, nose, lips, his tongue, all over his face. Someone next to me moaned "ugh," and I assume they also came.

When I had no cum left to leave on his face, my cocksucking cum slut husband licked his lips, took the cum off his face with his fingers, and dipped them in his mouth. I took my hand that had a bit of cum on it and put it in his mouth, and he sucked it hard. I pulled him up to his feet, with my free hand and dragged my tongue across his cheek, then pulled him close so we could kiss passionately. The people around us amusingly started clapping, making us both laugh. We looked around at all the happy faces, and it looked like a few people had their dicks out and came too. Romulus lifted his beer to us as a salute, making us laugh again.

My baby once again gets the gold.

Connor helped to pull up my underwear and jeans. Once they were on, he used the bottom of his shirt to wipe his face. I kissed him and said, "That was the hottest shit that has ever happened to me. Let's go."

I pulled him from the room so fast and through the crowded dance floor back up the stairs. When we got outside, it wasn't any cooler than inside and we were dripping in sweat. The guy who was at the desk took one look at us and said, "You need a cab, right? What hotel?"

We told him, and he called for one of the guys to come over. "Get these two back safely. They are friends of Romy," he told him.

The driver motioned for us to cross the street with him and opened the door to the Volvo. He started driving in the direction of the beach and resorts. We immediately started kissing in the cab. Amazingly, I was growing all over again, and Connor was still hard.

I pulled back and said, "Tell me what you want me to do." I rubbed his cock through his pants.

Connor said, in a very clear and commanding voice, "Put your mouth on this cock and make me cum, bitch."

I unbuckled his belt and pulled his pants and underwear down in one motion. I was half off the backseat as I deep-throated him, and he moaned loudly. He put both hands on my head and when I pulled up, he pushed me down again roughly, like I really was his bitch. We gave the driver another show, but neither of us gave a fuck. I put my fingers in his ass and sucked him hard until he yelled my name, "Jameeelll fuuuuck!" and came in my mouth, and I greedily swallowed all of him. Then I came up, and we kissed until our lips hurt as we pulled up in front of the hotel.

"How much?" I asked the driver, breathing hard.

He chuckled. "For that, it's on the house," he said with a heavy accent as well. I chuckled too but handed him a ten-dollar American bill anyway.

I pulled Connor out of the car and held his hand as we made our way through the resort to our room. We quietly stripped naked and got in the bed. This time I laid on his chest, and he rubbed my head.

I let my mind spin, then spoke. "Yeeeaaah, I'm going to say it out loud."

He chuckled. "Say what you gotta say, Mel."

"Soooo ... you've been to a sex club once or twice," I stated.

"Once or twice," Connor said. "Or three times."

I looked up at him and started cackling. "Oh my God, baby!"

"Jameeeelll," he whined my name. He had the audacity to turn red from embarrassment!

"Oh no, you don't. You don't get to act all shy right now. Not after that performance you just did, sucking my dick like that in public," I teased him.

"Uuuugh!" He groaned and put the pillow over his head.

I removed it from his face and played with his nipples. "So, have you gone all the way in a club like that? Full sex?"

He sighed, but then he looked me in the eyes and answered, "Yes."

"Threesomes?"

"Yes."

"Foursomes?" I raised both eyebrows.

"Yes."

Holy shit. I started chuckling. "What's the highest—"

"Six." He gave me the number before I finished the question. I started laughing again.

"Holy shit, Connor. Holy. Shit." I sat up and put my hand out. "Hi, I'm Jamel, nice to finally meet the real fucking Connor! Holy shit!" I yelled and started laughing again.

Connor slapped my hand away. "I'm not exactly proud of it, you know," he said sheepishly.

"Baby, you have nothing to be ashamed about with me," I told him, kissing his abs. "I told you a long time ago that you are free with me. Tell me anything. Be anyone. Do anything...." He didn't respond, but I knew he knew where I was going. "Like maybe a threesome with me."

He was quiet, then asked, "Like you, me, and our new island friend Romy?"

"If that's what you want." I shrugged.

"That's not what I want," he said abruptly. Then he softened. "It's just that ... I left that life behind when I met you. When I committed to you. You're the only man I ever want to be with."

"Okay," I said. "I won't bring it up ever again." I put my head back on his chest.

Connor was quiet again, then said, "You brought that up pretty quickly, Mel. Something tells me you aren't shy about having a threesome either. You know, since we're confessing and shit."

"I've had a threesome before. Once or twice," I admitted.

"Or three times," he said and laughed.

"Well, I haven't gone over three, Mr. Half A Dozen Cocks In My Face." I busted out laughing.

"Ugh, it was five plus me and I fucking hate you," Connor said with a groan.

I moved my body up and over him until we were face to face. "You fucking love me."

"I fucking love you," he repeated after me, lifting his arms around my waist.

I leaned down and asked sweetly on his lips, "You love me, baby?"

"With all my heart," he said back to me on my lips. Then he kissed me. "With all my mind." Another kiss. "With all my body." Kiss. "With all my soul." Kiss. "With every fiber of my being." One more kiss. "I love you, Jamel," he said, as he touched my face.

I rubbed my nose with his. "Is this still okay?"

"Always," he said, as he rubbed his nose back with mine.

We kissed, then I moved to the side of him and pulled him closer. As much as I wanted to make love to him, I knew it was not what he needed then. He needed to feel safe and cared for by me. To feel my unconditional love. To know that showing me that side of him wouldn't change how I felt about him.

And it doesn't, not one bit. I just might love him more for trusting me with that part of himself, that sexually adventurous side, and his confidence that I still love him with every fiber of my being too.

He moved into my chest curling up and clasped his hands together between us, proving my intuition right about what he needed from me. I put my arms and legs around him and held him tight.

"I love you," I whispered in his hair after a while. He responded by kissing my chest, already falling asleep.

CHAPTER 15

If We Were To Pick A Third

Jamel

We spent the day going from the pool to the beach. Back and forth every few hours, either laying under a beach umbrella, sleeping and reading, to horseplaying in the chlorinated water and swimming up to the in-pool bar for free drinks. Interestingly, I found him to be less self-conscious about being affectionate with me in public. It could be because we were in Aruba far away from home, or it could be because of what happened the night before. But either way, I welcomed it; Connor's gentle caressing of my arm as we walked together, laying his head on my chest on the sand as we laid in a T-formation reading our novels silently, holding onto me and kisses on my face as we floated together in the deep end of the pool. I wanted to make a joke about it, but I was afraid that it would make him shy and pull back from it.

In the evening, as we made our way back to our room, holding hands, we passed by the ice cream shop. We both looked in to see if Romy was there, and he was. The shop was busy and filled with patrons, so he didn't notice us. Then we looked at each other and laughed, again remembering last night.

We were on the balcony watching the sun set when my phone rang. Josh was video calling me. "Heeeey! Happy Anniversary!" he screamed into the phone.

Willy was right next to him. "Haaayy *feliz aniversario!*" he yelled too. I laughed at them.

Connor moved closer to me, hearing their drunken cheers for us. "It's tomorrow, guys, but thanks."

"No, it's not, it's..." Josh looked at Willy. "It's not the 17th?"

"*Coño, yo no sey,* I thought it was ... How long have we been here?" Will asked confused.

"Where are you?" I asked them.

"Well, Josh has the great idea to visit my homeland that I've never been to, so ... surprise!"

Connor looked astonished. "You're in Colombia?"

"*Si!*" they both said simultaneously and laughed.

"He just needed to get away," Willy said. "So, we just got on a plane and came a few days ago."

"Partying like rock stars," Josh said.

"Okay, well don't party too hard," I stated fatherly.

Josh was still not okay, but he was better when someone was around, especially if it was Will. He went back to the base to keep his structured, busy, and organized life, which helped, but Henry told me his C.O. was making him see a grief counselor, which he hated. Willy, true to his word, had quit his job and pretty much moved into Nick's house, got an apartment near the base, and went to see him at least once a week.

"Sure thing, Dad," Josh responded, rolling his eyes.

"Okay, we're going to call you back tomorrow and do this all over again," Willy said, making us both laugh. "Have fuuuuuun! Don't do anything I wouldn't do. I take that back, do *all* the things that I would do. You only live once, right!?"

"Right," Connor said, looking at me.

They hung up. He sat back in his chair and looked thoughtful. "What's on your mind?" I asked him and gently touched his thigh.

After a few moments, he asked me, "If we were to pick a third, who would it be?"

That wasn't what I expected him to say. I expected him to tell me that he wanted to go back to the club. The back room.

"I don't know," I replied. "It's not something that I've considered. Who would you want it to be?"

"Someone that we both trust," he said.

"Someone that we both love," I said. "And that loves us too."

"Yeah," he agreed. "Someone that, if something were to happen to the other, would take care of us."

"Sexually?" I grinned.

He smiled at me. "Yes, but not just that."

"I know what you mean," I said. "Like how Willy is taking care of Josh."

"Yeah, like that," he said softly. He was quiet again.

"I don't think we're thinking of the same person," I teased him. *I know exactly who he is thinking of.*

"No, I don't think we are."

"Because you're thinking of Jack," I told him.

He grinned slyly. "Obviously if he wasn't with Ethan, but yes he would be the obvious choice for me. Why, who would you say? Ethan?"

"Yes. Ethan would take care of you."

Connor scoffed. "Ethan pretty much tolerates me because of my friendship with Jack and his friendship with you. He hates my family and kinda dislikes me by extension."

I shook my head. "That's not true. Ethan considers you a friend. I know this."

"But not someone who would love me and want to take care of me. Jack would."

"Ethan would. If something ever happened to me, Ethan would take care of you. He'd do it for me. They both would."

He thought for a moment. "And vice versa? If something were to happen with one of them, would we take the other one in, make them a part of us?"

"If that's what they wanted or needed, yes, without a doubt."

Connor nodded, then laughed. "We should probably tell them of this guardianship plan that we have for them."

I laughed too. "Could you imagine either of their faces? 'Yeah, so Connor and I decided if one of you dies, we'll make the other a part of us and take care of you, physically, mentally and emotionally.' They would laugh in our faces."

"Don't forget sexually." He winked at me.

"You just want me to give you permission to fuck your first love." I grinned at him.

He laughed again. "I'm just saying. If we are taking care of them, then we gotta do it the whole way." I shoved his shoulder.

"You're right, and I would have no problem fucking Gorgeous Gay Jack." I smiled dreamily, expecting his shocked reaction.

His jaw hit the floor. "Mother. Fucker!" He shoved my shoulder, making me laugh loudly.

Then he said, "But would you really have sex with Ethan though? I mean, I would. Ethan is hot and not my best friend." He winked at me, and I shoved his shoulder again. "But would you?" He gave me a look of disgust, knowing how close we were.

I chuckled, then sighed. "Probably not. He's one of my closest friends right now. Closer to me than Dante. But maybe if you died tragically in Aruba and I was lonely..." I said with a straight face.

He turned around to face me, wide-eyed. "You're already killing me off!? What, a car accident or maybe a plane crash?"

"Hey, people go missing all the time," I said again with a straight face. His mouth dropped again, and I laughed. He shoved me lightly, but then put his hand on my leg. He stared out into the sunset.

I let him lose himself in his thoughts again, and then I said, "Tell me what you want, Connor. What you really want right now."

He looked me in my eyes, and we stared at each other. He opened his mouth, then closed it. Then opened it again. "I want to go back to the club." I nodded at him, holding his gaze and encouraging him to go on. "I want to get on the bed in the back room."

I nodded again. "Just you and me?"

Connor opened his mouth again, then turned his head forward. He said quietly, "That's up to you, Mel."

I turned his face back to me by his chin. "No, it's *our* decision. We make it together. I just need to know what you want." I let a moment pass. "You want a third with us?"

"Only if you want it too. You have to want it just as much as I do. Otherwise..."

"I do. But only if I get to do it with you. Equal footing. Otherwise, this wouldn't even be a conversation. You know this."

Connor stared at me, as if he was trying to figure me out. "I can't believe you're..." He trailed off again.

"Being so open with you?" I answered for him. "It's all I've ever wanted for you, Con. To feel like you could be yourself with me. We don't talk about it, but I know you're still struggling with being out fully. And although our sex life is amazing, I think you kind of miss the thrill of your sexual freedom. I think those two things have kept you from being completely you." I let him take in my words.

Connor looked away for a moment, then turned back to me. "Yeah. Maybe."

He looked down, but I again raised his chin up so his eyes met mine. "Do you realize this is the most physically open in public that you have been with me in these last three days than in the entire ten years we've been together? And that's because those two things are non-factors for you right now. I don't know

243

what will happen when we go home, but for now, don't hold back, baby. I'm right here with you. I got you. And I'm not going any-fucking-where." We both smiled, as we remembered our earlier days when he used to say it to me.

He nodded at me. "Okay, baby."

I kissed his lips. "So, we'll go back tonight."

"Yes."

"Then you should call to make sure he's going to be there tonight."

Connor smiled and returned the kiss on my lips. Then he got up to grab the card from the dresser and came back out to the balcony. When he dialed the number and held the phone to his ear, I stood up and held his waist, leaning in close with my head on the other side of him.

The man answered, "Yo, it's Romy!"

We could hear the background noise from the ice cream shop, so we knew he was still working.

"Romy," Connor said, as I kissed his neck. It was more red than purple, as the bruises from my hickies were going away. "It's Connor and Jamel. Will you be at the club tonight?"

"Connor! Yes, Blondie, good to hear from you. The club is closed tonight; we close on Sundays and Mondays."

"Oh, okay," he said. I could see his disappointment. It was already Sunday, and we were to fly out on Tuesday.

But then Romy said, "But I'm free tonight. I get off at midnight if you want some company. Talk to your husband and then come find me."

Connor's mouth opened slightly, and I knew why. Having a threesome in a public sex club was one thing, that's like performance art to him. But having a three-some privately was a lot more intimate.

He stared at me with those brilliant blue eyes of his. I took over. "We'll let you know, Romy," I said into the phone, then took it from him to hang up.

I wrapped my arms around my husband and looked in his eyes. "Yay or nay?"

Connor hesitated. "Can I think about it? We have a few hours."

"Okay," I kissed him again. "Let's have dinner, and then you let me know."

Connor

Jamel is scaring me with this.

It was almost too good to be true, that he wanted me to be sexually free, as long as I did it with him. For a recovering whore like me, that's like hitting the moth-erload. Like getting off of heroin but being offered methadone instead, under the care of a physician. Mel wanted to be my physician. But maybe it was also a test, to see if I would really fuck Romy. *Which if it is, he is in for a rude awakening, because if Jamel gives me the green light, I'm going to fuck the shit out of Romy, repeatedly.*

Except he had given me the green light, as long as he got to fuck him too. And I didn't know how I felt about that yet. Selfish as it sounds, Jamel was mine and I didn't want anyone else touching him. That was why I couldn't give him a straight yes. My mind was spinning in so many different directions, and I just needed to slow things down for us.

We went out to one of the restaurants at the resort for dinner and talked about other things. Afterward, we went on a walk on the beach again, holding hands silently, both lost in our own thoughts. We then went upstairs and found a movie to watch and laid in bed. But I wasn't watching; instead, I was scrolling through my phone, trying to understand how other serious couples do it, considering the proposition.

Setting boundaries and ground rules is a thing, so maybe Romy penetrating Mel is my deal-breaker. Also, I wouldn't want this to be a thing in our relationship. It was fine for now in a foreign country, since we were celebrating together, but the truth is I don't trust myself enough to have this become our regular thing. The best thing Jamel did was demand exclusivity from me right from the beginning. We are who we are to each other because I gave myself to him and only him fully, mentally, emotionally, and sexually. I still wanted us to be us after all was said and done.

True to his word, Mel didn't bring it up again, waiting for me to give the yay or nay. And if I never said yay, then it just wouldn't happen. I knew him enough to know that my silence on the issue meant no to him. So, after doing all the research I could, going on blogs and chat rooms and getting some advice, I sat up in the bed and said, "Yay."

He looked over at me and sat up too, waiting for me to talk. "But we have to talk first, set some ground rules that we both agree to. And if we can't agree, then we don't go through with it," I told him.

Jamel nodded. "Agreed."

He turned off the TV to give me his full attention. I moved to the end of the bed so I could face him and sat cross-legged. He moved closer to me and touched my leg.

"Tell me what you want," he said.

I stared at him for a long moment, still trying to decide if I should. "I want to be able to do everything. Everything. I don't want to hold back. But I don't want to feel like you're watching me, judging me."

"When have I ever made you feel that way, Connor?" he asked.

"You haven't, and that's why I love you. But you have no idea what you're in for Jamel. I can't explain it. I can only show you. I'm going to show you."

He smiled. "And I can't wait to see it. Experience it. Don't hold back." He rubbed my leg. "What else?"

I exhaled, then said, "This is going to sound kinda selfish, and at its worst, fucked up, but I don't want him fucking you."

He smiled again. "Okay."

"You sure you're okay with that?" I challenged him.

He looked at me slyly, tilted his head to the side, and said, "You know I'm a top, right?"

I started laughing. "Not with me you're not."

"Exactly," he said seriously. "That only happens when I care about someone deeply. You're the fourth, last and only. So, I'm really good with that rule. Trust me."

"Okay," I said, relieved. "Give me one of your rules."

Jamel thought about it for a moment. "But then that means you can't penetrate me either at any point during it. You say you want to do everything, and I'm cool with that. Except fuck me. We save that for after, when it's just the two of us."

Damn. There goes my one image of me fucking Mel while Romy fucked me. I can live without it.

"Okay," I agreed. "But that reminds me of something else. I want to Dom."

He fell backward on the bed, laughing. "I'm serious!" I exclaimed, although I found myself chuckling at his response. "What the fuck is so funny?"

"Tell me exactly what you mean by 'Dom'," he said, still laughing as he sat up. "Because suddenly you wanting to do 'everything' has me thinking you're about to have me handcuffed somewhere calling you Master Sergeant."

"I meeeeeean..." I cringed and smiled, and he laughed again.

"No, Connor."

"Fuck! Okay. That's too much, I gotta ease you into the Kink life. I get it, I get it." I laughed and he laughed with me.

"So, tell me how do you want to Dom? Explicitly," he said when the laughter died down.

"I'm not asking you to call me sir. I want to say what happens and when it happens. Don't question me. Don't hesitate. Don't say no. I'm in charge," I said very seriously.

Jamel nodded slowly. "Okay. I trust you completely."

That made my heart melt for him. "One more thing: I don't want anything to change between us. Can you promise me that?"

He pulled me into his lap. I straddled him on the bed and put my arms around his neck while he held my waist. We kissed like lovers, then he said, "I'm still so deep in love with you, Connor; there is no getting me out. Nothing is going to change how I feel about you. What about you?"

"Fuck, Jamel. I'm more in love with you in this moment than I have been the entire time we've been together. I fucking love that we are doing this together." I kissed him again. "And when it's done, it's done. This isn't going to be part of our regular life, threesomes and shit. Apparently, a lot of couples do this, a lot of gay couples at that, but I don't want that. I've outgrown this, trust me. I love our domesticated life. I don't need to have sexual freedom with multiple partners. I just need you. And I need to know that after all is said and done, you still love me, unconditionally."

He kissed my neck with every word. "Unconditionally. Unequivocally. Absolutely. Irrevocably. Undoubtedly. Assuredly. Emphatically. Indubitably."

"I love it when you use SAT words," I cooed.

Jamel pulled back to look in my face. "One more thing," he said. "Protection on at all times. He's still a stranger to us. We'll buy more than enough and switch out as often as needed."

I nodded, knowing I played fast and loose with my life way too many times when I was out there; grateful that Jamel was the complete opposite and always used condoms for the first thirty years of his life before he met me. "Agreed."

Jamel held me tighter and said, "I'm in the mood for ice cream. What about you?"

I smiled. "Same. Let's go get some ice cream."

♥

The shop was still crowded. We saw Romy taking orders at the register and stood in his line. He glanced down and locked eyes with me but made no other acknowledgement of familiarity. When we got to the front of the line, he smiled and said, "What can I do you for?"

"You're off at midnight?" I asked softly. He nodded. I nodded back and said, "I want cookies and cream in a waffle cone, three scoops." I looked him in the eyes.

He nodded again. Then Romy looked behind me at Jamel. "Do you want the same?" he asked. Something about that made me appreciate the island man.

"Yes. Three scoops." I heard Jamel say.

Romulus gave a huge, knowing smile as he wrote it down on his notepad. "What room am I charging this to?" he asked, without looking up.

While charging things to the room was pretty common at the resort, I'm pretty sure no one charged little things like ice cream. So, I knew what he was really asking: What room was he going to tonight.

"Room 804. That's where I want the bill to go."

"It will be there around thirty after," said Romy.

I nodded, but then Jamel said, "What's the charge?"

Romulus flipped his pad and wrote a number down, flipped the page back over to rip off both receipts and hand it to me. "$11.95 for your waffle cones," he said with a straight face.

I didn't look at it; I just handed it to Jamel. I forgot Romy was doing this for a price. It kinda took the magic out of it for me so I didn't want to know. Jamel looked at the second slip, then looked up at Romy, but typical Mel kept his face unreadable so I couldn't tell if it was a high price or not. Then he sighed through his nose and pulled out his wallet. He handed over a twenty-dollar bill for the ice cream and said, "Keep the change." He put both receipts in his pocket, and we stepped to the side so he could take the next order and get our waffle cones.

I turned around and looked at my amazing, beautiful husband. I wrapped my arms around him and put my chin on his shoulder. Jamel rubbed my back with one hand and kissed my cheek. I realized in that moment he was right, that I had been more affectionate with him and less aware of who was watching us lately. I gave into that feeling of wanting to be close to him, and fuck everyone else and their thoughts of our same-sex coupling. I wished we were this way all the time. *But I know the only reason we aren't is because of me.* I closed my eyes and held him tighter.

We stood like that until we heard Romy say softly, "Your order is up."

Jamel walked over to the counter. Romy handed him both cones, making sure their hands touched on purpose. I felt a pang of jealousy, then decided I was going to make him choke on my dick for that, and I immediately felt better.

After we stopped at a small novelty shop at the resort for the condoms and more alcohol, Jamel stopped at the ATM, pulling out wads of hundred-dollar bills. We kissed and touched each other on the way upstairs, getting more and more sexually aroused but knew we were going to save all the real stuff for the romp later. Then I remembered something else.

"Hey, Mel? We need a time-out code word."

He was a little confused. "What's that? So if one of us wants to tap out?"

"Yes, just a way to communicate that we don't want to do this anymore. And at any point, either you or I could say it and we both tap out."

"I like it. What's our code word?"

"Something simple like, 'Aruba.'"

He laughed. "Okay." He was thoughtful, then said, "How about a full phrase? Like, 'I love Aruba but.' The 'but' part is our way of knowing the other wants to stop the train."

I smiled. "I love it."

We waited until 11:30 p.m. and went to take showers together. I scrubbed every inch of him, and he did the same for me. When we got out, I put on my thin gray sweatpants that showed the outline of my bulge and a tank top. Mel began to do the same, but I told him, "No shirt. Let him see your chest."

He smiled at me. "Are we already beginning our role reversal, Corporal?"

"Yes," I told him seriously. I wanted him to lust after Jamel, but I was going to rock his fucking world first. Neither of them had any idea what they were in for.

"Okay," Mel said and took off his tank top.

We grabbed the tequila bottle, 100 proof, and a couple of shot glasses with Aruba on them that we bought from the novelty shop. I opened it and gave myself a shot, then poured him one. I walked over to Jamel as he sat on the bed, putting Vaseline on the heels and soles of his feet. I stood between his legs, and he made room for me, rubbing his hand up my thigh to my ass, then held onto my cheeks.

"Lift your head back and open your mouth," I ordered. He did immediately. "Don't swallow." I poured the liquor into his mouth and watched it pool up at the bottom of his throat, then I put my mouth over his. Immediately, we kissed and swallowed it together. "Good boy," I said and grinned.

"You're going to enjoy this shit," he said and laughed.

"About as much as you enjoy me calling you Big Daddy," I smiled knowingly.

Jamel laughed loudly. "God, I do love that."

I kissed his face gently and stepped back to the counter. I made myself another shot and turned around to face him, sipping it slower. He sat there and stared at me with those gray eyes of his and as usual, I got lost in them. We continued to stare at each other until we heard the knock on the door.

"Open it," I told him.

Jamel did, and Romulus came in with his bike in tow, a professional one that was easily a couple of hundred dollars, that had a fanny pack hanging off it. It looked like he went home to shower, then biked his way back to the resort. He must not live very far because it was only 12:30 a.m., right on time. Romy gave Jamel a dap as he moved his bike to the wall near the door. He looked over at me, and I nodded my head to him. Romy wore black, yellow, and green bicycle pants, like the kind Mel wore when he exercised, that showed off his huge cock, and a white loose tank top, the kind you can see his nipples through the side of it.

I poured another shot and held it out to him. Romy came closer and took it from me, touching my fingers, watching me watch him throw his head back and drink it. Then he turned around as Jamel resumed sitting on the edge of the bed, facing me, waiting for my instructions. Romy looked back at me, who was unsmiling, and quickly caught on to who was in charge here. I pointed at the bed with my chin. He went to sit on the edge of the bed next to Jamel but leaned back on his forearms.

"So, gentleman, where are you from?" he asked casually.

Jamel glanced at me, and I gave him a slight nod. He said, "Rhode Island."

"I've never heard of it. How close is it to New York? I have family there."

"About two-and-a-half hours north. Rhode Island is the smallest state. You ever been to New York?"

"Not since I was much younger, probably the age my daughter is now so I don't remember much of it."

"Oh, you have a daughter?" Mel asked, very interested in his life now. "How old?"

"She'll be six in a few months. Yeah, Joan is my pride and joy. The best thing I've ever done, you know? She's back home in Jamaica with her mum. We're not together anymore."

Jamel nodded. "I thought your accent was different than the others here. That's where you are originally from?"

Romy nodded back. "Yeah, I followed my brother here for work about five years ago, and just never left. Montego Bay resorts are nice, but I like the scene here better." He looked at me who was still watching this exchange. I wanted everyone to be nice and comfortable, so I let the conversation continue.

Romy turned back to Jamel. "What kind of work do you do?"

Jamel glanced at me again, but then turned back and said, "I work in construction, and Connor is a property manager."

He grinned. "Blue-collar rewarding work. I like it." Jamel chuckled and I didn't. "I meet a lot of people, but I find those who do good honest work, especially with their hands, are the best kind of people."

I saw him glance over at Jamel's hands that were still in his lap, then slowly survey his broad chest with his lion paw tattoo, then up his collarbone and neck, stopping at those full lips of my partner. *He wants Mel to fuck him so badly.*

Jamel asked, "How old are you, Romy?"

"Twenty-six," he told him. "And you?" Romy reached over and touched Jamel's leg.

Before Jamel could answer, I moved off the counter and came over with my shot of tequila. Romy immediately removed his hand and sat up. I stood between his legs just as I had done with Jamel a few moments earlier. I looked down at him as he looked up at me and got to see his features up close—his unblemished, golden brown skin, a very thin mustache forming on his full, light brown lips, dark brown eyes, thick eyebrows, ears that jutted out at the top, curly brown hair that was long enough for me to run my fingers through. He smelled sweet, some kinda orangey scent I couldn't place.

"Open your mouth," I said. He did. Right before I poured the drink in his mouth, I gave him the same instructions, "Don't swallow yet."

Like a good, little slut, he listened, letting it pool in his throat. I put my mouth over his and our tongues danced. He moaned a little when I sucked his tongue, hard. I pulled back first, and he was still moving his mouth like he wanted more. He glanced over at Jamel, but I palmed his face and turned him back to me roughly.

"Not him. Me," I demanded. Romy held eye contact and nodded.

I reached down and pulled off his tank top slowly, not breaking eye contact, and he raised his arms and allowed me to. Once done, I ran my fingers through his thick, curly brown hair. His eyes narrowed in satisfaction as I did this over and over again. He reached over and touched my thighs. I took his face in both my hands to lift his head up. I nibbled the tip of his ear first and kissed his lips softly, then I opened my mouth wider and put my tongue down his throat again. He moaned and pulled me closer.

I let him suck on my lips a bit, then I pulled back from him and stepped out from between his legs. He was surprised, leaving his hands hanging in the air. His dick was straining in his tights and his nipples were hard. I finally looked at Jamel, whose face was unreadable, even for me.

"Kiss him," I told my husband.

Jamel moved closer, and they started kissing, tonguing each other down. Watching Jamel give someone else those slow, sultry kisses he gave to me gave me a pang of jealousy again. *Romy is going to get punished for that too.*

"Touch his cock."

Mel reached over and rubbed the outline of Romy's cock, and he moaned again, then Romy reached up and touched Jamel's chest. I watched them, my own cock straining to come out and play. I pulled it out and started stroking it, coming closer. Jamel saw me first, pulled his tongue out of Romy's mouth, again leaving his mouth still open in midair, wanting more. Jamel wrapped his lips on me, sucking me off. It was Romy watching us, as he pulled his own cock out and started stroking it.

"I didn't tell you to do that, Romy," I spoke without looking at him, as I touched Jamel's head lovingly. Romy paused stroking himself and smiled. "Now you have to wait a bit longer. You're going to be a good, little slut for us, right?"

He nodded, hand still paused on his dick. "Don't move your hand. Now you just watch."

Jamel continued to blow me while Romy watched, hand tight on his own cock that was involuntarily twitching, but not stroking. I reached down and put my finger in the precum at the tip of his dick. He gasped at my touch and watched me suck my finger. His cum was a little sweet. I did it again, this time pressing a bit harder in the slit, and he moaned. I pulled back slowly from Jamel's mouth, looked at him, and then down at Romy's lap. He understood. Simultaneously, I moved closer to Romy whose mouth was ready and open, and he put his pretty, brown lips over my white-skinned cock.

It felt … Different. His suction wasn't as strong as Mel's, but there was something sensual about it, the way he twisted his mouth around as he went up and down. Then I felt him gasp, and we both looked down to see Jamel's pretty brown lips on Romy's cock, deep-throating him.

Romy moved like he wanted to come off me, so I grabbed his face roughly and pushed my dick down his throat. "You don't move until I tell you to," I ordered.

He moaned again and gagged but allowed it, one hand on my leg with the other on Mel's back. I pulled my dick out of his mouth so he could catch a breath, rubbed it on his face, then shoved his mouth right back on it, and he really gagged that time, tapping my hand harder than he intended to so I could let him out.

That's what he gets for touching my man without my permission.

Romy coughed up spit, which dripped from his mouth onto Mel's head, who was still deep-throating him. I lifted Mel's head up gently and kissed his mouth again, then pulled him to a standing position. I pulled down his pants and took them all the way off, then reached down and took mine off.

"You know what to do," I said to Romy.

Romy immediately got on his knees between us, sucked Mel off while stroking me, then switched. We moaned above him, letting him feast on both of our cocks as we kissed each other. He was indeed a pro.

After a bit, I told Jamel, "Go get a condom. I want you inside of me."

He obeyed, moved to the nightstand, and grabbed a condom and the first of many bottles of lube we would go through. While Romy continued to suck me off, Jamel got on his knees, spread my cheeks apart and rimmed and fingered me, making me shudder. He lubed my hole, put the condom on him, bent me over slightly and entered me. He reached around me with both hands, one on my waist and the other on my nipples, to hold me steady, pulled out halfway, then thrusted back in, sliding against my prostate. I closed my eyes and moved my waist back and forth, back to meet Jamel's groin and forward to meet Romy's mouth, enjoying the feeling of being sucked and fucked simultaneously. *God, it had been so long since I'd been serviced like that.* But after a while, I stopped them both when I was getting too close.

I pulled Romy off me first and said, "Take off your clothes and get on the bed." He did so, and I pulled out Jamel's dick and went to grab a condom. Then I turned to Mel. "Get him ready."

Jamel climbed on the bed and sucked Romy's hard brown nipples and left wet kisses all over his chest, as he made his way down to lick his cock while I put protection on. I went over, and Jamel moved to lay on the side of him. I moved Romy so that he was on all fours, face directly over Jamel's dick. I took off Mel's condom and again, Romy knew what to do. As he blew Mel, I moved behind him, coated his hole with lube, and noticed his lower back tattoo, in the shape of an island that wasn't Aruba. I kissed it sensually as I fingered him, and he moaned as he gave Jamel a blow job. I could feel my husband's eyes on me as I kissed up and down my new lover's spine, but by the time I looked up, his eyes were closed. I went back to kissing Romy's tattoo.

Eventually, I got on my knees on the bed and entered him slowly. It felt foreign, like this wasn't my home. But I knew I was just visiting. His hole was tight, and he moaned with Jamel's dick in his mouth as I bottomed out. I held his waist and began fucking him. I looked over at Jamel's face, whose eyes were still closed and he moaned in his throat, also running his hand through Romy's hair. He liked Romy's hair and blow job skills, I could tell.

I said loudly, "This is our fuck toy. Fuck his mouth, hard. Don't let him up."

Jamel opened his eyes and looked at me. He grabbed Romy's face steady and began to thrust upward. We thrusted at the same time, watching each other. It was so in sync that we might as well have been fucking each other, and Romy just happened to be in between. We both held onto the island man who completely submitted his body to us, and together we fucked him, slow at first, then faster, harder. If we were too much for him, I didn't know, nor did I care.

Mel slammed his face into his groin repeatedly, making him gag again but wouldn't let him up while I pounded into his backside. Romy grabbed the sheets tightly, choked again on Mel's ten-inch dick, and started cumming all over the sheets hands free, squeezing his rectum on me. I immediately started cumming, then I heard Mel moan his familiar moan and I knew he was cumming too. Romy couldn't handle it, cum and spit oozing from the side of his mouth all over Jamel's dick, and the sight of it made my toes curl and I came again.

When Mel finally let him go, Romy fell over panting and coughing, pulling himself from me. I took off the condom and tied it, threw it on the floor, then moved between Jamel's legs, and started to lick up all of the spit and cum Romy left behind as he caught his breath. Jamel looked down at me, and I saw his face was surprised. Romy came over and joined me, and together we licked up spit and cum off his dick and balls, kissed each other in between while Mel caressed both of our heads. Then I left Romy down there to finish cleaning up his mess as I made my way up Jamel's chest and finally to his mouth. We kissed, then he pulled back and looked into my eyes.

"Holy shit, Corporal," he said quietly.

We stared at each other, then we smiled together. Round one complete.

Romy moved off the bed to his fanny pack and pulled out a clear sandwich bag. In it was the same stuff we saw at the club, little white joints and pills. I asked him, "What are the pills?"

"X," he said, as he put one in his mouth. "You boys aren't playing. Something tells me I'm going to be here all night, so I want to be prepared."

Romulus held out the bag to me. The last time I smoked weed was a couple of months ago with Donny, who smokes it on the regular, but I haven't taken Ecstasy in over a decade, probably a whole year before I met Jamel. I took the bag from him, but then I looked at my husband.

"Give me a joint but I'm not taking X," said Jamel. "But you can if you want. Don't hold back."

I popped two little white pills in my mouth and said to my lover, "You're in charge now."

Jamel grinned at me.

♥ ♥ ♥ CHAPTER 16 ♥ ♥ ♥

QUALITY TIME

Connor

The rest of the night was a blur. After we finished a round of joints, we started out in a sandwich for round two, me on the bottom on my stomach, Romy inside of me, and Jamel inside of him. I remembered again it felt foreign, like I had an unknown visitor in my most private space. But when he started to move, all that was forgotten because he made himself at home and fucked me good. I lost track of time and space after that.

I remembered I got spit-roasted just like I wanted to, with my mouth on Romy's dick and Jamel pounding my ass. I remembered getting double penetrated at one point, riding Jamel's dick as Romy fucked me too. I forgot what that felt like, having two cocks in me, but my ass sure remembered because it was on fire in the morning. There was a lot of biting. And choking. I remembered Romy and I facing each other, me riding with his hand around my throat while Jamel thrusted him from behind, then I think we switched, because it blurred with me being behind while Romy was on Jamel. But Jamel wasn't going to be penetrated so maybe he was riding him, also double penetrated? Image after image almost like a dream that I couldn't separate from reality.

I opened my eyes. I was laying on my side, and my body felt like lead. I was on Jamel's arm as he was lying flat on his back. Romy was pressed tightly behind me, his arm draped across my chest and holding onto my genitals. My mouth was completely dry, and someone's dried-up cum was on my face, with remnants of cum still lingering in my throat. I slowly sat up and looked around. All twelve condoms were thrown around the floor, some tied and some not. The bottle of tequila was empty. It was definitely a flashback to my early twenties, waking up not remembering exactly what happened, just the bits and pieces of it all.

My head was pounding, and I was grateful for the couples' chocolate mud bath and massage we had scheduled for that day, because I could certainly use it. I removed Romy's hand to slide out of the bed, and both of them began to stir awake as I went to the bathroom. When I came out, I glanced at myself in the mirror and I had new purple hickies and bruises on my neck, as well as bite marks all over my body, shoulders, chest, inside of my thighs, probably on my ass too. I chuckled to myself at the wild night we had.

I went to the fridge and pulled out three water bottles. Romy sat up first, also looking as harried as I felt, with bite marks all over him. I handed Romy the water bottle and said, "Good morning."

"Hmmm ... morning." He took it, thankful. X dries you out completely so I knew he was parched.

Jamel laid on his side and lifted up on his elbow. I came to his side of the bed, kissed his lips and said, "Happy anniversary, baby."

He smiled and brought my face back to his. "Happy anniversary, baby," he repeated. We kissed softly again, and then I handed him a water bottle.

I sat at the bottom of the bed between their legs and crossed mine like a pretzel, my penis hanging lazily between my thighs. "Thank you," I told Romy.

Romy laughed. "I think I should be thanking the two of you. I haven't had that much fun in a while."

Jamel reached over and touched his thigh, caressing it. "Neither have we," he said. "This isn't something we do. And we're both grateful that it was with you."

Romy was looking into his eyes, and I knew he felt like he was drowning in them. The man had that effect on people. He moved closer and kissed my husband on the lips. Jamel hesitated slightly but allowed it. Then Romy looked over, locking eyes with me. I watched him crawl down the bed and pull my face toward his and kiss me next. His mouth tasted like stale cum, and I assumed mine did as well. Jamel came behind and started fingering his hole.

"One more for the road?" My lover looked past Romy and asked me.

I looked at him and said, "We don't have any more condoms."

"I have condoms," Romy said. "I always carry." He looked back and forth between us. "I'm clean, just so you know. I take what I do very seriously and get tested regularly. This is why I only work with couples because chances are they are clean too. But I also carry condoms."

Jamel looked over at me. *I guess I was in charge again.*

Even though my body felt like it had been hit by a MAC truck, my dick had no reservations and let it be known by standing attention. "Yeah, one more."

When Romy moved away from us, Jamel immediately came closer and kissed my face. He asked quietly, "Are you okay?"

I nodded. "You?" He nodded. "And us? We're okay?" I tried not to look as fearful as I felt. Jamel got to see me in rare form last night, and it might have scared him a little.

But Jamel nodded again. "Yes, baby. We're okay." He kissed me again. "Now let him ride you while I pound him too. We're going to fuck him together again."

Ah, so we did double penetrate him.

I laid down, and Jamel began to lick my already hard cock. Romy came over to help, and it was amazing seeing these two men worship my dick with their mouths and tongues. Jamel took one of the condoms from him and placed it on me, motioning for Romy to spread his cheeks. Mel lubed and fingered his hole. Romy sat on my chest and moved backward as Jamel guided me inside of him. Then Romy began to move like a belly dancer, making me moan out loud and annoyed at myself for getting high and missing this feeling while sober.

I found myself saying, "Holy shit, you can ride dick!"

They both laughed at me. "You've been yelling that all night," Jamel said. And they laughed again, making me laugh. "But he's not riding right now. He's getting fucked."

Romy barely had a chance to react when Jamel pushed him down by his neck and came to straddle my legs. He put a condom on, added an exuberant amount of lube to the condom and Romy again, then slowly inserted himself into the same hole I was already occupying. Romy started moaning and shaking. Jamel's dick is huge, and it felt like it was flattening my own hard cock. It didn't matter that we both had condoms on; our cocks were so close together we might as well have been frotting raw. He got most of his dick in, and then we moved together. When he pulled out, I pushed and when I pulled back, he thrusted in.

Romy started cursing in Patois, calling someone's mother a cunt as his eyes watered. Jamel held onto his waist but locked his eyes on me as he began to move faster inside him and against me. I laid still and gave up all the control to my man as he pumped harder and faster. I closed my eyes, stretched my hands out to the side of me, and allowed myself to get fucked.

Five minutes in, Romy started yelling, "Fuck fuck fuck" and came on my chest, streams shooting out of his untouched cock. I touched and tasted it. It was sweet, like all he did was eat ice cream. Jamel's eyes were closed as he began to move sporadically, one leg up and the other knee down, pounding into our fuck toy. Romy came again, and I dipped my hand into it and reached up until I could touch Jamel's lips and rubbed it there before I laid back down. Jamel licked his lips and moaned, making me smile. I kept scooping up Romy's sweet cum and licking my fingers; it made me so hot for him. My balls tightened, and I knew I was close too.

"I'll cum when you do," I moaned over Romy's loud, sexual sounds of pleasure and pain.

Jamel heard me. "I'm cumming baby, uuuugh. Cumming."

I could feel Jamel's dick flex and spurt, and my dick instantly started doing the same. We both moaned out our orgasms as one more cum strand flew out of Romy's cock, and I instantly scooped it up. When he was done, Jamel moved off him and laid down on the bed, catching his breath. Romy slowly removed me from inside of him by sliding upward, then moved to the other side of me. I laid there with my eyes closed. Then I felt someone move over me. I knew it was Mel, taking the condom off me, licking what was left of Romy's sweet-tasting semen off my chest, little by little, making his way up to my mouth. I reached my arms around his familiar body and held him as we kissed. By the time we remembered we weren't alone, Romy had already found his cycling pants and tank top.

"I hate to be crass, but we do have one more matter to attend to," he said.

Jamel got off me to go to the safe and pull out the money. I saw him count out four one-hundred-dollar bills and hand it to him. Romy said, "It's too much." He tried to give a hundred back.

Jamel held up his palm to stop him and said, "Keep the change. Buy your daughter something nice with it."

I smiled as Romy grinned at my husband. He kissed Jamel on the cheek. Romy then opened the door and left. Jamel locked it and came to lay beside me again at the bottom of the bed. I rolled over to lay on his chest. We didn't talk, just held each other and eventually fell asleep again.

♥

We took showers and made our way to the adult pool again, making out like teenagers at the deep end that we had all to ourselves, kissing and touching each other. Neither of us mentioned Romy or the threesome we just experienced together. Another male couple also came into the deep end, but they stayed on the other side of the pool, giving us privacy and wanting their own.

I wrapped my arms around Jamel's neck and said, "Let's move to Aruba."

He laughed out loud as he held me. "Yeah? We'll just quit our jobs, sell our house, and say goodbye to all our friends?"

I shrugged. "I can do Vet Buddies from anywhere. And I'm sure someone somewhere here needs a house to be built or electrical work."

Jamel chuckled. "Ty can take over the business." He kissed my neck.

"We'll put the house in Freddie's name. Or we'll sell the house to Ethan, so he can give it to EJ when he gets older. It's basically their damn house anyway."

"Then we can retire here. Right here in this community. Mai Tais every morning." He nibbled my ear.

"Making love on the beach every night."

"Sounds like paradise," he whispered in my ear.

"Anywhere with you is paradise, baby,"

He raised his head from my neck and looked at me. We kissed gently. "God, I love you Connor," he said on my lips.

I was about to say it back when I heard moaning. He heard it too. I turned around, and he looked past me to see the couple on the other side of the pool moving together, one facing the wall with his arms on the deck and the other one directly behind him, the water moving in waves around them. I turned back to Mel, and we started giggling softly.

"Maybe we should go and give them privacy," I suggested.

"Maybe we should join them," he suggested back.

I laughed. "Not unless it's you up against that wall." There was no way I was getting fucked for the next 72 hours, at least.

He turned me around so that my back was against the pool wall. "I got a better idea," he said.

He held onto the wall with one hand and palmed my bottom with the other, then pushed against me so that I had nowhere to go, and my hard dick was stuck against his abs.

"Fuck, Mel," I said breathlessly.

I lifted up my legs and wrapped them around his waist. He moved against me, up and down, stroking my dick with his own. I held onto his neck and let him work me, kissing and biting on my neck that was turning purple again. He knew what he was doing and wouldn't let up, and the moaning sounds that echoed across the pool were not helping my restraint. I started moving with him, building up the friction between us. I found myself moaning too, and I saw the Top turn his neck to lock eyes with me. He smirked, then began to fuck his Bottom faster. Something about the four of us men in this pool fucking sent me over the edge.

I cried out, "I'm cumming."

As I began to jizz right in the pool, I heard one of them say, "I'm cumming too."

This sent Mel over the edge, and he began cumming in the pool as well. He slowed to a stop but continued to hold me tight and I did the same, holding onto his neck. The couple on the other side finished as well, also still holding onto each other. White sperm began to float up around us, and we started laughing, moving it around to make it disappear.

"My body is exhausted," I told him. "I'm definitely not 23 anymore."

He looked up at the big clock over the bar. "We have two more hours until our massage. Let's hit the hot tub for a little while."

I nodded and we made our way to the adjacent hot tub. It was the right kind of hot and what I needed to soothe and soak. He sat down and I immediately sat down on his lap, leaned against his chest, closed my eyes, and let him hold me. After a while, the couple that was in the pool came to join us. They mimicked us, with the guy that was bottoming sitting on the Top's lap.

"No funny business in here," I said jokingly.

The Top laughed. "We just came here to relax after all that, just like you did." He had a southern accent.

"Where are you from?"

"New Mexico," the Bottom responded. "I'm Gary. That's Karl. Where are you from?"

"Rhode Island. I'm Connor. This is Jamel." Jamel raised his hand in acknowledgment. "So, there's a gay scene in New Mexico?"

"Oh, honey there is a queer scene everywhere; you just have to find it," Karl, the Top said.

Jamel nodded and said, "We found it here."

Gary asked excitedly, "Ooooh, you found The Underground?" We both nodded. "That's real raunchy gay, like no fucks given-type gay. But there are other regular club scenes like District 7. Who got you in, Antonio?"

"Romulus," I told them.

"Do we know him?" Gary asked Karl.

"Um ... I think so. Is he the one that works in the gift shop or the ice cream shop? Or the one that does the towels over there?" Karl pointed to the far end of the resort, closer to the beach.

"Ice cream shop," I said with a smile. Apparently, it was a whole operation.

"Oh yeah, he's nice. They are all really nice and know how to fuck," Karl said.

I laughed. "So you guys come here a lot?" I asked.

"No, just me," Karl said. "I come here for business and occasionally bring Gary down here. He's married with kids."

Gary looked embarrassed. "Shut up."

"What, it's not like we're ever going to see them again, darling; they literally live on the other side of the country," he reminded him. Karl turned back to

272

us. "Our relationship is complicated." Gary relaxed, as Karl played with his light brown hair, and asked us, "How long have you been together?"

We looked at each other and smiled, then said at the same time, "Ten years today."

Gary and Karl beamed at us, then said simultaneously, "Happy anniversary!"

Jamel leaned down as I leaned up, and we kissed. "Awww, that's what real love looks like," Karl said. "Whatever it is that you got, don't ever let it go."

I sat back against his chest as he held me tighter and said, "Never."

♥

Gary and Karl wanted to have dinner with us, but we already had anniversary dinner plans, a five-course meal served to us by candlelight on the beach. But we agreed to have breakfast with them in the morning, since our flight wasn't leaving until late afternoon. After our well-deserved spa treatments, we went back to the room and played around in the bed, kissing, touching, and a bit of sucking until it was time for dinner. We got dressed up for it: Mel wearing black dress pants that he cuffed at the end and a tight, dark green muscle shirt, and I wore white ankle pants with a red, white, and gold, button-down, short-sleeved shirt with the two top buttons opened.

Even before we walked out the door, Mel was already palming me, saying, "Fuck, your ass looks good in these pants," making me blush like only he can.

273

We dined on a secluded side of the beach, getting stuffed with lobster and sirloin, and never-ending wine as the sun set lower and lower in the sky. We were both pretty tipsy so I told him, "Let's walk."

We left our shoes at the table, and I reached my hand out to hold his before he could do it to me, which was something I rarely did. He smiled and took it, as I laced my fingers with his. We walked in silence for a while along the edge of the water, just like we did the first night. But I felt different somehow, like I was coming out of the trip more accepting of my sexuality than I was going in just four days ago. And I understood why. Being sexually attracted to men was like this huge secret for me for so many years. But not anymore. There was no secrecy, guilt, or shame around what we did, and I think that was a huge part of my newfound confidence. I was gay. And I celebrated that part of me on this trip with no fear, no restrictions, and with the most wonderful man by my side. It dawned on me that to live openly really just meant not to live my life in secrecy, and I was determined to do that moving forward. What that would look like when I got back home, I didn't know.

I broke the silence by saying, "I want to be different when we get back. More open about who I am. Freer in public with you."

"But whether you do or not, I'm okay with exactly who you are today," Mel said. "You don't have to hold my hand or kiss me in public for me to know that you love and care about me."

My loving husband was always so affirming. "But it's your love language," I reminded him. "And I've been slacking on it."

Jamel smiled. "Actually, Quality Time is. Just like we're doing right now. Just like we did this whole trip."

"Okay, but Mel, you've always given me what I needed. I know saying how you feel isn't something that you were used to doing before you met me. You're like your father in that way. But you do it anyway, for me."

He shrugged. "I got used to it. I can tell you exactly how I feel and give you random hugs too. Just like my mama." I laughed, missing Mama Denita's hugs, and I knew he did too.

"Still. It's time for me to step out of my comfort zone. I want to give you what you need too, what you deserve as a proud, gay husband. No more hidden love. I want to be the gay man that is happy to show you off as my husband, just like you did at Nick's funeral with me. I didn't even know how much I needed that until you did it to me. It made me so happy to be yours. So, I'm doing the same for you. I want to show you that I'm deeply devoted to you too. It's long overdue."

He kissed my cheek. "I love you."

"And I love you."

We walked on. "What do you want to do tonight, other than fuck me?" he said and laughed.

I chuckled and said, "Actually, I don't. We can just lay together if that's okay with you."

Jamel raised our hands to his mouth and kissed the back of mine. "That sounds like the perfect night."

We spent the night talking and laughing in the dark. I made love to my husband in the morning. Then we had brunch with our New Mexico friends, bought some souvenirs, and got on the plane to go back home to our domesticated life.

Connor and Jamel's love story continues...

BOOK CLUB QUESTIONS

♥ ♥ ♥   ♥ ♥ ♥

1. Jamel had a relationship with Nick that went back and forth from lovers to friends over twenty years, before ultimately deciding that friendship was best. What similarities did you see between their relationship and Connor and Afia's? What differences?

2. Nick's introduction to the storyline, just like Vinnie's, was in his death. Why do you feel the author did this?

3. Although mentioned that Connor talked to Nick a few times over the phone, they only met once in person at Connor and Jamel's wedding, nine years later. Was that intentional on Jamel's part, or did circumstances not allow them to meet until that time?

4. Has the military changed for the LGBTQ community since the repeal of Don't Ask Don't Tell? In what positive ways? In what negative ways?

5. What were your thoughts on the friendship and brotherhood between Jamel, Nicholas, Henry, and William? If you have a military background,

consider the friendship made while serving and the accuracy of it in the storyline.

6. Describe the impact Nick's death had on each of the characters: Jamel, Connor, Henry, and especially Josh. How did Josh's breakdown affect you?

7. What are your thoughts on the closeness between Jamel and Connor's sisters, and Connor and Jamel's brothers, at this stage of the series?

8. A occurring source of contention in their relationship, and many other relationships, is having children together. Discuss infertility, child-rearing, and the sensitivity and pressure many couples feel around the topic.

9. Jamel is constantly managing Connor's emotional outbursts by staying calm and being rational, since the beginning of their relationship. Does Jamel's point of view of how emotionally taxing it is to him change your perspective on their relationship?

10. It was important to the characters to choose a vacation spot that was diverse and gay-friendly. How important is that to you as the reader?

11. Was the decision to have a threesome mutual? Or did one influence the other?

12. Discuss Connor's thoughts and promise to Jamel at the end, to no longer live his life in secrecy, guilt, and shame about his sexuality, and to be more publicly open with his affection for Jamel.

AUTHOR BIO

♥ ♥ ♥   ♥ ♥ ♥

Wife, mother, partner, daughter, sister, friend, social worker, life skills coach, and part-time erotic romance novelist, Eskay Kabba finds the complexity of human nature and her characters reflect the notion that no one is all good or all bad, but we are all just trying to find love in hard places. Eskay pens erotic romance novels that celebrates the LGBTQ community, people of color, and interracial relationships. When not writing about the throes of passion, Eskay finds joy in spending time with her family and loved ones, reading dystopia and fantasy series, and binging popular shows from a streaming app. Eskay. Kabba@gmail.com

More books from 4 Horsemen Publications

LGBT Erotica

Dominic N. Ashen
Steel & Thunder
Storms & Sacrifice
Secrets & Spires
Arenas & Monsters
My Three Orc Dads: a Novella

What Makes Me a Whore?
A Breach in Confidentiality
Back Door Pass
My European Adventure
An Unexpected Affair
Finding True Love

Eskay Kabba
Hidden Love
Not So Hidden

Leo Sparx
Before Alexander
Claiming Alexander
Taming Alexander
Saving Alexander
The Case of Armando

Grayson Ace
How I Got Here
First Year Out of the Closet
You're Only a Top?
You're Only a Bottom?
I Think I'm a Serial Swiper
Lookin in All the Wrong Places

Robert Lewis
Someone to Love
Someone to Come Home To

LGBT Romance

Eskay Kabba
Hidden Love
Not So Hidden
Signs of Affection

Mikaél's Moment: Type 6
Stephan's Resurgence: Type 5
Anastasia's Arrival: Type 6

Lucas LaMont
Roman's Reckoning: Type 6

Stormie Skyes
Check Yes, No, or Maybe

Discover more at 4HorsemenPublications.com

www.ingramcontent.com/pod-product-compliance
Lightning Source LLC
Chambersburg PA
CBHW050029120726
47903CB00006B/1974